Lame

4|r||

D0590819

WITHDRAWN

The Tree of Death

Also by Brian Eastman in the
Rosemary and Thyme series:

And No Birds Sing

THE TREE OF DEATH

A Rosemary and Thyme Mystery

BRIAN EASTMAN
with
REBECCA TOPE

First edition published in Great Britain in 2005 by
Allison & Busby Limited
Bon Marché Centre
241-251 Ferndale Road
London SW9 8BJ
http://www.allisonandbusby.com

A catalogue record for this book is available from
the British Library.

10 9 8 7 6 5 4 3 2 1

ISBN 0 7490 8272 0

Printed and bound in Wales by
Creative Print and Design, Ebbw Vale

BRIAN EASTMAN heads one of the UK's leading independent production companies, Carnival Films, and has produced a wide variety of TV programmes and feature films including Agatha Christie's *Poirot, Jeeves and Wooster, Shadowlands* and *Traffik*. He created, and produces, *Rosemary and Thyme* for ITV.

Chapter One

Laura hadn't seen Keith Briggs since he was sixteen. Now, ten years later, as he welcomed her to his new home, he had changed dramatically from the awkward teenager she remembered. She smiled to herself at the idea that she might ever have predicted that he would one day wear a dog collar.

'Suits you!' she said, indicating the white band.

Keith pulled a rueful face. 'I'm glad you think so,' he said. 'I thought you might be in agreement with my mother.'

Keith's mother, Sandy, was Laura's first cousin, and very much the rebel of the family. Her wholly negative reaction when her son had announced his intention to seek ordination reverberated across the hundred miles between them. The wounded feelings were still raw and bleeding, which explained Laura's visit, to try to find some grounds for compromise.

'No, I don't agree with her,' she told him. 'I think it's rather splendid to have a vicar in the family. And it's very nice of you to invite me to stay. I've been really looking forward to it. Isn't it a beautiful day!'

'They say it's the last one for a while. Here we are – this is my humble abode.'

She studied the building carefully: a good-sized house of attractive old stone, in a small hamlet, it was more than many young vicars could expect these days. A lot had changed since the vast rambling vicarages she remembered from her childhood, but Keith had been luckier than most. Even so, she was already realising that his new life was far from easy. Like most clergymen in the country, he had to care for five or six parishes, with never a moment to call his own. And Laura suspected that he received a lot less respect from his parishioners than he might have enjoyed a century earlier.

'This is very pleasant,' she said, inspecting the house from the driveway outside.

'Looks are deceptive, I'm afraid,' he said. 'The man before me had five children, and very little interest in discipline, from all appearances. This house was built in 1905, and to be honest, I don't think it's had much done to it since.'

Laura laughed. 'Well, it certainly has plenty of potential. You'll have to brush up on your DIY skills.'

Keith clutched at his own hair, in a gesture that was more than half serious. 'Time, Laura!' he wailed. 'There's never any time.'

Inside, Laura could see the problems. Most of the walls had been scribbled on by an obviously manic three-year-old. The carpets were threadbare and the heating system rudimentary. But the ceilings were high, and the main room had decorated cornices and a rose around the light fitting. An art nouveau fireplace caught her eye. 'What a gorgeous thing!' she exclaimed.

Keith nodded. 'I'm lucky it wasn't ripped out during the Seventies. But I'm afraid you won't find anything to admire in the kitchen.'

He was right; the kitchen left Laura speechless. Keith laughed at her expression.

'I'm actually very fortunate,' he repeated, as if he had already acquired a habit of counting his blessings several times a day. 'This is a lovely part of the country. My parish is five separate villages, spread over quite a big area. It's going to take me ages to get the hang of them all. Baffington's the biggest – and the prettiest. I still feel I've stumbled onto the lid of a chocolate box every time I go there. It has quite a good-sized congregation, and it's where my parish secretary lives. As far as the people of Baffington are concerned, I'm their full-time vicar and the other parishes can go without. Unfortunately, they've had their way for years, and the other four have very much lost heart.'

'I see,' smiled Laura. 'Very Christian.'

'I'll just have to do all I can to improve their spiritual health, won't I.' He squared his shoulders, and Laura thought he looked dreadfully young. She couldn't remember the last time she'd met a vicar under forty-five.

'So – what's the plan?' she asked. 'Don't let me get in your way. You've obviously got masses to do.'

'Masses?' he repeated, cocking his head sideways. 'I think you'll find that's the other lot.'

The joke reminded Laura of the teenager Keith had been, immersed in the more serious end of science fiction and fantasy in films and books, always thoughtful and questioning. He'd enjoyed playing with words, even then. 'Very funny,' she said, affectionately.

'So, you've seen my mother, have you?' he asked her, in a quick change of subject. 'Does she know you're here?'

Laura gave him a direct look. 'Yes, she knows. She's hoping I'll argue her case, seeing as how I'm the same generation as her. I'm more of a kind of aunt to you, in her eyes.'

Keith groaned. 'Can't she understand it's far too late now? It's done. I'm here. It's my life, as well as my vocation and my source of income. It's who I am.'

'She finds it all dreadfully embarrassing,' Laura explained. 'She's always been such a rationalist.'

'Yes, yes, I know,' he said impatiently. 'I didn't do it deliberately to snub her. Surely she must see that? I admire her work and her strength of mind, I always have. But I'm grown up now. I must follow my own course.'

Laura sighed. 'To be honest with you, I think she's dug herself into such a deep hole she needs somebody like me to get her out of it, without losing too much face. I hope we can think of a way to mend a few bridges, while I'm here.'

Keith laughed. 'Sounds as if you'll be very busy – being a ladder as well as a bridge-mender.'

Laura joined his merriment. 'Oh, Keith, you haven't changed,' she said happily.

He coloured slightly at this, and shook his head. 'I think you'll find I have,' he said with a hint of a sigh. 'Life is really rather earnest these days.'

Laura regarded him sternly. 'That may be true, but you mustn't let it get out of balance. You have to have some fun, as well – or you'll grow old before your time.'

'You're right,' he agreed, not quite convincingly. 'Now, let's bring your bag in, and have some tea, and then I'll take you to see Baffington.'

* * *

An hour later, on the road to Baffington, Laura asked, 'How long have you been here now? Can you give me a character sketch of all your main parishioners yet?'

He laughed. 'I've been here exactly a month. The main event this week is the Baffington Fête. It's a fundraiser for the church, and I'm supposed to be the chief organiser. Quite honestly, I haven't got the least idea of what I'm meant to do. They didn't cover fête organising on my theology course. There was a move to make some sort of historical pageant out of it, but it hasn't worked out. All to do with village politics, I suspect. One or two people seem particularly disappointed about it, and I can't help feeling they blame me.'

'I'm sure that isn't so. Besides, fêtes are easy,' Laura breezed. 'You'll see – the whole thing'll run by itself. People just turn up on the day with their old books and jigsaws, and somebody produces one of those wiggly wire things and a battery, and a local farmer brings his pig for you to guess the weight – and it's all up and running like clockwork. When is it?'

'Day after tomorrow,' said Keith gloomily. 'And I think your optimism is seriously misplaced. As far as I can tell, the whole village is sulking about something. I'll be surprised if more than four people and a duck turn up. Even the weather forecast is against us. It's going to rain, apparently.'

'Well, at least that can't possibly be your fault. And as far as the other things are concerned, you haven't been here long enough to make a difference.'

Baffington was six miles from Keith's home, and a stunningly pretty village. There was a stillness to it, a calm oasis of Englishness that continued to exist in every region of the country, but was less easy to find in recent times. The road wound down a steep hill, arriving at the short village street, with a Green on one side, church and pub on the other. Many of the houses appeared to be several centuries old, and a small stream ran merrily under an ancient brick wall which bordered a raised grassed-over area. 'That's the Glebe field,' said Keith. 'Preserved in perpetuity from being built on, and very much treasured by the residents.' The church was small, solid and timeless, at least as much as Laura could see of it, surrounded as it was by a very large overgrown churchyard and screened by a massive tree.

'Why is the graveyard so big?' she queried.

'According to Mr Danvers, our local historian, it goes back to the Black Death. This area was badly affected, and they created the burial ground according to need. There's some sort of charter that ensures it can't be encroached on for any other use, the same as the Glebe. We're the envy of all the churches in the diocese. Unlike them, we'll never run out of grave space.'

The tree that concealed the church proved to be a huge old yew, standing between the lych-gate and the church itself, completely dominating the scene. Laura stared at it for a moment, wondering why it made her feel suddenly gloomy, even slightly apprehensive.

'It's usually a chestnut tree in the middle of a village, isn't it?' she said. 'With a smithy set up underneath it.'

Keith shook his head vaguely. Laura realised that he had already accepted the village as it was and no longer saw it with an appraising eye. For him the yew tree had become a fact of life, almost invisible and certainly not to be criticised.

Next to the churchyard stood the charming Holly Tree pub, and across the small village green was a row of cottages that had to be over two centuries in age. A large house lorded it over the others, standing on a rise a few hundred yards distant, with a gravel driveway and a number of outbuildings. There was a fairytale air to it, with large trees shielding much of it from view. Except, thought Laura, it was more a tale from the Brothers Grimm than one of the more cheerful storytellers.

She returned her attention to the village green. All the cottages had well-kept gardens, brightly coloured and tidily arranged. 'No work for Rosemary and me here, then,' thought Laura, mindful that they were currently without any commissions. Rosemary, her partner in their gardening business, was spending the week searching out some more jobs. 'Our trouble is, we're too efficient,' Laura had joked. 'We've done ourselves out of work.' But there was always something, and neither was too worried about the temporary lull.

'We'll have a look at the church later on,' said Keith. 'First I need to go and see Harriet.'

'Harriet?'

'The parish secretary. I told you she lives here, and has done all her life. She's devoted to Baffington.'

'How old is she?' It was a question Laura found herself asking a lot recently.

'Oh, slightly under thirty. I suppose she's rather an aberration these days, staying in the place she grew up, but she's made herself indispensable in all sorts of ways. That's her house. She inherited it from her parents, who both died in their fifties, a few years ago.' He pointed to a small cottage set back a little way from the centre of the village. They approached it down a short path.

Laura sighed admiringly. 'I love the way these villages have grown up, all higgledy-piggledy. Not a straight line to be seen. And there are always more houses than you first think.' She turned her head from side to side. 'It's actually quite a good size, isn't it.'

'Population of eighty-nine, at the last count. That includes a few farms as well. Sixteen of them are regular churchgoers, which, believe me, is quite an impressive proportion.'

'Doesn't Harriet have a proper job? Will she be in on a Thursday afternoon?'

'She works from home some of the time. She's actually very busy. She's a sort of Girl Friday to several people – does the paperwork for some of the farms, acts as research assistant for our local celebrity —'

'Who?'

'Oh – the chap who lives in the big house. The historian I mentioned just now. He writes books. You might possibly have heard of him – Franklin Danvers?'

Laura shook her head. 'Not really my subject,' she admitted.

'Never mind – neither had I when I came here. He's the one who wants to put on a medieval village pageant. Not so long ago, he'd have been known as the local squire, but I suppose we don't use that word these days.'

They were at Harriet's garden gate when the serenity was

shattered by raised voices.

'Just drop it, will you!' shouted a man. 'You never leave me alone. I tell you – I've had enough of it. I'm getting out of here.'

'No! Malcolm! Come back. I'm sorry. Oh, Malcolm please!'

Laura and Keith looked at each other in alarm. 'What's going on?' she whispered. 'Sounds rather personal.'

The vicar shrugged helplessly. 'Maybe we ought to – um —'

'Too late,' said Laura, as the man came rapidly down the garden path towards them, followed by a very attractive young woman. The four of them became entangled around the gate to the considerable embarrassment of all concerned.

'Oh! Vicar!' said Harriet, in great confusion. She looked from Keith to the man she'd called Malcolm, as if expecting something from one or both of them.

'Get out of my way!' snarled Malcolm unpleasantly. 'Here's a job for you,' he added to the vicar. 'One of your lost lambs needs a shoulder to cry on. And it isn't going to be mine. I've had enough of it.'

Laura stood back, before he had a chance to push her aside. The three of them watched Malcolm stride down the lane and out of sight.

'Er —' said Keith to Harriet. 'Maybe I should come another time?'

'No, no,' she said weakly. 'I'll be all right. That must have sounded awful. I'm ever so sorry. What a spectacle!'

She was wiping her eyes with a tissue, and struggling to control her breathing. 'So undignified.'

'Never mind dignity,' said Laura. 'Let's get you inside, and you can tell us all about it.'

Harriet gave her a look of alarm.

'Oh, this is my – cousin, I suppose,' said Keith. 'I always called you Auntie Laura, didn't I, when I was little?'

'I'm your first cousin once removed,' Laura told him. 'So I think you'd better drop the Auntie. I've come to see how he's settling in,' she said to Harriet, with a friendly smile

'Are you all right?' Keith asked Harriet nervously. 'I mean —'

'Yes, I'm fine. Did you want me for some work? I'm supposed

to be going to Franklin's in about an hour. But I've told him the fête has to take priority this week, and I'll have to spend more time on that.' She heaved a big sigh. 'It's going to be a washout, I'm afraid. In more ways than one.'

'Actually,' Keith said, confidingly, 'I'm praying for a deluge. If the whole thing is cancelled because of the weather, we might be less humiliated. Though I still don't quite understand what's gone wrong. Didn't you say it all went brilliantly last year?'

'I've explained,' said Harriet patiently. 'Joyce Weaverspoon's ill, and without Joyce nothing really happens. Besides that, the Suttons aren't taking much of a part this year.' She shuddered convulsively, and looked at Laura. 'That was Malcolm Sutton you just met. You might not believe it, seeing him like that, but he's always been the life and soul of the village fête. We've relied on him to bring some friends along and organise games for the children. Malcolm's usually a lot of fun,' she sighed.

'So what happened?' asked Laura.

'I'm not really sure. He's been having awful rows with his father. The usual sort of stuff – Malcolm's taking too long to settle down, he's dropped out of three different courses in the past five years, and now he says he wants to buy and sell antiques.'

'What's wrong with that?'

Harriet pulled a face. 'Most of his antiques are fakes,' she said.

'Oh dear.'

Harriet went on, miserably, 'He's got on the wrong side of Mr Danvers over it. Antiques are important to him as sources of history – the way things were made and so forth. And now it looks as if it's all over between Malcolm and me.' She looked sadly at the vicar. 'I was hoping we'd give you your first wedding to officiate at, but now —' a stray tear trickled down her cheek.

'Must be in the stars,' said Laura. 'So much going wrong, all at once.' Belatedly she realised that this might not be the best thing to say to a vicar. Presumably it wasn't the stars in control of events, the way he saw it. 'Well – you know what I mean.'

'They miss the old vicar, I'm afraid,' said Keith bravely. 'He had quite a way with him, I gather. Saw trouble coming and headed it off. I don't know where he found the time.'

'You're doing very well,' Harriet said encouragingly – and rather generously, in Laura's view. 'It's just such a pity about the dratted fete.'

'Can't we cancel it?' Keith asked. Laura had the impression he'd asked this several times before.

'Only if there's a non-stop downpour from first light. Even then, we could move it all into the village hall. It's been done before.'

'But the village hall is being decorated,' he reminded her.

'That wouldn't stop us. Honestly, Keith, it really doesn't matter. Nobody actually cares. Except Franklin Danvers, of course. He'll indulge in quite a lot of I-told-you-so, I'm afraid.'

Laura was beginning to find this parochial chit-chat mildly tedious, and wondered whether they'd object to her going off for a little walk. She started moving towards the door.

'I'll leave you to it,' she said. 'I thought I'd have a little explore. I'll come back in half an hour or so, shall I?'

'Oh!' Keith looked agitated. 'This must be dull for you.'

'Not a bit. It's fascinating. But I'd truly like to wander about a bit. I've been on a train all morning. I need the exercise.'

She made her escape, reminding herself that if the village only took ten minutes to explore, she could drop into The Holly Tree for a cup of tea.

As it turned out, she was somewhat longer than the promised thirty minutes. She found herself following a winding country lane out of the village, for no better reason than that she could see a picture-book cottage on the next bend, with a luxuriant garden, and it drew her like a magnet. As she admired it over the low stone wall, she heard a noise a short way along the road ahead and turned to investigate.

It was a voice she recognised. The man who had been shouting at Harriet was on the other side of a hedge, snarling and snapping, 'Go home! Get away! How many times must I tell you?' There followed a thud and a yelp of pain and bewilderment. Laura moved closer, peering through the vegetation. A yellow labrador was crouching at Malcolm Sutton's feet, evidently having just been kicked.

'Hey!' cried Laura, in outrage. 'Don't do that!'

He couldn't see her at first, looking round in confusion. 'Who's that?' he demanded.

'Never mind who I am. What do you think you're doing, abusing that poor animal?'

'I'm teaching him a lesson. He belongs to my family, anyhow. I can do what I like.'

'I think you'll find you're entirely mistaken about that,' she told him. 'You don't deserve a dog if that's the way you treat him.'

'He's not mine, anyway. He belongs to my sister. She's spoilt him. He knows he isn't allowed to stray from home. He's the most brainless specimen I've ever met.'

'He looks perfectly all right to me.' Laura had moved to a gateway, where she and Malcolm had a clear view of each other. The labrador crept towards her, still crouched low, glancing frequently at Malcolm. 'Here, boy,' Laura encouraged. 'He won't hurt you again.'

'For goodness' sake!' the man exploded. 'What gives you the right to interfere? The dog's going to get run over or shot if he thinks he can wander anywhere he likes. He's got to learn.'

'Perhaps he just thought he'd come to greet you. Perhaps, despite your treatment of him, he still loves you. Dogs are like that, aren't they. Loyal to the end, often against their own interest.'

To her surprise, Malcolm's face crumpled into an expression of pain. 'No, you've got that wrong,' he said. 'Bobby doesn't like me at all. He never has. My father bought him for my sister, and he's devoted to them both. But he's never had any time for me. Not surprising, really – he's just adopted the general attitude of the family. Well,' he added, with a burst of defiance, 'I've had enough of it. They won't have to put up with me any longer. I'm getting out of here.'

'I got the impression that Harriet would miss you,' Laura ventured.

He shrugged. 'She'll get over it.'

'So when are you leaving?'

He shook his head. 'I don't know exactly. Why are you asking all these questions? Who the devil are you?'

'Just a nosy old visitor,' she said. Then she looked at him again, seeing a man in his early thirties, still unsure of his role in life, antagonistic to everybody and everything. The sort of son every parent dreads producing, by some fatal error in the upbringing, or circumstance beyond their control. Laura's own son had never shown any signs of going the same way – but her daughter had. 'Won't your father miss you, if you go?' she asked gently.

'It'll be because of him,' Malcolm snarled. 'On at me the whole time. Nagging and criticising. I can never do a thing right in his eyes. He'll be well rid of me.'

'Have you told him you're leaving?'

'I'm going to look for him now, as it happens, and get it over with once and for all,' he said, lifting his head up and taking a deep breath.

'So you can take your dog home, and try to treat him kindly,' she suggested. 'Where do you live?'

'It's called Brockett's Farm,' he said absently. 'Over there.' He pointed across the fields, to where a handsome red brick farmstead could be seen on the side of a hill, about a quarter of a mile away.

'Gosh!' Laura said admiringly. 'It looks quite a spread.'

'Three hundred acres. Been in the family since Doomsday, just about.' He kicked at a stone, making the dog flinch. 'You'd think, wouldn't you, that after all those generations of fathers and sons, we'd have found a way to work it out – without all this trouble.' He looked forlorn to Laura's motherly eye. 'The truth is, my sister's the real farmer. I can't be bothered with it. It's mucky and old-fashioned and there's no money in it any more.'

'So what's your passion?' she asked him.

He looked at her, a frown between his eyes. 'Passion?'

'What gets your heart thumping, what gets you out of bed in the morning?'

His glance scanned the rolling hills, bathed in summer sunshine. 'Not a bloody thing,' he said.

* * *

Keith and Harriet were waiting for her, outside the church. 'Sorry!' she panted. 'I got talking —' she stopped, remembering the angry exchange between Harriet and Malcolm, and wary of hurting the young woman's feeling. 'It's a very pretty village,' she went on. 'Very peaceful.'

Harriet made a snorting noise. 'You wouldn't say that if you knew the people,' she said.

Keith met Laura's eye and pulled a comically alarmed face. 'Every community has its little conflicts,' he said. 'I don't think Baffington's anything out of the ordinary.'

Laura looked around, at the village green and the overgrown churchyard; the big house dominated it all, and her eye eventually settled on the hanging baskets of The Holly Tree. Perhaps, she acknowledged to herself, it was all slightly unreal. A feeling took hold of her that there was far more going on beneath the surface than a casual visitor could ever hope to perceive.

The day of the fête was cloudy, with flurries of drizzle. The sort of weather that was neither one thing nor the other, as Laura remarked.

'The worst possible,' groaned Keith. 'The optimists are going to say it's sure to clear up and we can carry on outside, and the pessimists will argue for taking it all into the village hall. What about you, Laura? Which side would you be on?'

'Carry on outside,' she said. 'It shows a better spirit.'

'Yes! I'll phone Harriet and tell her, then.'

The villagers assembled on the green, preparing their stalls with dogged stoicism. Most wore cagoules with hoods, as if setting out for a Ten Tors Walk. Franklin Danvers, local bigwig, sat in a large red four-wheel drive, awaiting his moment. He was to officially open the proceedings with a short speech, promptly at two o'clock.

'He doesn't look very happy,' Laura observed, peering shamelessly through the windscreen. 'And why is he in his car anyway, when it's only a hundred yards to his house?'

'I think he wants to make a point,' said Keith.

At five minutes to two, another car arrived, parking on the far side of the green and disgorging three people. Laura watched as they stood stiffly beside their vehicle. She recognised the disaffected Malcolm Sutton, and assumed the others were his father and sister.

Harriet, busy with some last-minute arrangements, did not at first notice the arrival of the Sutton family. But when Malcolm's loud voice came across the grass to her, she dropped what she was doing and stood up straight, as if transfixed.

'I don't damn well care!' he shouted at his father. 'Do what you like. It makes no difference to me.'

Such a public display of family disharmony struck Laura as very uncivilised. She noticed the sister cringing with embarrassment, and the father scarlet with outrage. She was strongly tempted to march over and tell Malcolm to behave himself.

But before she could move, he had climbed back into the car. 'You can walk home,' he called, as he started to reverse the vehicle. 'I'm off. You can fetch the car from the station.'

The older man made a gesture to stop him, but his daughter put a hand on his arm, saying something that was probably 'Let him go.'

Laura turned to Keith. 'What a display! Can you work out what's happening?'

'No, but I'd better see if I can help, I suppose.'

'You can't. It's two o'clock, look.' Laura pointed up at the church tower, where the clock was chiming the hour. 'Your celebrity's going to want to make his speech.'

With military promptness, Mr Danvers had got out of his car and was standing on a small rostrum, head held high, waiting for a respectful silence.

'Ladies and gentlemen!' he began in ringing tones. 'Although I fear it cannot be denied that there has been much about this event that has been inauspicious, it is with high hopes that I stand here before you to perform the opening rituals. As you all know, profits from this afternoon's proceedings will go towards the repair of the stonework in the church tower, as well as other necessary maintenance. The church is the core and hub of our community, as has been the case for many hundreds of years. The history is a fascinating one, of course. Dedicated to St Thomas in the year 1317, at a time of great turbulence and anxiety, the church would have been a haven of consolation and reassurance. Remember, the Black Death arrived in England not too long afterwards, and then the great battles of the period followed on its heels...'

'Ohhh,' moaned Keith softly to Laura. 'Stop him, somebody, before he starts telling us about the reasons for the Battle of Poitiers.'

'Is he mad?' Laura asked, in all sincerity.

'No, not really. He's making a pitch for his blessed Medieval Fayre next summer, I think.'

Danvers was in full swing by this time. '...We in Baffington are extremely fortunate in having virtually intact records from the fourteenth century until the present day. For this we can thank the church itself, and the genius of the local clergy who preserved so much, where others managed to lose theirs...'

'You can hardly blame them for wars and floods,' muttered Keith. 'It's sheer fluke that Baffington managed to avoid that sort of catastrophe.'

'Look,' Laura nudged him. 'Harriet to the rescue!'

Harriet Luke had edged closer to Danvers, and was doing her best to catch his eye. Finally succeeding, she wagged her head at him, and indicated the restless assembly of villagers. He slowly took the hint.

'Well – be that as it may. I must now perform my duty and privilege, and declare this annual Baffington summer fête open.'

The scattered applause from the dozen or so present cut him short, but not before he had raised his voice and added, 'And next year, I trust we can all enjoy a full-scale Medieval Fayre, in due commemoration of the crucial place our village holds in the history of this fair land!'

'He is definitely bonkers,' said Laura. 'I don't care what you say.'

'Even if he is, next summer he'll get his pageant or Fayre or whatever he wants to call it,' sighed Keith. 'We might as well get used to the idea right now.'

The fête lasted for roughly twenty-five minutes before the storm clouds gathered, and the whole event was rained off. Laura managed to spend four pounds on a tombola in which she won nothing, a paperback book she would probably never read, and a hopelessly shaky venture on the wiggly wire where a bell rang when you touched it with your travelling loop.

As the rain beat down, and people scurried to gather their wares and run for shelter, there was a commotion in the middle of the green. 'Call an ambulance!' came a carrying voice, bringing Laura to a sudden halt as she tried to find cover.

Turning quickly, she saw a man lying stretched out on the wet grass, and two or three people kneeling at his side. Without thinking, she rushed to join them.

'It's his heart!' cried a young woman. 'Oh, somebody, help him!'

Several people were clutching mobile phones, looking at each other to ascertain who would actually make the 999 call. Laura crouched over the man, her first aid training automatically asserting itself.

No pulse, no sign of breathing. Poor colour, and unresponsive pupils. 'I'm afraid —' she began, before Keith joined them and interrupted.

'Marie,' he said, addressing the distraught young woman, 'what happened?'

Laura looked again at the victim, and realised it was the angry father of Malcolm Sutton. She had not noticed him during her tour of the stalls, and had forgotten all about the family squabble she had witnessed.

'He's been feeling ill all day,' said his daughter, looking from face to face as people clustered round. 'I took him to The Holly Tree after Malcolm went off in the car, but he said he wanted to be outside. He thought he might breathe more easily. Then he just sort of – collapsed.' Her face was tragic, as if this was the final blow in a long list of disasters. Her wet hair hung lank around her face, increasing the impression of calamity.

'I'm afraid it doesn't look very good,' Laura managed to warn her.

'The ambulance won't be long,' said a man in the crowd.

'But somebody should be doing something,' said the desperate Marie. 'Mouth-to-mouth, or something.'

'I'm afraid…' said Laura again, loosening the man's collar, and placing a hand over his failed heart, '…it's rather late for any of that.'

'My God!' said Keith, finally realising the truth. 'You surely don't mean…?'

'There's no heartbeat,' said Laura. 'And it's already been three or four minutes at least. I'm ever so sorry, but…'

'He's dead,' supplied Marie, suddenly calm. 'Isn't he?'

'I'm afraid so,' nodded Laura.

Marie Sutton took a few steps back. Her hands were clasped together. 'He knew this would happen. He even made a new will, only two days ago. Because of Malcolm, you see…' She looked round, and her eyes locked onto Harriet Luke, standing a few feet away. 'He was so angry with Malcolm that he wrote him out of his will.'

Harriet met Marie's eyes, every bit as stricken by the afternoon's events. 'He won't come back, you know – not even for the funeral,' she said warningly.

'I know,' Marie nodded. 'And I'm glad. We're well rid of him. This is all his fault!'

All at once, the siren of an ambulance could be heard in the distance. Laura got to her feet, only to find herself face to face with Mr Danvers, the local squire and historian. He was looking at Marie Sutton fixedly.

'Terrible, terrible,' he muttered. 'Poor old Sutton.' Then he turned his gaze onto Harriet Luke. 'Well, well, well,' he added.

Chapter Two

Rosemary Boxer drove her elderly Land Rover into the hotel car park, where it was suddenly desperately conspicuous amongst all the BMWs and Saabs. Even the Discoveries and Shoguns were in a completely different social league. 'You'd have thought people with an interest in the environment might drive something more modest,' she muttered to herself.

To her relief, she found the hotel itself was a lot less intimidating. Embellished with bits of trellis and pot plants in the foyer, it had a sprawling ground floor, which led the guests from a lounge area, via the bar, to the dining section. All very open plan and relaxed, she decided. Long corridors of identically unmemorable rooms filled another chunk of the ground floor, as well as two further storeys above. In the information pack that Rosemary was clutching, a brochure informed her that there were over three hundred guestrooms and four conference rooms.

The girl at the reception desk smiled welcomingly, and asked for her name.

'Boxer, Rosemary.'

The keyboard was tapped, and her room identified. 'Will you be wanting a wake up call? Newspaper? There's internet connection in the room, and the TV is Pay As You View. Ninety-nine channels.' The spiel poured from her lips without passing her brain. Rosemary merely shook her head wordlessly.

In the room she had a hot shower and changed into a smart outfit that she had packed with unprecedented care, to avoid creases. It felt tight and strange after such a long time spent in jeans and sloppy sweatshirts. There was to be a welcoming speech in the Apricot Conference Room before the evening meal. And then, halfway through the next morning, Rosemary would be called upon to deliver a paper on 'Fungal Infections and Climate Change'.

'But why me?' she had wailed, when Professor Henry Owens had phoned her to request that she speak. 'I left all that nearly two years ago.'

'Because we wanted a fresh face, and somebody with a bit of passion. I know it's a subject you care about, and you can't tell me you've forgotten it all.'

'I think I have,' she said doubtfully.

'Well, you've got eight weeks to do your homework. I can recommend a few good websites, and there was a brilliant article in *Nature* last month. It's rather well paid, I might add.'

She had been fairly easily persuaded after that. The subject was, in fact, well within her comfort zone, as the Professor would say. She had noticed an increase in fungal damage in plants over the past year or so, and wondered whether it could be as a result of the warmer, damper climate that much of the British Isles seemed to be experiencing. If she could find some statistics and illustrations, she thought she might manage to assemble a reasonable presentation.

'I can't fill more than an hour, though,' she'd warned.

'No problem,' said the Professor. 'I'll send you an information pack.' Which, to his credit, he had done within the week.

Rosemary had spent almost all her working life as a college lecturer. She was used to standing in front of audiences, trying to capture their attention while conveying information. Students, however, were very different from an international collection of top experts, all with their own agendas and priorities. There were still people, even in important scientific posts, who did not believe in global warming. There were some who predicted an imminent ice age, which was only being staved off by carbon dioxide emissions – leading to the logical conclusion that the more humankind heated the planet, the better. They, Rosemary surmised, were probably the owners of the monster four-by-fours out in the car park.

All of which meant that she was scared. Reading through her speech, it seemed hopelessly amateurish and thin. She wouldn't be telling them anything they didn't already know. Who was she, after all? Just a jobbing gardener who had dropped out of the academic world and really had forgotten a great deal in the process.

She went down to the reception that would start the

proceedings, knowing she would feel even worse after meeting some of the people who were to be her audience next day.

It was every bit as bad as she'd feared. About ninety per cent male, middle-aged, serious, the gathered delegates seemed to form a solid wall of intimidation when Rosemary walked into the Apricot Room. It felt as if every one of them looked at her, as she slipped into a seat at the end of a row near the back, for no other reason than that she was female. She knew there were plenty of women in the world of plant pathology – it was just that even now they found it difficult to get away for weekend conferences. Weekends were precious oases of time for most of them where you caught up with sleep and shopping and washing and then some more sleep.

The podium seemed to be a long way away, and she tried to imagine herself standing there, striving to avoid total humiliation as she showed them pictures of phytophthera and echtomycorhizals and told them earnestly that she had personally encountered instances of such infestations in English gardens over the past year.

The opening speech, by Professor Owens himself, was short and unexpectedly entertaining. People laughed and began to seem more human. Then, with an almost unseemly haste, they got up and made for the bar.

Suddenly Rosemary was confronted by a familiar face. 'Professor Hashim!' she cried, almost flinging herself at him. 'How wonderful to see you!' Then she remembered that he was a world authority on plant diseases, and would be witness to her pathetic performance in the morning. 'But – you should be doing the fungus talk, not me.'

'Not at all,' said the handsome bearded academic. 'In fact, it was I who suggested you to Henry.'

Rosemary stared at him, feeling a painful mixture of pride and anger. 'Did you?' she spluttered.

They had been together at conferences before, over the years. In fact, there had been one memorable occasion when one thing had led to another, and they had become rather more than fellow delegates. The memory returned to Rosemary in a flood, making her blush. Was that why he'd engineered her presence here now? Was he hoping for a repeat?

Evidently not. 'Come here, my dear,' he said, reaching for one of the few other women in the place. 'Meet my old friend Miss Boxer. Rosemary, this is my wife, Jasmine.'

Jasmine Hashim was oriental, young and overwhelmingly beautiful. She also looked rather clever. Rosemary held out her hand as steadily as she could.

'Pleased to meet you,' she said.

'And don't think she's here only as an appendage,' said the Professor. 'Her paper on "Sustainable Methods of Land Irrigation" comes directly after yours.'

'Gosh!' said Rosemary weakly. 'That sounds fascinating.'

'I hope to make it interesting,' said the young woman in a clear businesslike voice, before taking her husband's arm possessively. 'I think we might go in to dinner now. I see people are beginning to move.'

Amir Hashim gave Rosemary a look that shouted 'It was nice with you, but see how much better I've done for myself now' and allowed himself to be escorted away by his lovely wife. Rosemary watched them go with a pang. They might at least have suggested she take a place at the same table.

As it was, she spent the meal between two biochemists who spoke across her and found fault with the food. They managed not to ask her who she was, or what her area of interest might be, but when forcing themselves to address a few words to her, seemed to assume that she must have been sent by some obscure institution to learn what she could. A younger man with floppy fair hair, on the far side of the table, raised her spirits only slightly when he sent amused glances across to her. The room was much too noisy and the table far too wide for any conversation to take place between them.

As soon as possible, she escaped to her room, and looked again at her lecture notes. At least, she told herself, by this time tomorrow, it'll all be forgotten. The astonishing Jasmine Hashim would have obliterated all memory of Rosemary Boxer.

* * *

On the whole, it went rather better than she had feared. Two minutes into the presentation her hands stopped shaking, and her voice lost its terrified squeak. The listeners appeared to be absorbed in what she had to tell them, and at least half of them laughed at a slightly forced joke she made towards the end.

Then came the questions. The first two or three were merely confirming her perception that fungal infestations in indigenous species were indisputably on the increase. Then a large bearded man challenged her findings, proposing that the fluctuations in temperature were simply random, and scarcely significant. 'After all, the Romans grew grapes in the north of England,' he said. Rosemary had expected something along these lines, replying blandly that by the time absolute certainty had been reached, it would probably be too late to rectify the situation.

Then another hand went up, and a man asked, 'So – what do you propose we do about it?'

'Global warming, you mean?' Rosemary asked.

'No. Increased levels of fungal diseases. What's the remedy?'

'Well – fungicides, mainly,' Rosemary said, trying to see him more clearly in the sea of faces. 'And isolation of affected plant populations.'

'Wouldn't it be preferable to research ways of making the plants themselves more resistant?'

'Well,' Rosemary gave this some rapid thought. 'Of course, we would normally expect them to adapt and become resistant. The trouble is, this all seems to be happening rather quickly and they are unlikely to be able to keep up.'

As the man spoke again, she realised that he was the one who had watched her across the dining table, the previous evening. 'You're admitting that there is no solution,' he accused, rising a little in his seat. 'It's a counsel of despair. There you are, telling us that all kinds of tropical-style infestations are going to decimate our trees and crops, but the only hope is that somehow the plants will fight back by themselves.'

A restless muttering was swelling in the hall. Rosemary had a feeling they were agreeing with her questioner.

'Not at all,' she countered angrily. 'It all comes down to proper management. Horticulturalists and others will be working to maximise the chances of every affected species. Besides,' she added, 'that isn't what I'm here to talk about. All I've been trying to do is present you with an up-to-date picture of the current situation.'

Another man shouted out, 'So what do you suggest?' obviously aimed at the questioner.

At this, Rosemary's interrogator stood up, and twisted to look behind him. 'To me it's obvious,' he said. 'We have to give the plants much more proactive help. We have to establish extensive breeding programmes, control the habitat, and create totally adverse conditions for the fungi.' He stopped abruptly, leaving Rosemary with the strong impression that he could have said a lot more if he'd chosen to.

Still annoyed, Rosemary gave him a long straight look, before saying in a ringing voice, 'That sounds to me as if you think human beings have infinite power. We can't play God, much as we might like to.'

The look on the young man's face made her shiver. Although he did not speak again, his expression seemed to say, 'Oh can't we?'

Seconds later, the Chairman announced that there was no time for further questions, and there would be a short break for coffee before returning to hear the renowned Director of Ecological Science from Kuala Lumpur University, Miss Jasmine Shia Luang.

Rosemary waited until the hall was almost empty before gathering her notes and pictures together. She had decided to skip coffee, and take her things back to her room, before returning to hear the next presentation. Her mind was blank with relief. She might even be able to enjoy the rest of the conference now. But she was headed off before she could make her escape.

'I'm sorry if I sounded aggressive just then,' said a familiar voice. 'I didn't really mean to.'

It was her questioner. She smiled graciously at him. 'That's all right,' she said. 'All part of the job.'

He held out his hand in a boyish gesture. 'Shake on it?' he

coaxed. 'No hard feelings?'

She took the hand, which was dry and very much alive. A handshake could tell such a lot about the person, she mused. This one was strong, not too competitive, and pleasantly warm. She looked into his face with fresh interest.

'Will you sit next to me at lunch?' he asked, again with a little-boy appeal that was hard to resist. 'I promise to be more interesting than those stuffed shirts last night.'

'All right then,' she agreed. 'If you also promise not to argue about fungicides.'

'I do,' he said seriously. 'I promise to avoid all mention of plants, absolutely.'

He kept his promise rather too comprehensively, quickly embarking on questions about her outside interests, her childhood and travel experiences – seeming to know unerringly just which topics made for friendly and stimulating conversation. Rosemary went along with him happily enough, though perversely hoping to discover more about his work and his ideas about climate change.

His name badge identified him as Redland Linton from Knussens, a well-known company producing medications and remedies for a range of human ailments, all based on natural ingredients. Rosemary tried to reconcile what she knew of his company with the implications of his assertions after her talk. She had taken him to be advocating aggressive breeding programmes, habitat control and comprehensive human intervention, whereas Knussens were at pains to stress their ecological credentials, with their well-known slogan of 'Nature's Way'. Perhaps, she thought, it was not such a conflict as she assumed, but more a difference in emphasis. After all, everybody accepted that the ecology could not safely be left entirely to its own devices. The folksy image of Knussens operatives wandering through the rain forest with hand-woven collecting baskets, gathering leaves and seeds, which featured in some of their commercials, was obviously far from accurate. It was a successful multinational enterprise, and therefore inevitably using technology and sound business practice.

Despite her earlier demand that they avoid the subject, she found herself eager to quiz Linton about the philosophy behind his company, and his own standpoint. He had clearly felt strongly about her presentation and she would have liked to understand his reasons.

But she was never to get the chance. A tap on her shoulder spun her round to find one of the hotel staff leaning discreetly towards her. 'Miss Boxer?' she asked. 'I'm sorry to disturb you, but there's a message for you.'

Wildly, Rosemary thought of all the things that could be important enough to drag her from her conference. The obvious one was her mother – had she collapsed, or had an accident?

'Oh!' she gasped. 'What is it?'

'I hope we got it right,' said the girl, handing her a slip of paper. 'Sasha's on reception at the moment, and her English still isn't too great.'

Rosemary read the scribbled words with difficulty.

Pleese come back as soon as u can. Urgent commission, start Mon morning, Bafflettn Villig. The vicar my cousin. Laura.

'Bafflettn Villig?' Rosemary said.

Redford Linton leaned shamelessly over her shoulder to have a read. 'There's a place called Baffington, only a few miles from where I work,' he suggested helpfully. 'Maybe it's that.'

'I suppose I'll find out soon enough,' she sighed. 'Laura did visit a cousin last year who was a vicar. It must be the same chap. I don't remember where he lives, though.' She looked at the hotel girl, still standing to attention behind her. 'Thank you,' she said.

'Does this mean you'll be checking out today?' asked the girl.

Rosemary thought quickly. 'No,' she said, decisively. 'I'll stay tonight, as planned, and leave first thing tomorrow morning. I'm not missing the Grand Dinner for anything.'

'Thank you, madam,' said the girl.

The dinner was a lot more enjoyable than the previous evening's meal had been. Rosemary had made the acquaintance of a number of people by the end of the day, besides Redland Linton. One was a man called David Billington, whose shaggy hair and creased trousers marked him as a genuine ecology enthusiast, working outdoors and very much aware of many of the more urgent issues.

'I did like your talk,' he told her. 'And the way you handled the Knussens chap.'

'Thanks,' she acknowledged. 'Actually, I had lunch with him, and he's really quite sweet.'

'Ah, good,' said David Billington, making an elaborate show of taking her point. 'You won't be needing my backing then, if he picks another fight with you.'

Rosemary laughed. 'I hope not. But he is a bit of a paradox,' she went on. 'I mean, Knussens are meant to be so pure and natural. He didn't sound quite that way to me.'

'That's what I thought.' David lowered his voice. 'But the word is, they're finding it harder and harder to sustain the purity of their products. Or maybe I should say, they seem to be less and less inclined to try. It's a bit like organic farming – there's always such a huge temptation to cheat.'

Rosemary gave this some thought, but before she could reply, the conversation had moved on. Instead, she found herself wondering what she should pack for the mysterious commission Laura had landed them with, and where exactly Bafflettn might be.

By mutual agreement, Rosemary took the place next to Linton at the Grand Dinner, relieved to find that there was no pre-arranged seating order. She remembered with a brief pang the way she and Professor Hashim had sneaked into the empty dining room at their conference, hurriedly swapping name cards so they could be together. A degree of rather amusing chaos had ensued, when two people who had been feuding for decades suddenly found themselves adjacent.

Linton was good-looking, young, attentive, and Rosemary was flattered. She was also intrigued by a number of contradictions that were emerging. He clearly felt it was his turn to talk about himself, having given her the floor at lunch. He described travels to remote parts of south-east Asia and central America, where there were still countless plants that had never properly been analysed for their therapeutic potential. With her enthusiastic encouragement, he described some of his discoveries.

Then, having been interrupted by the arrival of the main course, he switched subjects completely, and went on to tell her about his brand new town house on an eighteenth-century wharf in Bristol which had been thoroughly refurbished, with all the latest technical gadgetry.

Rosemary enjoyed it all unreservedly. The feeling of lightness that followed the delivery of her talk had persisted all day. Linton was excellent company, even if he was talking so much about himself. In a short lull, she jumped in with a question about Knussens, and his exact role in the company. He shook his head. 'Oh, no,' he protested. 'I'm definitely not going to talk shop now. Although if you are happy to talk about plants, I'd love to hear just what it is that you do for a living now.'

With an easy good humour, she obliged, telling him how she and Laura had met by accident, at a moment when they were both at a crossroads in their lives. How they had shared a passion for gardening, as well as considerable skill. 'She does more of the hands-on stuff, usually, while I muck about with designs and microscopes and checking things on the computer.'

'You're the brains and she's the brawn,' he nodded.

Rosemary almost choked on the wine she had just sipped. Violently she shook her head. 'Gosh no. Laura's got far more brain than I have. She was a police officer in her twenties, and she's as sharp as a pruning knife when it comes to people. And I'm no slouch when it comes to the work – after all, a lot of it takes two pairs of hands, anyway. It's just – well, sometimes there's a natural division of labour, and that's when I come over all academic, and she rolls up her sleeves and shins up a tree.'

Linton laughed at the picture this presented. 'I think I get it now,' he said.

In the bar afterwards, David Billington reappeared, one eyebrow cocked in a silent question, when Linton had moved away to speak to another delegate. Rosemary giggled and let him buy her a Drambuie, before returning to her solitary soulless room for an early night. Her last thoughts before drifting off to sleep were of Linton's strong warm handshake and his easy conversation, and what a welcome change it made, to be able to spend an evening in the company of a good-looking man.

Chapter Three

Two days later, Laura was once again standing outside the churchyard with the Reverend Keith Briggs, introducing him to Rosemary. 'It seems a long time since I was last here,' she said.

'Eleven months,' Keith said. 'I can't say that much has changed.'

'Funny the things you forget,' Laura said thoughtfully.

'Such as?' Rosemary asked.

'Well, I suppose I must have noticed this great straggling holly tree, but I have no recollection of it at all.' She looked up at the dark prickly mass that took up a lot of space between the pub and the churchyard.

'I don't see how you could miss it,' said Rosemary. 'And the name of the pub gives you quite a big clue, as well.'

'It's because of the yew tree,' Laura realised. 'It dominates everything. I swear it's grown since last year.'

Keith interrupted. 'Come and see the churchyard,' he urged them. 'I'm afraid you've got a daunting job ahead of you.'

'So – what brought this on?' Laura asked him. 'I don't remember you worrying about the churchyard last year.'

Keith sighed. 'It's all because of Franklin Danvers. I'm sure you remember him, don't you?'

'Oh, yes!' Laura agreed. 'I could never forget that tedious speech he made, while everybody stood around in the drizzle.'

'It sounds as if I've got quite a bit of catching up to do,' said Rosemary. 'Did you meet the entire village last time you were here?'

'Almost,' Laura nodded. 'Harriet Luke, Marie and Malcolm Sutton, the dreaded Danvers, and others whose names I didn't catch. Did Malcolm ever come back?' she asked Keith.

'Never mind all that now,' he said, almost dancing with impatience. 'We have to get on with the job. I'm sorry, but it's so urgent, you see. I really wanted you here a month ago.'

'Come on then,' said Laura. 'Show us the worst.'

'Oh, gosh!' breathed Rosemary, once they had pushed their way through the long grass just inside the lych-gate, and stood amongst the graves. The yew tree, with huge downward-drooping branches, formed a closed-in shadowy area all of its own. Nothing grew within several feet of it, the ground covered in dead needles that had fallen from its branches for decades, creating a springy mattress of barren ground.

Rosemary stood just outside the tree's curtilage. 'This is – well —' She gazed in awe at the seemingly vast area of overgrown land. 'It's so big,' she said. 'With more at the back of the church.'

'It's a jungle,' Keith admitted. 'But you can probably leave some of the long grass behind the church. Just clear the path that leads to the little gate.'

'You'd better show us,' Rosemary said. The vicar obligingly escorted them around the side of the church, where the main part of the churchyard stretched away to their left, and onto an almost invisible path that ran crookedly across a narrower patch of jungle. He pointed out a small gate.

'It isn't used very much,' he said. 'But it is useful as a short cut for the people who live in Goldfinch Lane. That includes Harriet. She comes this way quite often, and regularly complains about brambles across the path.'

'How on earth did it get like this?' Laura burst out. 'It can't have been touched for years.'

'It's all down to the multiple parish situation,' Keith explained. 'I know it's a disgrace, but there simply isn't time for that sort of maintenance work, with so many people to minister to. Things like tidying the churchyards always slip down to the bottom of the list. Even now, if it wasn't for Mr Danvers insisting…well, I should be grateful to him, of course. He's going to pay for most of it himself.'

They were retracing their steps, as Keith castigated himself for the condition of his churchyard. Laura found herself quite enjoying the swish of long grass against her legs, and the appearance of several wild flowers amongst the undergrowth. Finally they were standing once more beneath the enormous yew tree.

'Does all this have something to do with the Medieval Fayre?' asked Laura.

'Of course it does – look!' sang out Rosemary, pointing to a notice pinned to the trunk of the tree. She read it out aloud: "Grand Baffington Medieval Fayre, June 25th to 27th. To include displays of archery, falconry, battle re-enactments and authentic contemporary comestibles. Costumes available for loan. Multiple venues, including the Village Green, Highview House, St Thomas's Church and the Glebe field. To conclude with a Grand Banquet on Sunday 27th in the Great Hall at Highview." Wow! That sounds very ambitious. Three days of jollifications.' She looked at Keith. 'Do I detect an enthusiast behind all this?'

Keith nodded. 'Franklin Danvers. He's potty about all things medieval. He writes books about the period, and goes on grand-scale re-enactments. He lives up there.' He pointed to the large house that Laura had admired on her last visit. 'He's even got an estate manager who's also an expert archer. They encourage each other.'

'It all sounds terribly English,' smiled Rosemary. 'And pretty good fun.'

Laura had gone quiet, one hand placed lightly on the bark of the yew tree. 'This is quite a specimen,' she murmured. 'Must be centuries old.' She shivered. 'I never like them, though. Yews, I mean. They call it the tree of death, you know. Full of bad omens.'

Keith and Rosemary both looked at her sceptically.

'It's a bit sick, if you ask me,' Rosemary observed. 'There's a lot of dead wood to cut away, if it's to survive much longer. And look at the rest of the place.' She swept a critical gaze around the churchyard. 'I don't want to be rude, but it really has been neglected, hasn't it.'

'First requirement is a herd of goats,' said Laura. 'They'd soon get the grass down for you. I suppose that would be how they dealt with it in earlier times.'

'Oh no!' Rosemary disagreed. 'Absolutely not. Quite the opposite, in fact. Every churchyard would have had a stone wall or stout hedge to enclose it, precisely to keep the animals out. They'd poison themselves, otherwise, eating the yew spines.

Although, oddly enough, the berries aren't poisonous at all.'

'Oh? I always thought the yews were planted in order to poison the animals, and teach them not to come into the sacred grounds,' said Keith. 'Am I being very ignorant?'

'A bit,' said Rosemary gently. 'The yews are symbolic, you see. Laura's right – they did stand for death, at least partly. But they date back before Christianity, marking sacred places of worship before churches were built on the same sites.'

'Steady on!' Laura pleaded. 'You're doing your lecturer act again.'

'No, no, it's fascinating,' Keith objected. 'I've already learned something.'

'This is all very good to hear – people discussing history,' came a voice from the lych-gate. 'Although I'm not sure any of you has quite got it right. Yew, you see, is the wood used for making longbows. And the English made the greatest use of that weapon in warfare. Only the English have the close association between churches and yew trees.'

A man stepped into view, and Laura recognised Franklin Danvers, who must have been standing quietly listening to them for some minutes. He was smiling widely, and looked very prosperous and pleased with himself. Something about his manner prompted her to argue with him.

'But —' she began. 'Wouldn't they need to fell the trees to make the bows? And why should the church especially be involved?'

'Well, perhaps it isn't quite as simple as I implied,' he conceded. 'I know there was a brisk import trade of yew from southern Europe, as well. Perhaps you'd introduce us, Keith?' he turned to the vicar.

'Yes, of course – although you might remember my cousin Laura Thyme, from last year?'

Danvers looked blank, not at all to Laura's surprise.

Keith stumbled on. 'So, this is Mr Franklin Danvers,' he told Rosemary. 'Franklin, this is Miss Rosemary Boxer, who works with Laura. They're just having a look at the job we've got lined up for them in here.'

'Quite a task, I'm afraid,' beamed Danvers. 'Do you think you can manage it in time?'

'Deadline June 25th, I see,' said Rosemary, squaring her shoulders. 'It's tight, given the state it's in, but I expect we can cope. Keith still has to explain exactly what he wants us to do.'

Franklin Danvers raised his eyebrows at Keith, who said hurriedly, 'Actually, Rosemary, it isn't so much me as Franklin who'll be doing that.'

'Oh.' Rosemary glanced at Laura. 'Sorry. We didn't realise.'

Danvers gave a reassuring laugh. 'Don't worry your head about it,' he said. 'Keith and I are in complete accord over the whole project. We both think it's a dreadful shame that the churchyard's potential as a key focal point for the village has been so neglected.'

'It's certainly enormous,' Rosemary murmured.

'And Keith told me why, when I was here last year,' Laura said brightly. 'All to do with the Black Death, I gather.' She looked to Danvers for his confirmation that she was right. He nodded approvingly, and she went on, 'This Medieval Fayre is all your pigeon, then? I remember you mentioning it last year.'

'It's been a year in the planning,' he nodded. 'The whole village is to be involved, as well as some specialists from outside. We're really going to put Baffington on the map. You won't be familiar with the Battle of Baffington, I assume?'

'Well, no,' Laura and Rosemary said in unison.

'Time to remind everyone of it, then,' he said, rubbing his hands, and showing no sign of hearing the stifled sigh that emerged from the Reverend Keith Briggs. Danvers went on to inform Rosemary that he had an old print of the churchyard, showing it as it had been almost two centuries earlier. 'I know we're aiming for a medieval atmosphere, but there are some pleasing details you might want to replicate, despite it being somewhat anachronistic,' he said, obscurely. At their puzzled looks, he added impatiently, 'The print is from 1804. My Fayre is essentially fourteenth and fifteenth century. Quite a discrepancy, I admit.'

'Oh – right,' said Rosemary, exchanging a glance with Laura, both of them having noted the 'my'. 'Thanks very much.'

'Think nothing of it. Now I must be off. So much to do, you

see.' And he hurried away, leaving Keith to continue their tour of the churchyard.

As they finished their inspection, another familiar figure met them on the road outside. 'Oh, hello!' said Laura. 'It's Harriet, isn't it?'

'Nice to see you again,' the young woman smiled. 'I hope we haven't landed you with an impossible task. I'm afraid we're a bit embarrassed by the state we've let things get into. Keith probably explained that we just don't have the resources for proper maintenance at the moment. If it hadn't been for Franklin's generosity, we'd never have got around to it at all. Would we, Keith?'

If anything, Harriet was more attractive than Laura remembered. Her curly dark hair set off perfect skin and big brown eyes, creating an impression of real beauty. She seemed a lot more relaxed and cheerful than she had the previous summer, as well as considerably more friendly towards the vicar. Laura found herself hoping that in the process of recovering from the broken relationship with Malcolm Sutton Harriet might have turned to Keith. It might be an old-fashioned idea, but Laura felt he could definitely do with a wife, and Harriet was an obvious candidate.

Keith hastened to agree with her remark about Danvers. 'I was just saying the same thing,' he confirmed. 'Now, why don't we all pop into The Holly Tree for some tea?'

Laura had explained to Rosemary, before they arrived, that Keith's home was some distance from Baffington, situated as it was in another of his village parishes. Where he might normally have invited them in for a drink, he was constrained to use the local hostelry instead. But they had reckoned without Harriet.

'Oh, no,' she said, quickly. 'Come to my cottage for a bit, if you like. We should probably talk through the timetable while you're here, anyway.'

Having accepted her offer gratefully, the little group walked down the village street to the narrow lane that led to Harriet's cottage. Rosemary exclaimed at the prettiness of the village, as they went.

'It's been a real community effort,' Keith agreed. 'I must say, they have all thrown themselves into this Fayre with a will.'

'It's fun, Keith,' Harriet said, slightly reproachfully. 'I think we're all enjoying it far more than we expected to. It's bringing the whole village together.'

'I don't think poor Marie Sutton would agree with you,' Keith said.

Laura was quick to pick up this reference to the sad-looking girl who had witnessed her father's sudden death at the last village fête. 'Why? What's the matter with her?'

Rosemary, only half listening, hung back, to admire a particularly spectacular cottage garden between The Holly Tree and the lane leading to Harriet's home. A mass of golden marjoram had been used to splendid effect near the front door, which had Rosemary fishing in her shoulder-bag for pencil and pad to jot it down as a design idea for the future.

The other three moved on, still discussing Marie Sutton, leaving Rosemary behind for a few moments. As she made her jotted notes, a minicab drove up to the door of The Holly Tree and a man got out. Rosemary merely gave him a casual glance, noting the briefcase and single travel bag. Must be some sort of salesman, she concluded, inattentively. Then she watched as he stood still on the threshold of the pub and scanned the village green and surrounding houses. It seemed to Rosemary that he cast a particularly poisonous glance at the imposing Highview House, home of Franklin Danvers.

Then Laura called her, and she hurried to catch up with the others, forgetting the new arrival completely.

Tea was a basic and rather rushed affair, with Harriet obviously juggling a thousand and one tasks, her mind full of lists and meetings and obligations. 'I see you still work for the vicar and the squire,' said Laura.

'That's right,' Harriet nodded. 'And they've been fighting over me more than usual in the past few weeks. Don't forget, Keith,' she said to the vicar, 'we're due at archery practice in ten minutes. Lyall won't like it if we're late.'

'Archery?' Laura raised her eyebrows. 'The real thing, you mean?'

'Absolutely,' Keith told her. 'Mr Danvers has got a marvellous collection of longbows and all the paraphernalia that goes with it. Quivers and gloves as well as dozens of arrows. All totally authentic. That man never does anything by halves, and never runs out of energy. He makes me feel completely inadequate, most of the time.' He sighed.

'Is Lyall the estate manager?' asked Laura.

'That's right. He's a useful chap, very willing to turn a hand to anything. I think Danvers rescued him somehow. He's rather shy and a bit of a loner, but he's been earning people's respect recently.'

'Rescued him?' Laura echoed. 'That sounds very romantic. Like Heathcliff being fished out of the gutters of Liverpool.'

'Well, I don't think it was quite like that,' Keith smiled. 'Lyall was in the army, and after his discharge, he wasn't sure what to do next. Danvers meets a lot of different people on his re-enactments, and Lyall was his spear-bearer or something, a year or so ago. They got talking, and Franklin offered him a job.'

Harriet interrupted impatiently. 'It wasn't a bit romantic,' she said. 'Lyall had recently left the army after eighteen years, and he needed a job. Franklin needed a manager. It was all perfectly straightforward. I should know – I had to deal with all the tax and insurance and salaries. He's got all the right qualifications, as it happens.'

Keith held up his hands. 'I stand corrected,' he said. 'I didn't mean to impugn the good Lyall's character,' he added mildly. 'As I said before, he's a thoroughly useful person to have around.'

They spent a few minutes over the tea and biscuits, which Harriet produced almost instantly. Rosemary and Laura had the impression that they had walked into a situation of controlled chaos, the Fayre deadline rushing towards the whole village like a tidal wave. It also seemed as if Harriet Luke, rather than Franklin Danvers, was responsible for the actual practical organisation.

'Now, we must be off,' Harriet announced briskly, the moment the last teacup was drained. 'I suggest you two come along and watch – it's on the Glebe field, up the hill past the church. That's assuming you don't want to get started on the churchyard today?'

'We should probably have a look at that old picture Mr Danvers mentioned, before we do anything else,' Rosemary decided. 'Will he be at the archery?'

'Sure to be,' said Harriet. 'He wants to pick out the best shots. There's to be a contest on the day, you see. Like Robin Hood challenging the Sheriff of Nottingham.' She paused, and then laughed. 'Except Franklin hates Robin Hood because he doesn't think any of the legends are real history. I suggest you don't mention the name in his hearing during the practice.'

Harriet and Keith hurried off, leaving Rosemary and Laura to make their own way, after another good long look at the churchyard.

'What do you think?' Laura asked, as she stood beneath the huge yew tree.

'What do I think about what?'

'Everything. Keith, Harriet, Danvers, Baffington.'

'Oh. Well, I think your Keith ought to snap the lovely Harriet up quickly. It's a mystery to me why she's still single, with those looks. And she does seem quite fond of him.'

Laura laughed. 'My very thoughts, just a little while ago. But tell me – why is it you're always match-making, when you've never tied the knot yourself?'

'Good question,' Rosemary pulled a rueful face. 'I suppose I just want to see everybody happy.'

'Nonsense,' Laura chuckled. 'You're just trying to get everybody neat and tidy like one of our gardens. No straggling, no uninvited intruders. So, what else? About Baffington, I mean?'

'I think it's all going to be quite good fun. I can't wait for the Fayre, even if it does mean we'll have to work our socks off to get the job done in time. You have to respect that Danvers chap, knowing so much, and mobilising everybody to participate. He seems positively inspiring.'

'Hmm,' Laura said dubiously. 'You might think differently once you've heard one of his lectures. I'm not sure he's completely sane, to be honest.'

Rosemary shook her head. 'He's just a typically English obsessive. We're sure to learn a lot about the Middle Ages. That can't be bad, can it?'

'I suppose not. But the whole place still has a creepy feel to me. Probably because of what happened last year, with that poor Mr Sutton dying before my eyes, and his horrid son being so aggressive. I told you about him, didn't I?'

'The one Harriet Luke was seeing? Who went off in some sort of rage? I wonder if anybody's seen him here since.'

'We can ask Mr Danvers, when we go to look at his picture. What about this churchyard, eh? Seems a shame, somehow, to chop down all this jungle. It's like the forest around the Sleeping Beauty at the moment. Look at those brambles!'

'You're not suggesting we leave them, I hope.' Rosemary was severe. 'Brambles are the devil's work, and you know it.'

'I'm not so sure about that,' Laura demurred. 'I think the yew tree has a prior claim to that description.'

'You really don't like the poor thing, do you?'

Laura shook her head. 'It's dark and gloomy, and casts a very big shadow. It's also poisonous, and half dead. No, I don't like it one little bit.'

'Oh, that's mean of you. It'll look wonderful when it's been trimmed and shaped a bit. I think it has real character. Now – let's go and find the Glebe field and see how the archers are shaping up.'

Chapter Four

There were several villagers armed with longbows, lined up facing a row of targets, when Laura and Rosemary arrived. A dark man with a strong neck and broad shoulders was standing behind Harriet, as she familiarised herself with a longbow.

'That must be Lyall,' said Laura.

'You didn't meet him last year, then?' Rosemary asked.

'No, he wasn't here then. Rather handsome, in a brooding sort of way, don't you think?'

Rosemary cocked her head appraisingly. 'Not really my type,' she pronounced. 'He looks moody to me.'

Gordon Lyall was instructing Harriet carefully. 'That's right,' he said. 'Hold it tight, but don't clench your fingers. Like this —' He lifted his own bow, and fitted an arrow to the bowstring. With a fluid movement, he turned sideways, pulled back the string and sent the arrow whizzing into the golden heart of a target several yards away. It landed with an impressively powerful thwack that made Laura think for the first time in her life about what it might be like to be on the receiving end of such a weapon. Some of the people clapped.

Harriet had been watching her instructor's hands, and scrupulously arranged her own in imitation. Lyall made a small correction, folding his own fingers over hers for a moment. 'Take it slowly,' he murmured. 'Get your sight line, hold the string as far back as you can, feel the tension. Feel that arrow wanting to hit the gold. Then, just open your fingers, and off she flies.'

The arrow suited action to words, and Harriet's first attempt struck the outer circle of the target, but didn't embed itself. 'Not bad,' said Lyall. 'Try again. Pull back further this time.'

Harriet used all six arrows in the quiver on her back, each shot better than the last.

Rosemary and Laura were entranced. 'It's poetry,' sighed Rosemary. 'I had no idea it could be so – I don't know. What's the word?'

'Magical?'

'Not quite. Visceral, I think is what I mean. The archer and the bow all one entity. Lyall's a fantastic teacher, isn't he. So calm and encouraging.'

They followed closely as Lyall moved down the line to the vicar, who had been given a slightly larger bow than Harriet's, and was wearing a rather comical pair of leather gauntlets. 'Take them off,' Lyall ordered him. 'You need to be able to feel what you're doing.'

Rather to Laura's surprise, Keith made almost as good an archer as Harriet had done. In the course of his first six arrows, he developed a graceful sureness of movement that was a delight to watch.

'Very good indeed,' Lyall approved, taking in Harriet as well as Keith. 'At this rate, we'll easily beat those Frenchies.'

Franklin Danvers, standing nearby, smiled approvingly. 'We'd better,' he said. 'If we're to keep the history accurate.'

Laura drifted closer to him. 'Exactly which battle will you be re-enacting?' she asked him.

Danvers took a deep breath. 'The Battle of Baffington, of course.' He raised an arm and pointed westwards, where a small hill was covered with trees. 'The site is over there, as far as I can ascertain. It took place in the early stages of the Wars of the Roses, in the fifteenth century, and was in reality no more than a minor skirmish. There are almost no reliable records, but I have managed to discover a few salient facts.'

'Fifteenth century?' Laura repeated, trying to keep abreast of the various dates Danvers tossed around.

He nodded impatiently. 'Not a lot of choice, to be honest. The fact is there were no battles on English soil between the eleventh and the fifteenth centuries. Plenty in Scotland, one or two in Wales, but nothing in England.'

Laura tried to look receptive. 'That's really interesting,' she said. 'I'm afraid my knowledge of that period is dreadfully hazy.'

Danvers sighed. 'You're not the only one. Do you know, the general level of ignorance shocks me, it really does. Hardly anybody these days can distinguish between the Hundred Years War and the Wars of the Roses.'

'Shocking,' said Laura faintly, before managing to change the subject. 'Oh, look, somebody else is having an archery lesson now.'

Lyall's attentions had moved to a young woman who Laura recognised as Marie Sutton. She held her bow rigidly, her shoulders hunched and face screwed up. 'Just pull back steadily,' said the instructor, in a low soothing voice. 'Keep going. Pull…more…'

Suddenly his pupil took her hand from the bowstring, and let the bow drop by her side. 'I can't do it!' she cried. 'It's too dangerous. Somebody might get killed.'

'Seems a bit of a wimp to me,' muttered Rosemary, to which Laura nodded cautious agreement.

Franklin Danvers stepped up to Marie, and put a hand on her arm, reassuringly. 'Don't worry, Marie, you don't have to do it if you don't want to. But honestly, it's all perfectly safe. Lyall has it all under control. As long as everyone does as he says, there isn't the slightest danger.'

Lyall hesitated for a moment, his eyes on Marie's face, plainly checking that she was all right, and not about to throw another wobbly. Then he moved along the line, explaining to a middle-aged woman in a tweed skirt about a thing called the 'nock' which was used to hold the arrow steady on the bowstring before it was fired. 'Be careful with them,' he cautioned. 'They fall off very easily, and get lost. And that would be a shame, because they're all handmade out of horn.'

Once everybody had had a turn, Lyall suggested a repeat practice, in their own time, using the arrows they had each been allocated. Once again, Harriet and Keith both showed a natural talent, hitting their targets even more centrally with every try.

Franklin Danvers moved away from Marie Sutton, who had not seemed anxious for his attention, and strolled over to Laura and Rosemary. 'When this is over, perhaps you'd like to come up to the house, and see that print I mentioned? It's only three or four minutes' walk from here. Shall we say in about forty-five minutes? I've got something I need to do first, but I'll be ready for you by then.'

'We'll be there,' said Rosemary cheerily, as Danvers began to depart at a brisk pace.

They stayed until the end of the practice, enjoying the way the villagers were gaining so rapidly in skill and confidence. When the time was up, Lyall explained that everyone was permitted to take their longbow home with them for practice, on condition they obeyed the basic rules which he proceeded to recount. 'Never aim at a living creature. Not even a bird. Always collect your arrows again. Keep the bow dry. I'll see you all again this time next week, and I'll want a full set of bows and arrows returned to me then. Well done, everybody. You're an excellent bunch of archers.'

'Bunch,' Rosemary whispered. 'Is that the technical term, then?'

Laura merely snorted.

The Danvers residence was an imposing if asymmetrical mansion, clearly assuming the role of 'the Big House' within the village.

'Very nice,' Rosemary said approvingly. 'Looks pretty old, as well. How long have you lived here?'

'I bought it ten years ago, in an awful state. When I embarked on the restoration, I realised the central part is fourteenth century,' he boasted. 'With no less than four additions at subsequent points in time. It's ended up with tremendous character, don't you think?'

'Definitely,' said Laura, eyeing the odd-shaped gable at one end. 'Rather like Gormenghast, in fact.'

'Hmm?' queried Danvers, absently. 'Where's that?'

'It's in a book,' said Laura. 'It doesn't matter.'

But she had underestimated Franklin Danvers, who clearly didn't like to think there was something he hadn't read. 'Oh? What sort of book?'

'A kind of fantasy, I suppose. By Mervyn Peake. It's terribly funny. I'm surprised Keith hasn't mentioned it. It used to be one of his great favourites.'

'Oh, fantasy.' Danvers dismissed this with barely disguised contempt.

He ushered them into a spacious hall, with a minstrels' gallery projecting from one end. The whole area was lined with displays worthy of any museum. Stands of halberds and pikes and other sharp-edged weapons stood on all sides. Dozens of arrows were mounted on vertical boards, all with businesslike metal tips. Laura idly fingered one, pulling back quickly when she realised how sharp it was. As well as weapons, there was armour, costumes and very old books.

'My goodness!' breathed Rosemary. 'This is amazing. And I suppose this will be where you hold the Great Banquet at the end of the Fayre?'

'That's right,' he nodded.

'But how will you clear a space?' Laura wondered.

Danvers bridled slightly. 'Harriet has all that side of things under control. Some things will be moved up to the gallery, and the rest ranged along two of the walls.'

Rosemary renewed her murmurs of admiration, worried that Danvers was becoming irritated by questions concerning practical details. 'All this stuff must be extremely valuable,' she said.

He shrugged. 'It's all very precious to me, of course,' he said. 'But my interest is really much more than just a hobby. I admit the hardware has started to get a bit out of control, although it's all crucial for my researches too.' He indicated a small stack of books on a central table, which Rosemary politely went to examine. They all had Franklin Danvers' name on the cover, and dealt with medieval battles.

Laura joined them, reading the titles of the books aloud. 'Crecy, Poitiers, Agincourt – well, well, you do know your subject, don't you!'

The man fingered the books affectionately. 'This is the best,' he said, patting the one on the Battle of Poitiers. 'I had some excellent assistance with it.' He opened the book at the front, to show the dedication.

Rosemary read it aloud. '"For Harriet, with grateful thanks for your invaluable help." That's very nice. She must have been pleased.'

'She was quite overwhelmed,' he said. 'But it's no less than she deserved. She developed a real commitment to this book, which was tremendously encouraging for me, of course.'

'It's always good to work as a team,' agreed Rosemary, rather vaguely. 'So you'd describe yourself as a military historian, would you?'

'Actually, I've started to drift away from the military side, and have a new project in mind.' He was plainly overflowing with the need to divulge his next enterprise. Rosemary made an interested sound.

'I thought I might establish a Medieval Museum at Brockett's Farm, with a large section devoted to agriculture. It would be the perfect setting, and the visitors would really put Baffington on the map. There'd be a falconry centre, and a lot of the acreage would be farmed according to medieval methods. It's ambitious, I know, but I'm really fired up about it.'

'Brockett's Farm,' echoed Laura. 'I know that name. Isn't it where the Suttons live?'

'It's where Marie Sutton lives,' he corrected. 'She's all on her own now. You remember her father died, of course?'

'I certainly do,' Laura said.

'Well, her brother never came back, not even for the funeral, and hasn't been heard of since. Marie inherited the farm outright, anyway – luckily for her, the old man changed his will only days before the heart attack. She's been dithering about what to do, ever since. Her obvious course of action would be to sell it. There are three hundred acres, including a mature woodland consisting mostly of yew trees. It's worth enough to give her security for life, if she invested wisely, and as things are, she's really not managing to keep up with all the work.'

Laura remembered something Malcolm Sutton had said to her, the previous year. 'But I thought she loved the place,' she protested. 'And hasn't it been in the family for centuries?'

'I'm afraid the poor girl can't afford to be sentimental. There's very little money coming in, and no prospect of an improvement. The reality is that she has very little choice.'

'So you've made her an offer for it, have you?' Rosemary put in.

'Several times,' he said, with obvious irritation. 'And I never get a straight answer. The uncertainty is making things very difficult, I don't mind telling you.'

'I suppose she's been hoping Malcolm would show up again, and at least help her to make the right decision,' Laura suggested. Danvers merely tutted at the mention of Marie's rebellious brother.

'He'd be within his rights to contest the will, I should think,' said Laura, going off at a tangent. 'He must be feeling very cheated, surely?'

'Nobody knows what he's feeling, but there's not a soul in Baffington who wants him back.'

'Not even Harriet Luke?' asked Laura, innocently.

Danvers bridled. 'Absolutely not. The swine broke the poor girl's heart. Why would she ever want to see him again?'

'Oh, well,' said Laura vaguely. 'You know what women are like.'

Danvers made no answer to that, but left the room saying he was going to find the print of the churchyard.

'If you ask me,' Rosemary whispered, 'he doesn't have much idea at all of what women are like. There's no sign of any female touches here, for a start.'

'True,' agreed Laura. 'How old would you say he is?'

'Mid-forties, I'd guess. Too old to change his ways, that's for sure.'

'Hmm,' said Laura doubtfully. She looked around at the oak panelling and the wood-blocked floor. 'He's certainly spared no expense on doing this place up.'

'And that lovely gallery,' Rosemary pointed. 'I bet that wasn't there when he arrived. Do you think he has people playing medieval music up there?'

'Sure to,' said Laura.

'Here it is!' Danvers announced, sweeping back into the hall. 'Have a good look. The vicar will agree with me, I'm sure, that it would be marvellous if you could return the churchyard to something close to this.'

Rosemary and Laura bent over the picture. The yew tree was there, dominating one side of the churchyard, but looking much healthier than the present day reality. Small hedges separated different areas, and several attractive shrubs were scattered amongst the graves. Unusually, there was also statuary that did not appear to be part of grave memorials. Not so much weeping angels as more classical figures, including cherubs and something that might have been a satyr. 'Statues!' said Rosemary. 'What happened to them, I wonder?'

'They were cleared away about a century ago, as being unsuitable.'

'I'd be surprised if Keith thought any differently now,' Laura said. 'I mean – the church has very strict rules about the style and material of headstones these days. I imagine that extends to statues, doesn't it?'

'No need to worry about that,' Danvers assured her. 'We won't contravene any church regulations. Any difficulties – just refer to me. All right?'

'Right,' said Rosemary, with a mock salute.

Nervously, Laura watched Danvers for any sign of offence, but he appeared to take it in good part. After a short silence, she and Rosemary turned to go.

'Oh – just one more thing,' the historian said. They both looked at him, while he seemed to be thinking rapidly. 'This evening – in the village hall – there's a public meeting. It occurs to me that your horticultural expertise might come in useful.'

'Oh?' said Laura. 'Why's that?'

'One of the big drug companies is sending a chap to talk to us about the potential there is in the bark of yew trees, or some such nonsense.'

Rosemary gave him a reproving look. 'It isn't nonsense, Mr Danvers. Yew bark does contain a chemical that's been shown to work on malignant tumours.'

Danvers shook his head impatiently. 'Be that as it may, the fact is, they want to buy Brockett's Farm, to exploit the yew wood, as well as starting some sort of tree nursery there, with new young yews. This man that's coming is sure to blind us with science, or persuade us we'll be doing a public service if we let them start up here. He'll try to convince us that we won't notice a thing. He's been crawling around Marie for weeks now, doing all he can to influence her.'

'So he's in direct competition with you and your museum, then?' Laura realised. 'It isn't just a matter of Marie trying to decide whether or not to sell the farm to you. Is there anybody else with his eye on it?'

Danvers wriggled his shoulders uncomfortably. 'Obviously, if she put it on the open market, there might be a great deal of interest. That's why I've been trying to persuade her that a simple private sale to me, with no agents or media interest, would be so much less painful for her.'

'But possibly less profitable as well?' Rosemary ventured.

Instead of taking offence at this, Danvers surprised them by giving a tolerant smile. 'You misjudge me,' he said. 'I'm not trying to get it on the cheap.'

'But the drug company might outbid you, just the same,' Laura remarked.

'I'm not too worried. Even Marie Sutton wouldn't be fool enough to sell out to big business. She'd hate to see her precious ancestral pile turned into laboratories and polytunnels and all that stuff.'

'Well, we'll be there for the meeting,' said Rosemary. 'It sounds fascinating.'

'Meanwhile, we must get down to some work,' said Laura. 'I've been trying to make a mental list of everything that needs to be done, and it's alarmingly long.'

Rosemary grimaced. 'Me too,' she said, holding up a finger for each task as she listed it. 'Clear the undergrowth; trim the yew tree; create new ornamental hedges; plant shrubs; find statues and put them in place; smarten up the front wall and perhaps plant climbers alongside it. Goodness, I'm going to run out of fingers at this rate.'

'Well, shout if you need some help,' said Danvers expansively. 'I can probably lend you Lyall for the odd hour or two, if you get desperate.'

'Thanks,' said Rosemary. 'And now we'll get out of your way.'

* * *

Much of their talk was of Franklin Danvers as they walked back to The Holly Tree, where they were to stay. 'If you ask me,' mused Laura, 'he resents the Suttons because they've been here for generations, and he's a newcomer. All this stuff about re-enacting the Battle of Baffington is typical. I bet the real locals think it's all a big laugh.'

'That Marie seems rather a drip. She doesn't get out much, I suppose.'

Laura nodded. 'She's just a typical country girl.'

'Except for the little matter of sitting on a farm that has to be worth close to a million. I wouldn't say that's very typical. What was her brother like?'

'Rather good-looking, actually. And fairly fit, I'd say, even if he was living a life of debauchery.'

'Life of debauchery? Really? How do you know?'

'Last year, after her father died, I spent a little time with Marie, just letting her talk – you know. She said quite a lot about her family, some of it she probably wishes she hadn't mentioned afterwards. But she needn't worry. I've forgotten most of it.'

'Except for the debauchery. Isn't it a wonderful word! So old-fashioned and judgmental.'

'And not altogether accurate, I'm sure. Malcolm seems to be the person everybody disapproves of. His father cut him off, thinking he'd never have the stamina to take on the farm, or settle down and behave responsibly. But Harriet had certainly fallen for him. She was devastated when he told her he was going away and not coming back.'

'I can see how he might seem rather a misfit in this place,' Rosemary said, looking around at the quiet village. 'Where is everybody?'

'Not back from work yet, presumably. Most villages are deserted during the week, nowadays. They probably all appear on Saturdays and Sundays, mowing their lawns and cleaning their cars.'

'Mm,' said Rosemary. 'You think we're in for rather a dull time, then, do you?'

'I wouldn't tempt fate by even suggesting it,' shuddered Laura.

Chapter Five

The public meeting at the village hall was very well attended. Harriet Luke and Keith Briggs sat on the small platform at one end of the room. Harriet had a notepad in front of her and an empty chair beside her, obviously intended for the speaker. There was a screen set up, and a complicated-looking machine on the table. Franklin Danvers was in the body of the hall, making the point that he was simply one of the concerned residents, with no special position. Rosemary and Laura had taken the seats next to him. He was restless, turning round to scan the rows behind him, obviously looking for someone.

'Where's Marie Sutton?' he muttered. 'Shouldn't she be here?'

Rosemary barely heard him, leaning close to catch his words. Before she could respond, Danvers had switched his attention to someone else behind him, but she muttered into his ear, 'Maybe she couldn't face it, seeing how shy she is.'

Interest in the future of Brockett's Farm was obviously very high, with an animated buzz of anticipation as the villagers waited for proceedings to start. Finally, a man appeared from a small room close to the platform, jumping athletically onto the platform. Rosemary gasped, unable to believe her eyes.

'What?' Laura hissed. 'What's the matter?'

'I know him. He's from Knussens. He's called Redland Linton. Nobody said it was them who want to buy the farm. Gosh!' Her head was spinning with the coincidence of seeing him again so soon. 'Good-looking, isn't he?' she added in a whisper. 'I'd forgotten already how attractive he is.'

'He hasn't seen you yet,' Laura whispered back. 'Maybe you ought to wave?'

'Don't be ridiculous,' blushed Rosemary.

Linton was obviously accustomed to public speaking. He stood at the front of the platform, exuding confidence and camaraderie, introducing himself, and thanking everybody for coming. Expecting some disapproval, he seemed to be hoping to disarm everybody with his friendly smile. But the villagers were not so easily seduced. One man called out, 'Get on with it, then!'

With a tolerant smile, Linton moved to the gadget on the table, and clicked a button. Onto the screen came a bright image of the Knussens logo, with 'Nature's Way' emblazoned across the middle of it.

He started his presentation, projecting his voice to the back of the hall, still quite undaunted. Rosemary found herself admiring his performance, matching it with the pleasant time she'd spent with him only two days earlier.

'I would like to assure you, ladies and gentlemen,' he said, 'that the intentions of my employers are completely benign. There have been a number of highly inaccurate rumours going around, and my job is to scotch them and give you the true picture.'

One or two villagers made muttered remarks, obviously expressing scepticism, but nobody actually interrupted.

'Now – the really exciting aspect of the proposed Brockett's Farm facility is the presence on the land of several mature yew trees. We plan to harvest the bark of those trees, as well as propagate more identical trees, with a view to developing a revolutionary new anti-cancer therapy, which will, we hope, bring enormous benefits to people everywhere, and Baffington in particular.'

'Phooey,' Rosemary murmured, reminded of the things Linton had said following her own speech at the conference. 'Is he trying to claim that this is something new?'

In the seat next to her, Danvers heard what she'd said, and turned excitedly towards her. But before he could ask her to elaborate, the door at the back of the hall banged open, and a latecomer entered.

The general intake of breath was dramatic as over half the people present turned round and recognised the newcomer. Rosemary craned her neck to see past Laura. She immediately realised it was the man who had arrived at The Holly Tree earlier in the day, by taxi.

'Who is he?' she asked Laura.

'That,' Laura told her, in a low voice, 'is the runaway Malcolm Sutton.'

Everybody started muttering and whispering at once, with

wide excited eyes. Malcolm edged his way onto one of the few empty seats near the back, and sat down, careful to avoid meeting anyone's eye.

'Return of the black sheep, eh?' said Rosemary. 'Ten out of ten for timing, anyway.'

At a loss to understand just what was happening, Redland Linton stood on his platform, waiting for quiet to resume. He looked to Harriet for a signal, but she was transfixed by the newcomer, her eyes enormous, a rosy glow suffusing both cheeks, and an unconscious smile playing on her lips. 'Well – as I was saying,' Linton pressed on, 'it is with a total concern for the integrity of the farm, and everything it has meant over the years, that we —'

'All right, that's enough,' called Malcolm suddenly. 'You needn't go on, because you're not getting the farm.' He hoisted a briefcase onto his knees and opened it. 'I'm afraid I have quite other ideas.'

Franklin Danvers stood up, his face furious. 'And just what makes you think you have any say over what happens to the farm? You forfeited any claim long ago, when you went against your father's wishes in every possible way. It amazes me that you have the nerve to show your face here again. The whole village had hoped they were shot of you forever.'

'Look at Harriet!' Rosemary whispered to Laura.

Laura looked. 'I think it's safe to say she's pleased to see him,' she said. 'In spite of everything.'

Malcolm was also looking at Harriet, but with no reflecting fondness. 'Note that down, Harriet,' he said nastily. ' "A short speech of welcome was made by Mr Danvers." ' He gave a brief snort of bitter laughter, before taking more papers from his briefcase.

Rosemary was examining other faces in the hall. 'Look at Lyall!' she said. Laura obediently turned round, making no effort to hide her curiosity. Gordon Lyall was staring venomously at Sutton, his face red with anger. 'Wow!' breathed Laura. 'This chap's causing quite a sensation, isn't he!'

Danvers was struggling to remain in control. A patronising

sneer entered his voice. 'So just what is it that's brought you back where you know you're not wanted?'

Malcolm Sutton was not readily intimidated. 'This is my home,' he said. 'My sister – who is now my only surviving relative – lives here.'

'So where is she?' Danvers demanded. 'What have you done with her?'

This time Malcolm's laugh was genuine. 'Done with her? My, my, what a man you are for melodrama, Mr Danvers. Marie was perfectly happy for me to come here this evening as her representative. Our ideas about Brockett's Farm are identical. We will have no truck with Knussens and their so-called natural remedies. Neither, I might add, have we any intention of permitting you to turn it into some toytown theme park full of mock jousting and spit-roasted pigs.'

Sensing defeat, Redland Linton sat down, and left the field to Danvers. Nobody was interested in him any more.

'I won't believe that until Marie herself says it,' insisted Danvers. 'It was my impression that she regarded my plans extremely favourably.' Malcolm gave a rude snigger at this claim, which Laura thought had some justification. Danvers seemed to her to be indulging in some wishful thinking on this matter. Surely Marie would have accepted his offer by this time if she really did favour his plans over those of Knussens.

Danvers ignored Sutton's insolent sneer, and simply carried on, his voice getting louder. 'Perhaps,' he insisted, 'you haven't properly understood the nature of what I intend. My plans are for a museum, not a theme park.' He drew breath to go into more detail, but Sutton roughly cut through his words.

'Then you've been fooling yourself,' he said, 'if you think Marie's bought your idea. Besides, she didn't know what I'd been working on until today.'

'Oh?' The entire assembly of villagers was holding its breath by this point. Even Laura and Rosemary had stopped whispering to each other, or watching everybody's reactions. Like the whole gathering, they were hypnotised by Malcolm Sutton.

'I have been in serious discussion with the County Council

Planning Office, as it happens. You might not be aware of a recent change to their policy regarding rural development. They actually issued a revised Local Plan only last week. I have a copy here —' he waved a thick spiral-bound document in the air. 'And it says, in plain terms, that new residential development is to be permitted, given certain conditions regarding affordable accommodation, dum-di-da, especially within the curtilage of existing settlements. Brockett's Farm fits the bill exactly. I calculate that a modest development of around twenty new homes could quite easily be managed. That makes the land worth about a hundred times more than it would be as agricultural. Marie and I will be comfortable for the rest of our lives.'

Before he finished, there was uproar. The blasphemy of suggesting a new housing estate in Baffington caused near apoplexy amongst the village residents. Several objections were shouted, with the words 'Water!' 'Traffic!' 'Schools!' echoing around the hall.

Danvers tried in vain to restore order, forgetting his assumed role as ordinary member of the public, and continue his argument with the interloper. Sutton, having dropped his bombshell, made his escape before the villagers could lynch him. As he went, he caught Harriet's eye, and mouthed 'Holly Tree' at her, with an inviting smile. She nodded back, then turned her attention to the notes in front of her, still looking very flushed.

Danvers and Keith Briggs stood either side of Rosemary and Laura, watching the hubbub slowly subside. People came up to them both, demanding reassurance. 'Don't worry, don't worry,' Keith muttered repeatedly, with no effect. After a few moments, he was dragged away by a particularly agitated woman who insisted he call a meeting as a matter of urgency.

Gordon Lyall approached his employer, his face full of confusion. 'That's Marie's brother, is it?' he asked.

'Obviously,' Danvers snapped impatiently.

'You've never met him?' Laura asked, trying to soften Danvers' rudeness.

Lyall shook his head. 'I've only been here for eight months. Sutton had done a runner a while before that.'

Redland Linton then joined the group. Rosemary moved her head, catching his eye and watching his surprise as he recognised her. 'Good grief!' he exclaimed. 'Fancy meeting you here!'

'Hello again,' she smiled.

'But – why are you here?'

Briefly, she explained about the churchyard commission. 'Bafflettn Villig, remember? You guessed right – it was Baffington. This is Laura, my partner in the business.'

'Pleased to meet you,' said Laura. 'I'm afraid your presentation never quite got under way, did it?'

Linton made a rueful face. 'Rather a wasted evening, I admit. But I'm not downhearted. Compared to a new housing estate, a nice inconspicuous tree nursery should go down rather well with the locals.'

'You do sound confident,' Laura observed.

'Never give up, that's my motto,' he said, straightening his tie and smiling bravely. 'Nothing's certain until the contracts are signed and the cheques cleared, in my experience. A lot can happen in the meantime.'

Danvers made a sort of growl, hearing Linton's words, and after a polite nod to Laura and Rosemary, began to head for the door.

'He's not happy, is he?' Laura said.

'He's not the only one,' Rosemary pointed out.

The crowd was jostling them on all sides, as people tried to get out and air their views on the green or in The Holly Tree. Bowing to the pressure, Laura, Rosemary and Linton allowed themselves to be swept out of the hall. 'I'll come back for my equipment later,' he said. 'I suppose it'll be all right.'

'I take it you'd never seen Malcolm Sutton before,' Laura asked him.

Linton shook his head. 'I had no idea who he was until he mentioned Brockett's Farm as being his home. Marie had spoken of him, of course, and frankly I had been slightly bothered about his role, all along. As loose cannons go, though, he's certainly made a spectacular show.'

'And yet you don't seem worried,' Laura persisted.

Linton shrugged. 'I don't see any reason to be. I can wait, if I have to. All this will simmer down, and I'll be ready for when it does.'

Outside, they joined the vicar, who seemed completely bemused. 'A housing estate!' he said, as if his thoughts could get no further than this extraordinary idea. 'It would probably double the population.'

'If you ask me, Malcolm was just making mischief,' Laura said. 'After all, there are few things more likely to arouse strong feelings in the English countryside these days than a suggestion of new houses.'

Keith frowned. 'I wish I could believe that, but I'm afraid it's all a lot more serious than you realise. It sounded to me as if Sutton has really done his homework. If he carried these plans through, it would be the ruin of Baffington.' He turned towards the church, staring at it as if it might be the last time he ever saw it. 'There'd have to be so much new provision for such a big increase in population, you see.'

Laura patted his arm. 'Relax,' she ordered him. 'Nothing's going to happen overnight. And before you know it, there'll be a Village Action Group formed, and they'll come up with ten excellent reasons why nothing new can be built on Brockett's Farm. There's bound to be rare bats or ancient Druid temples in the way of any new building, if you look for them hard enough.'

Keith did his best to smile, but it was a feeble effort.

Rosemary had been watching Harriet Luke, who was walking as if in a trance towards where Malcolm Sutton stood on the edge of the village green. 'Hmm – this looks interesting,' she murmured.

Franklin Danvers, like the vicar, was being besieged on all sides by clamouring neighbours. But he was saying very little, his face blank. Laura nudged Rosemary. 'What price his Medieval Museum now, I wonder?' she said.

Rosemary watched Danvers for a moment. 'He looks like a man in shock. I saw that Malcolm Sutton earlier on, you know. He arrived at the pub in a taxi, with a travel bag. I don't think he's staying at the farm with his sister, although he did say he'd spoken to her.'

'I imagine there are quite a few bridges to be mended between Marie and her brother, after what happened last year,' said Laura. 'He must have told her he would take her place at the meeting – possibly thinking that would earn him some goodwill from her.'

'She'll forgive him, you'll see,' said Rosemary. 'Time heals, and he is her only living relative.'

'That might be so. But one thing was definite – she completely blamed Malcolm for what happened to her father. It's hard to believe she's changed her mind about that now.'

'If Malcolm's promising to make millions for her, she might well be prepared to overlook past grievances.'

'Mmm,' said Laura doubtfully.

It was still light, a warm summer evening which brought to mind barbecues on the patio, and cold white wine in pub gardens. Rosemary breathed in deeply, turning her head to catch the scented air. 'Somebody's got a *lonicera americana* around here,' she said. 'Gorgeous!'

Laura sniffed noisily. 'I can only smell fried chicken and garlic,' she said. 'The pub must be open for food. I assume that'll be where we're eating this evening?'

'Guess so,' Rosemary shrugged, without moving.

People were still gathered in small groups on the road between the village hall and the church, with some of them evidently intending to call in at The Holly Tree before going home. Franklin Danvers had joined up with Lyall, who looked as if he would like to get away. The vicar was listening to the same outraged woman as before, as she explained how she had moved to Baffington precisely to escape modern housing estates and noisy children. Redland Linton had not yet left, but hovered at Keith's elbow. Everybody looked unsettled, casting twitchy glances at each other, as well as at the couple who were the true object of universal curiosity.

Harriet Luke and Malcolm Sutton had moved closer to the doorway of the pub, apparently undecided as to whether to go inside. They were speaking too quietly for anybody to overhear, but with plain body language. He was asking for forgiveness, and she was performing that age-old female dance, which said, 'Your chances are reasonably good, but first you have to be ritually humiliated and made to suffer.' She looked into his eyes, her own large and slightly moist, to ensure that he understood how much he'd hurt her. As he leaned down towards her, she stepped back, indicating a lack of trust. He tentatively reached out a hand, letting it rest lightly on her forearm. She appeared not to notice it for a few seconds, before pulling away.

Then at a sudden sharp word from her, full of accusation, he turned and walked a little way up the hill leading towards Highview House. Having watched him for a moment, Harriet started after him. 'Oops! Bad move,' muttered Rosemary, voicing the feelings of many observers.

Harriet spoke to Malcolm's back, and he stopped. A few more words, and they took each other's hands, clasping tightly, smiling.

'That man's got a bloody nerve,' growled Franklin Danvers, loud enough for Rosemary and Laura to hear, as well as a few others.

His manager nodded in wordless agreement, and even Keith mumbled something that sounded like a similar sentiment.

'You can say one thing for Harriet,' said Laura admiringly, 'she certainly has her pick of the men around here. Look at them!'

Rosemary looked. Danvers, Lyall, Keith and one or two others were all magnetised by the little drama before them. 'Lucky girl,' she said softly.

'If you ask me,' Laura replied, 'you can have too much of a good thing. It can only lead to trouble.'

Rosemary laughed. 'Nonsense. Let the girl have her fun. Besides, it looks as if she's going to end up with the one she really wants, after all.'

Laura raised her eyebrows. 'And you think that'll make her happy, do you? When anybody can see what a rotter he is.'

The encounter between Harriet and Malcolm was clearly at an end. She gave him a cautious smile, patted his upper arm briskly, and said 'See you,' before walking away towards her cottage.

'That's more like it,' Rosemary approved. 'Don't throw yourself at him too quickly.'

'It isn't going to happen,' Laura insisted. 'She's moved on

since she last saw Malcolm. And he'd be no good for her.'

'You know what they say about the love of a good woman,' Rosemary smiled indulgently. 'She could be the making of him, you'll see.'

Over the next hour, the village returned to its normal peace and quiet. Keith, after a short consultation with Redland Linton, disappeared from sight. Lyall and Danvers returned to Highview House; Harriet too was nowhere to be seen. 'Where did they all go?' wondered Rosemary.

'Keith's car is still over there, look,' Laura pointed out. 'He can't be far away. Probably been dragged off by that hysterical woman to write a letter to the MP.'

Rosemary giggled. 'Poor man! And do you think Harriet's sneaked off to be with Sutton?'

'Could be,' Laura nodded. But when they went into the bar of The Holly Tree, Malcolm was sitting all alone with a glass of whisky, looking undaunted but pensive.

'Plotting his next move,' whispered Rosemary.

Studiously, they avoided him, devoting themselves to their plan of campaign for the churchyard next morning, first over a drink, and then moving to the dining room for a very welcome meal.

'We'd better get an early night,' said Laura. 'It's going to be a full day tomorrow.'

Rosemary readily agreed. 'One of us is going to have to climb that yew tree and cut out the dead wood,' she said. 'Until we get that done, we won't be able to start on the paths and hedges. We don't want branches landing on anything we've already got straight. Especially not our new little hedges that I've got planned.'

'Right,' said Laura. 'I'm itching to go and find some statuary to match what's in Mr Danvers' picture.'

'Well, you'll have to wait,' said Rosemary.

At the foot of the stairs, they passed Malcolm Sutton, the pub's public telephone clamped to his ear. He was twisting the cord around his fingers, oblivious to everything but his conversation.

'Will you come and meet me somewhere, then?' he was saying. 'Oh, I don't know. What about the churchyard? What time? It'll be light for at least another half-hour yet. Yes, fine. Yes. All right, Sunshine, I'll be there. See you in the churchyard.'

It was well before eight next morning when Laura and Rosemary arrived in the churchyard for work, having been first down for breakfast. 'These lovely summer mornings,' breathed Rosemary. 'Don't you just itch to get outside?'

Laura, rather less enthusiastic, reminded her that it wasn't so many hours ago that Rosemary had been waxing lyrical about the lovely summer evening.

'I just like summer, that's all,' laughed her friend.

Keith had given them a free hand, explaining that he would be fully occupied with his parish works, with two weddings scheduled for the coming Saturday in two of the smaller villages, as well as confirmation classes, hospital visits and a funeral on Friday morning. 'I'm afraid you won't be seeing very much of me while you're here,' he said. 'But I will make a point of preparing a meal for you at the vicarage, perhaps one day next week.'

The yew tree seemed even more dominant and threatening to Laura, as they went in through the lych-gate. She stared up at it in some trepidation, knowing she was likely to be the one to have to climb up and cut out the dead branches.

'I still don't like the dratted thing,' she said.

'By the time we've finished here, you'll have changed your mind,' Rosemary assured her.

'Oh look at this!' Laura paused, admiring a perfect spider's web slung between two tall grassheads. 'Isn't it gorgeous!' Dew sparkled in the gossamer.

Laura carefully hooked one side of the web with her forefinger, and wound it round and round.

'So why spoil it?' Rosemary demanded.

'It's lucky.'

'You could have fooled me. What about the poor spider? You just ruined her day.'

Laura walked into the overgrown graveyard, still playing with the web. The flash of sunlight on metal caught her eye, and she bent down.

'Good Lord!' she gasped. 'What's this?'

Rosemary was following behind her. 'What? Some other innocent insect to interfere with, I suppose.'

'Far from it. It's a gun.'

'What?'

Laura pointed at the ground where the weapon lay naked on the brown cushion formed by the yew's shadow. Her early training as a police officer ensured that she did not pick it up or even touch it. 'A rather nice modern pistol,' she elaborated. 'No silencer, so I think we can assume it hasn't been fired. I don't know about you, but I'm sure I would have heard it if it had gone off during the night. I could be wrong, but I think that's our bedroom window just up there.' She indicated the side of The Holly Tree, where a window overlooked the churchyard.

'Um – Laura,' came a small voice, further round the large trunk of the yew tree. 'Come here.'

Something in Rosemary's voice told Laura what she was likely to see. 'Oh, no,' she breathed, as a pair of large trainers came into view. 'Who is it?'

'See for yourself.'

Laura looked, automatically registering the important details. A man, lying on his back, eyes wide open, staring sightlessly at the sky. One hand was clasped around the shaft of a stout arrow, its red and blue flight feathers somehow alien in the greens of the neglected graveyard. The business end of the arrow was invisible, buried deep in the victim's heart.

'Malcolm Sutton,' said Laura. 'Murdered beneath the tree of death.'

'So much for lucky cobwebs,' Rosemary groaned.

Chapter Six

Gerald Winthrop, church organist, had been the first of the people of Baffington to become aware that something cataclysmic had happened. He watched the two women hired to clean up the churchyard come running through the lych-gate, their eyes wide with shock or excitement. He watched them go stumbling into The Holly Tree, and heard raised voices as they shouted for Jim, the landlord.

Mr Winthrop got to his feet from where he had been sitting on the village green, and slowly approached the lych-gate. Before he could go through it, the smaller of the two women came back, pushing herself in front of him. 'No, no,' she cried, 'you can't go in there. It's – I mean – something's happened. It shouldn't be disturbed.'

A feeling of dread came over him. Whatever was in the churchyard was going to turn his life – and the lives of everybody in the village – upside down. He could feel it in the air. What's more, he realised, it had started the day before, when Malcolm Sutton had walked into the village hall. He had known then that everything was about to change.

'Oh, my word,' he said to the woman. 'Whatever can have happened?'

She gave him a narrow look. 'I don't think I can tell you yet,' she said, tilting her chin importantly. 'You'll find out soon enough. I'm afraid it's something very nasty.'

Mr Winthrop found himself not particularly eager to know the details. Never a man to relish unpleasantness, he gave the woman a polite smile, and turned back towards the green. 'If there's nothing I can do,' he murmured, 'perhaps I should just get out of the way.'

That seemed to surprise her. 'Oh!' she said. 'Well, yes. Although —'

He paused, fighting to maintain his mild demeanour. His insides were knotting, seething with worry. Mentally he was praying that his hard-won equanimity was not about to be rocked by the horror in the churchyard. Vain prayers, he knew.

Life in Baffington had already changed and Gerald Winthrop knew he wouldn't be the only one to suffer.

The police arrived quickly, and there followed an hour or more of activity, during which they taped off half the churchyard. Shortly before ten o'clock, Laura and Rosemary were requested to present themselves for interview in a back room of The Holly Tree pub. Malcolm's briefcase had been retrieved from his room upstairs, as well as his travel bag, both laid out with their contents on a side table. A pleasant-looking Detective Inspector ushered the two into the room and firmly closed the door.

Laura had fully recovered from the shock, and was overflowing with impressions and suggestions. Almost before she sat down, she was asking, 'Have you found the bow that shot the deadly arrow yet?'

The man looked at her slowly, a mixture of irritation and amusement on his face.

'There is a tradition, Madam, that the police ask the questions in this sort of situation.'

'Yes, yes, I know that,' she dismissed. 'I've been a police officer myself. My ex-husband and son are both still in the force.'

'Ah,' sighed the man, who had introduced himself as DI Flannery. Rosemary suppressed a giggle at the wealth of feeling in the single syllable. Understanding, resignation, wariness were all there, plus a hint of something warmer and softer.

'Well?' Laura prompted.

'Well, no, we have not yet found the bow. Just the arrow.'

'You could hardly miss that, could you?'

'I suppose you know where the arrow came from,' Rosemary put in.

'Apparently from the direction of the church, to judge by the position of the body. It would have been easy for somebody to hide in that overgrown jungle. We're searching for flattened grass, footprints, that sort of thing.'

'No, no,' said Rosemary, flapping a hand. 'I didn't mean that. I meant – where did it come from originally? That is, did you know that Franklin Danvers has a large collection of bows and arrows? The one in Malcolm Sutton's chest almost certainly came from there.'

'Is your husband a copper as well?' Flannery asked.

'Oh, no. I'm not married.'

Flannery glanced at Laura, with a half smile. 'Neither am I, as of two years ago.'

Laura fidgeted in the chair, unsure as to whether to make clear just what her marital status was. The man didn't seem to have heard the ex. Rosemary cleared her throat, which only added to Laura's discomfort.

Flannery straightened his spine, and looked down at his notes. 'Right,' he said. 'Now then —' and he ran through a number of routine questions concerning their discovery of the body, their reasons for being in Baffington, and their last sighting of Malcolm Sutton alive.

Laura and Rosemary answered confidently, if slightly impatiently. To their minds, the man was not addressing the most important issues.

At last, he got to more interesting areas. 'Would either of you have an idea as to whether anybody in this village might have something against Mr Sutton?' he asked, leaning back in his chair and looking from one to the other.

Rosemary leaned closer to the desk, resting both hands on it, eyes wide. 'Now you're asking!' she approved. 'How long have you got? This could take some time.'

Laura interrupted, claiming a superior grasp of police procedure, deliberately adopting some of what she could recall of the jargon. Briskly she recounted the events of the public meeting of the previous evening. 'It was all over in less than half an hour,' she said. 'But in that time, almost everybody there had decided they'd love to murder Malcolm Sutton – because of his plans for a housing estate, you see.'

'And most of them had just been taught how to use a bow and arrow,' Rosemary added excitedly.

Flannery scribbled busily as the two supplied names, motives, opportunities and access to weaponry. 'Harriet Luke,' he repeated, 'Gordon Lyall, Redland Linton – hang on a minute.

Who did you say Linton was?'

They explained about Knussens and the exploitation of its yew trees for some sort of medical purpose. Then Laura went back to her first encounter with Sutton the previous year. 'He really wasn't a very nice man,' she concluded.

'But Harriet looked as if she might give him a second chance,' Rosemary said.

'Except – what if we missed something later on? While we were having dinner?' Laura narrowed her eyes. 'Harriet was an ace shot with the bow, wasn't she?'

'So was your cousin, the vicar, come to that,' Rosemary argued. 'I can't believe Harriet would have killed Malcolm.'

'She might,' muttered Flannery. 'A woman scorned, and all that. Plus there's this business with the new houses. What would she have felt about that?'

'Enraged, probably,' Laura admitted. 'She's completely devoted to this village and its history. But the same goes for practically everybody else.'

Flannery sighed. 'Well, I must admit it's useful to have an outside view, so to speak,' he told them. 'You seem to have got to know everybody with remarkable rapidity.'

'Oh, not really,' smiled Laura modestly. 'Just ordinary little conversations can reveal such a lot, you see.'

'Oh, yes,' the detective agreed, rather vaguely.

'You'll have to find out who could have been near the church at about nine-thirty last night,' said Laura. 'We last saw the deceased at nine. He was speaking on the phone in the pub, as we went upstairs after dinner. Do you have an estimated time of death?'

Flannery pursed his lips. 'You no doubt are aware, Mrs Thyme, that it is virtually impossible to ascertain the time of death beyond the very roughest of guesses. On that detail, Agatha Christie and her friends have a lot to answer for.'

'I understand that,' Laura agreed readily. 'But you must know whether or not rigor had set in. That would give you quite a good idea.'

Rosemary flinched at this rather too graphic conversation,

while the Detective Inspector looked at Laura for a long moment. Then he apparently came to some decision. 'I don't normally disclose the findings of our pathologist or forensic officers,' he said deliberately. 'But given that you have some professional experience —'

'Oh, come on,' Rosemary said impatiently. 'Stop being so stuffy and tell us what you think.'

'Rosemary!' Laura gave her a horrified look. 'Don't be so rude.'

'That's all right,' said the man, visibly relaxing. 'It's rather refreshing to be told off by two such attractive ladies. Now, as I was about to say, we believe the man died approximately ten to twelve hours before you found the body. And I mean approximately. The leeway is considerable.'

'Yes, yes,' said Laura dismissively. 'But it means you'd do well to find out who could have been near the churchyard just as it was getting dark last night.'

Flannery nodded with exaggerated patience. 'Yes, Mrs Thyme. I believe you're right there,' he said, with a twinkling smile to dilute the sarcasm. He closed his notebook, and pushed back his chair. 'Well, that'll be all for the moment. Lots to do.'

'Oh yes,' Laura agreed. 'The first few hours are crucial, aren't they? Gather as much information as you can before the trail goes cold.'

'Something like that,' he agreed, with another smile.

They left the room, and walked through the bar. Lyall was on a stool with a beer in his hand, and three other vaguely familiar local people sat around a table near the window. Silence fell as the police detective entered. He reached for Laura's hand and shook it heartily. 'Thank you very much, ladies,' he said. 'You've been extremely helpful.' Then he looked around the room. 'Would you be Mr Lyall?' he asked the man on the stool.

Lyall nodded, his face flushing.

'Would you be kind enough to come through, then, while I ask you a few questions? Just an informal little chat, at this stage, you understand. It won't take long.'

Lyall got up heavily, looking at Laura's face intently before following Flannery into the back room.

'Hmm,' said Laura, when the men had closed the door behind themselves. 'He must be worried.'

'Why?' Rosemary raised her eyebrows.

'Because he's the best archer in the place, isn't he?'

'Yes, but —' Laura hushed her with a warning look, as two more people came into the pub. Rosemary turned to see who they were.

'Oh – Keith!' she smiled. 'And Harriet. This must be dreadful for you, Vicar – with it happening in the churchyard like that. Almost blasphemous, I suppose, when you think about it.'

Keith looked drawn and shocked. 'I can hardly believe it,' he said.

Harriet put a hand on his arm. 'It's hard for us all,' she reminded him, with an obvious effort to keep her emotions under control.

He patted her hand distractedly. 'Oh, Harriet, I know. I realise you had – well, feelings, for him. It must be so much worse for you. And after last night —'

Harriet interrupted him quickly. 'Oh, the meeting, you mean. Yes, well, I suppose that's the reason for what happened. Somebody must have decided that if Malcolm were to be disposed of, his ideas about a housing estate would never happen.'

Keith looked briefly puzzled, before one of the villagers at the window table called him over. 'Sorry,' he said to Laura and Rosemary, with a helpless shrug. 'I don't know when I'll get a chance for a proper chat with you.'

'Don't worry,' Laura told him. 'Although —' she hesitated, '— we are wondering where this leaves us. I don't expect we'll be allowed to get to work in the churchyard for another day or two.'

Keith frowned. 'I suppose that's right. Well – isn't there something else you could be doing? They might let you start on the far corner, the other side of the church. It's big enough, in all conscience. You'd be well away from the area they're examining if you stay over on that side.'

Rosemary nudged Laura. 'Yes, they might,' she agreed. 'We

could clear away that patch of docks and brambles, and maybe our friendly local Detective Inspector will keep an eye on us.'

They went outside, unsure of what they might be allowed to do. As they left, they passed the public telephone, jogging Rosemary's memory. 'Oh!' she said, 'We forgot to tell the police about Sunshine.'

'Pardon?'

'You remember. Malcolm on the phone in here. He was talking to somebody he called Sunshine, and arranging to meet them in the churchyard. How could we have forgotten?'

'Sunshine,' Laura repeated, sceptically. 'It's hard to believe that could be anybody in this village, don't you think?'

'Possibly. But we should still have told him. Should we go back now and put him straight?'

Laura paused to consider, and then shook her head. 'I don't think so. We did tell him we saw Malcolm phoning somebody – that's the important bit. And we don't know if Malcolm called everybody Sunshine. Like "Mate" or "Boyo".'

'Boyo?'

'You know what I mean.'

'We ought to check with Mr Danvers that we're still going to be needed,' Laura realised, as they stood outside the church lych-gate. 'What if the whole Fayre is cancelled because of all this?'

Rosemary blew out her cheeks. 'You can't be serious,' she said. 'If I know Franklin Danvers, he isn't going to let a little thing like a murder get in his way.'

'All the same, I think we ought to check. We can go up to his house now, and see if he's there.'

The walk up to Highview House was short and steep, passing the Glebe field on the right, and accompanied by the stream that ran through Baffington. Police cars were still parked around the green, and three or four local residents were gathered near the village hall, clearly discussing the dramatic events of the morning.

Franklin Danvers was quickly found, bending over a terracotta pot containing a young fig tree, close to the front door of his house. Automatically, Rosemary stepped nearer, giving the plant a rapid expert appraisal. 'Looks very vigorous,' she said.

He turned his head without straightening, and grunted his agreement. Wasting no time, Laura explained why they'd come. Danvers gave her an uncomprehending stare. 'Cancel the Fayre?' he said, as if she'd suggested they all take a day trip to Venus. 'Whatever for?'

'Well…' she said weakly. 'We just wondered.'

'Absolutely out of the question,' he said briskly. 'It's gone much too far for that.' A thought seemed to strike him. 'Let me show you one or two things, while you're here. Maybe then you'll understand that the idea of cancelling is ridiculous.'

He led the way into a large garden behind the house, and was striding purposefully down a path towards a low brick building, when Rosemary was distracted by the plants on all sides.

'Hang on a minute,' she pleaded. 'You've got some very interesting things here.'

Laura and Danvers paused on the path. 'Well –' said Danvers. 'I'm really quite busy. Perhaps we should leave this for another time, after all.'

'Oh, no!' said Rosemary. 'We're here now. And who knows when there'll be another chance? We've already lost most of the morning, and we can't be sure when the police will allow us into the churchyard to get started.'

'Please lead on,' Laura coaxed him. 'Rosemary can comment on your garden as we go.' She gave her friend a warning look, which Rosemary ignored.

Danvers slowed his pace, speaking over his shoulder, obviously proud of his garden. 'There's nothing here that would not have been here in the Middle Ages, of course,' he said. 'All fine old English plants.'

'Acanthus?' Rosemary noted, with a twitch of one eyebrow. 'You call that English?'

'It was brought here by the Romans, which means it would have been here in my period.'

'True,' Rosemary conceded. 'And agrimony is certainly authentic.' She pointed to a sweep of modest-looking yellow flower spikes.

'They used it as a remedy for snakebites,' Danvers laughed. 'Or so the story goes.'

'And who maintains all this?' Laura asked him.

'I do most of it myself,' he said. 'Although I have a man who comes in one morning a week. I only let him do the heavy work. I can't trust anybody to get it right, you see. They will insist on pulling up things that are meant to be here.'

Rosemary laughed. 'One man's weed is another man's prize exhibit,' she agreed, with another glance at the agrimony. 'You haven't made it all over to knot gardens and herbs, I see,' she went on. 'That's what I would have expected.'

'Much too obvious,' he said, with a superior smirk. 'And I seldom show it to anybody, either. This is my own private place, where I come when I feel jangled, or when I want to compose another section of one of my books.'

'Then we're privileged, aren't we,' said Laura.

They arrived at the outbuilding after ten minutes of garden appreciation, and Danvers produced a key. 'Lyall prefers that we keep it locked,' he explained. 'There's some rather irreplaceable material in here.'

As soon as they stepped inside, the fragrance of freshly planed wood, combined with linseed and a hot animal smell made Rosemary and Laura lift their heads and inhale deeply. 'Oh, this reminds me of so many things,' Laura said, delightedly. 'I grew up on a farm, you know. But this isn't exactly farm smells, it's – well —' She gave up even trying to describe how she felt in this paradise of memories. The sights that met them were almost as pleasurable: piles of wood shavings, stacks of glossy longbows, the paraphernalia of woodworking.

'It's all so wonderfully medieval,' said Rosemary, making the others laugh.

'That is the general idea,' said Danvers. 'We aim to use only the materials that would have been available during that period, you see.'

Suddenly there was a large shadow across the window, and Gordon Lyall appeared in the doorway. His head was lowered in an aggressive stance. His eyes were fixed on Danvers, and his cheeks were flushed.

'Ah – there you are,' said his employer. 'I'm just showing these ladies —'

'Right,' the man said, thickly, plainly in a vile mood.

'Your interview didn't last long,' Rosemary remarked lightly. 'With the Detective Inspector, I mean.'

Lyall hadn't taken his eyes off Danvers since he'd arrived, and did not do so now. There seemed to be an antagonism between the two that went deeper than the invasion of the workshop, or the annoyance of a local murder. Then Danvers gave himself a shake, and smiled. 'Let you off lightly, did they?' he said.

Lyall blinked. 'What?' he demanded.

'Oh, nothing. Just a silly joke. I suppose I ought to go and present myself in a little while. Did they give you any message for me?'

Lyall shook his head. Then, with an effort, he said, 'They've got the vicar in there now, and Harriet's waiting to go next. All they want to know is when we saw Sutton last, and what we were doing yesterday evening.'

'And whether you saw anything unusual,' Laura prompted. 'They'll have wanted to know that.'

Lyall merely nodded, as if the whole matter was essentially uninteresting to him.

'Well, that gives us a few minutes to talk you through what we do in here,' said Danvers briskly. 'Lyall – you explain it to them, will you?'

'Explain?' he queried, as if this was a very strange idea.

'Never mind,' Rosemary said quickly. 'We can see for ourselves. Perhaps we could ask you one or two questions, though. Like, what on earth is this?'

She pointed to a black wood-burning stove, lighted despite the summer season. On top of it sat a heavy flat-bottomed pan. Peering in, she saw large grey objects immersed in a glutinous fluid. The hot smell that had hit them as they'd entered the barn emanated from it.

'Hooves,' said Lyall shortly.

'Pardon?'

Before he could elucidate, Laura had joined Rosemary. 'Yes!' she confirmed. 'Cow's hooves. They used to boil them down to make glue, didn't they? Does it really work? Where do you get them?'

Danvers gave a snort. 'Don't ask,' he said. 'With all the regulations involving the disposal of animals, it's not easy.'

'Yes, it works,' said Lyall. 'They need a lot of cooking, though.'

'And what has to be glued?' asked Rosemary.

'Bowstrings – see.' Lyall pointed to another bench, where lengths of some hairy string-like material lay curled in a shallow basin. 'Hemp,' he told them. 'Soaked in glue for strength.'

Laura had drifted to a tub on the floor containing more animal products. 'Horns!' she exclaimed.

'Right. We make the nocks out of them, just for a few of the arrows. We've had to compromise and use some plastic ones as well. They're so easily lost, that's the trouble.'

'And you have to get the horns on the black market as well, do you?' Laura said jokingly to Danvers. For reply, he merely rolled his eyes at the ceiling and smiled faintly.

There were bundles of arrows neatly arranged on another bench, all apparently hand-turned on a lathe which had to be operated by foot.

Lyall ducked his head in mild embarrassment when questioned about the lathe. 'That is a slight cheat,' he confessed. 'It should be attached to springy sticks, stuck into the ground. Instead, I'm afraid I've resurrected an eighteenth-century machine that somebody offered us a few months ago.'

Danvers hurried to the rescue. 'Wood-turning is a subject all on its own,' he said. 'Did you know that Victorian aristocrats often adopted it as a hobby? They would make all manner of monstrosities in their spare time. It's always been a fascinating activity, you see – shaping the raw wood in so many different ways.'

'It's all absolutely wonderful,' Rosemary enthused, making another circuit of the whole shed. 'I suppose everything these days is made of plastic and nylon. This is so – real!'

'I'm glad you like it,' Danvers said. 'The credit all goes to Lyall. I'm just the academic. I could never have got it all together without Lyall's practical expertise. I wouldn't have had any idea of how to get hold of hemp, for example.'

'That was Harriet,' Lyall said. 'She did the sourcing.'

'True, perfectly true,' Danvers agreed. 'Harriet has been a marvel. But she never takes the credit. She insists that it's all my doing, I'm the one with the ideas, the driving force.' His face adopted a fond expression. 'She keeps my enthusiasm up when it falters, you see.'

'And does it falter often?' Laura asked gently.

Danvers looked away, staring fixedly as the tub of cattle horn. 'Sometimes,' he admitted. 'I do get low from time to time.'

'Harriet's good at that,' said Lyall. 'They call it facilitating, these days. She's a clever facilitator, is Miss Luke.' He had already returned to work, bent over a bench, slowly planing a handsome piece of yew, following the grain, pausing to stroke it with his hand every few seconds.

Danvers seemed about to say something, and then changed his mind. His gaze rested on his manager for a long moment, as if trying to extract the answer to a question he couldn't bring himself to ask.

'Well,' he said at last. 'We'll leave you to get on with it. Time to join the queue for my police interview.' He gave a high-pitched laugh, and ushered Rosemary and Laura out of the shed.

Chapter Seven

DI Paul Flannery was summoned to the usual session with his Superintendent, early that afternoon. He had his preliminary notes already prepared, from the half dozen brief interviews he had conducted in Baffington that morning.

The Superintendent was a man of few words, who seldom uttered a complete sentence. 'Initial impressions?' he barked, almost before Flannery had taken a chair.

It was impossible not to respond in similarly terse fashion. 'Tight-knit village,' he reported. 'Lord of the manor, employing an estate manager and part-time admin assistant. Names of Lyall and Harriet Luke. Luke had a relationship with the victim. There's a young vicar, only there for a year, and a sister of the deceased. Something complicated about the family farm being up for sale, and a herbal product business wanting to buy it. Two gardening women, brought in to clean up the churchyard – they found the body. Cause of death was an arrow fired at fairly close range, penetrating the heart with considerable force.'

'Victim. Who was he?'

'Malcolm Sutton, aged thirty-four. Left the village a year ago, and not seen since. Planned to sell off the farm for housing development. He announced this at a meeting last night, which ended in uproar. He was last seen by the two women, at nine o'clock.'

The Super held up a hand. 'These two women – they were the last to see him, and the first to find his body?'

Flannery shook his head. 'It's not what you're thinking,' he said. 'They've only been in the village for one day. One of them's been a copper herself. She was married to another, and mother to a PC. She's one of us. Nice lady,' he added, softly.

'Girlfriend? Something Luke.'

'Harriet. She's in a right old state. Very shocked.'

'Scared?'

'Possibly.'

'Carrying on with the estate manager?'

'Nobody's said anything, but it's not impossible. Both un-attached, good-looking, working together.'

'He won't have been happy when Sutton showed up again, then?'

Flannery sighed. 'Nobody was happy, sir. That's the thing. The whole village seems to have had a reason to want the bloke dead.'

'Start with the girlfriend,' the Super advised.

Rosemary and Laura had difficulty in gaining access to the churchyard to start work. Franklin Danvers had shouted at two young police officers on their behalf, demanding to have the logic of closing the entire area explained to him. Laura had soothed their ruffled feelings with sympathetic smiles, and a promise that she understood exactly what they needed to do.

'Just the same,' she said, 'I think we could safely start work on the hedge over there without disturbing you.' She pointed to the far corner of the churchyard, beyond the area of police interest.

'You'd have to walk over the pathways,' the constable argued. 'We need to keep it clear.'

'We could use the little gate at the back,' Laura suggested. 'And you'd be able to keep a close eye on us. The thing is, the village does need to know the Fayre will be going ahead as planned, in spite of what's happened. And seeing us getting on with the work would reassure them.'

It sounded a feeble argument to her own ears, but it appeared to work. The constable went away to consult his sergeant, and came back with detailed instructions as to just how and where they could work.

The main focus of police attention involved the area between the lych-gate and the church door, taking in the yew tree and about twenty graves.

'They must think the killer was standing over there,' said Laura, pointing at the front of the church. 'Maybe crouched behind that big tomb.'

'You mean the last resting place of Sir Isaac Wimpey,' said Rosemary. 'It's certainly big enough to conceal a whole battalion of archers.'

'I don't think archers come in battalions,' said Laura. 'But I take the point. On the other hand, there are any number of equally good hiding places in here. You'd think the local kids would find it irresistible for games of cowboys and Indians, or whatever it is these days.'

'I don't think kids play outside at all these days,' said Rosemary. 'And besides, now I think of it, I doubt if there are many people under eighteen in this village.'

'If there are, I haven't seen them.'

They collected billhook, loppers and wheelbarrow from Rosemary's Land Rover, and finally set to work on a corner of the jungle, as far as possible from the forensic work going on around the yew tree. The day was overcast but mild, and the work satisfying. They were determined to make a visible impact at least on one corner, before awarding themselves a brief lunch break, falling into their habitual teamwork almost without discussion.

Laura was wheeling the tenth barrowful of straggling undergrowth to a growing heap inside the churchyard wall when Franklin Danvers hailed her from the other side of the wall. He had evidently completed his testimony to the police, and was looking positively jaunty.

'That's the ticket,' he said approvingly. 'I can see we've struck gold with you two. To be frank, I don't think any of us fully appreciated the scale of the task when we asked you here.' He gazed at the small area they had so far cleared, with some surprise.

'We'll cope,' panted Laura, forking the refuse into a tidier pile. 'Is there somewhere we can recycle this lot? It would make good mulch if somebody had a garden shredder.'

'Marie has one,' he said, after a moment's thought. 'Up at Brockett's Farm.'

'Well, we can hardly go and ask her, can we?' Laura said, impatiently. 'Under the circumstances.'

Danvers narrowed his eyes, as if about to tell her a secret. He leaned over the wall. 'I think you'll find she won't have any objection to visitors. There was very little love lost between her and her brother. I telephoned her a little while ago, and she sounded as if she'd be glad of a chat with somebody.'

'Oh?' Laura struggled to make sense of this strange piece of information. 'Well, perhaps we will go over there later on today, then. Did you hear that?' She had turned to Rosemary who had come to join them, scenting an interesting conversation at thirty yards. Rosemary shook her head, and Laura explained.

'A shredder would be useful,' Rosemary agreed. 'And maybe I could have a look at those famous yew trees. I'm interested in what Redland Linton started to say about them.'

Laura glanced towards the big yew in the churchyard, still surrounded by police tape. 'Did the police say whether they'd found the bow that the murderer used?' she asked Danvers.

'No – and it's not going to be easy. Several people asked if they could keep the ones they used yesterday, for practice in the gardens. Just at the moment, there are longbows scattered all over Baffington, any one of which could have been used to kill Sutton.'

'Then they ought to be collected up,' said Laura.

Danvers nodded, vaguely. 'I think they've asked Lyall to see to that,' he said.

'But there'll be no incriminating evidence – not like a gun,' said Laura. 'It wouldn't be possible to show which bow had fired a particular arrow, would it?'

'Absolutely not,' said Danvers.

'Do you keep a particular set of arrows with their own bow?' Rosemary persisted. 'The one that did the dreadful deed had red and blue feathers. Were they all like that?'

'Flights, not feathers,' he corrected. 'And yes – the colours are the same for all of them. We took them from the coat of arms of the Dukes of Baffington. It was one of Harriet's best pieces of research, discovering that family. They died out after three generations, in 1502, and were completely forgotten until now. Did I mention how indispensable Harriet has been in digging up all sorts of gems of local history?'

'Yes, you did. It's all quite fascinating,' murmured Laura, with a glance at Rosemary.

'So – do you think somebody walked off with a longbow after the practice, intending to use it to kill Malcolm Sutton?' Rosemary asked.

'Very likely,' Danvers nodded. His casual manner irritated Laura. With the whole of Baffington almost hysterical with shock, here was their effective leader calmly discussing weaponry and ancient battles as if nothing had happened.

But her irritation was mixed with curiosity and genuine interest in the subject. There was something that didn't fit, in what they had just discussed. 'That doesn't work,' she said. 'At that stage, nobody knew that Malcolm was back in Baffington, did they?' She cocked her head questioningly at him. 'See what I mean?'

Danvers nibbled thoughtfully at his lower lip. 'Well…' he began.

'Actually,' said Rosemary, 'I saw Malcolm arriving yesterday, just before we went for tea at Harriet's. If I saw him, it's quite likely that somebody else will have done.'

'That's a point,' said Laura.

'That's right,' Danvers confirmed, but he looked suddenly preoccupied. 'This is getting complicated, isn't it. I hope it isn't going to impact on the Fayre. That would be a real tragedy.' Without waiting for a reply, he walked away, heading back towards his house on the hill.

'Oh yes,' muttered Rosemary to his back. 'Much more tragic than the cold-blooded murder of a man in his prime.'

At Highview House later that afternoon, three people were standing in the Great Hall, discussing the forthcoming banquet. Two of them were obviously distracted by insistent thoughts that had nothing to do with the Medieval Fayre.

'Come on, you two,' pleaded Franklin Danvers. 'Concentrate.'

Harriet Luke gritted her teeth, making a muscle jump at the corner of her jaw. 'I don't believe you sometimes,' she said. 'Don't you ever think about other people? Have you forgotten what happened in the night?'

Danvers tutted impatiently. 'Of course I haven't forgotten. But there's nothing I can do to change it, so the best thing is for us to look to the positive. The Fayre will be very therapeutic for the whole village, and the Banquet has to be the climax of the whole event. Lyall —' he turned to the other person ' – can we be sure that a whole bullock can be roasted properly on a spit? I've only heard of pigs and sheep being done successfully.'

Lyall rolled his eyes at Harriet, before replying. 'There is an element of risk,' he admitted. 'Keeping an even heat through such a thickness of meat won't be easy. And modern bullocks weigh more than twice what they would have done in medieval times. We might try a calf instead.'

Danvers took a whistling intake of breath. 'Not veal,' he said. 'Most of the village would refuse to eat it on the grounds of cruelty.'

Harriet gave a soft moan. Both men looked at her in alarm. 'I'm sorry,' she said, pressing a hand across her mouth. 'I can't go on with this today. I'm much too upset.'

'But Harriet —' Danvers began.

'Leave her alone,' Lyall said, suddenly sharp. 'Don't be such a slave driver.'

'She doesn't need you to defend her. Not from me, at any rate.' Danvers was suddenly furious, thwarted in his plans, made to feel in the wrong. 'I have always found that the best thing to do when there's trouble is to keep on with the routine. That's all I want – for things to carry on as closely as possible to how they were before. After all,' he burst out vehemently, 'what was Sutton to us, anyway? Nothing but a nuisance. Why should we let him wreck things for us by getting himself killed the moment he returns to the village?'

Lyall merely shook his head in mute protest. Harriet stared at Danvers. 'You – you,' she spluttered. 'You callous beast.'

Danvers flinched. 'Harriet,' he pleaded, his voice much softer, 'don't say that. I'm not callous – far from it. You know that's true. You know —'

'That's enough,' she said. 'I'm going home now before I say too much. If I'm feeling up to it, I'll see you both tomorrow.'

At roughly the same time, Keith Briggs was telephoned by Marie Sutton as he hurriedly made himself cheese on toast back at his large lonely vicarage, having missed lunch completely.

'Vicar?' she began, in a low voice, 'I just wanted to thank you for your help this morning. It can't have been very pleasant for you.'

'Please don't thank me,' he said awkwardly. 'It's all part of my job. At least, the police seem to think it is.' He found he could not quite avoid a fleeting thread of resentment at having been asked to identify the body of Malcolm Sutton, shortly after it was found in the churchyard. More, he liked to think, from the manner in which the request had been made than the fact itself.

'Well, it was good of you,' Marie repeated. 'I don't suppose the police were very sensitive, if the ones who came here were anything to judge by. And didn't they move quickly! I was still having breakfast when they turned up here to tell me the news.'

'I ought to have called on you before now,' Keith apologised. 'It's just that there seems to be so much happening, all at once. The whole village is in uproar, and they all seem to want to tell me about it.'

'Oh, please don't worry about me. It's not as if – well, you can hardly call me a regular churchgoer.' She laughed dryly.

'That doesn't matter – really, it doesn't,' he assured her. 'It would never even cross my mind. Anyway, how are you? I mean, the shock, and everything?'

'Oh, I don't know. I don't think it's really sunk in yet. It's all been so fast. I had no idea Malcolm was coming home, until suddenly there he was, making trouble for everybody again, upsetting poor Harriet, and ruining Redland's presentation – and then there he was dead. My head feels like cotton wool. I can't get on with anything. The dog thinks I've gone crazy.'

'Your brother certainly knew how to make his presence felt,' Keith agreed. 'Now – would you like me to come over later on today? I just have one or two things —'

'No, really. It's very kind of you, but I'm sure you have more important calls on your time. I'll be all right.'

'Well, if you're sure. You know where I am, if you want me.'

'Thank you.'

He put the receiver down, thinking how little he knew his parishioners, even after a year in the job.

* * *

After another session of jungle clearance, Laura remembered the suggestion of borrowing a shredder from Marie Sutton. She mentioned it to Rosemary, who jumped at the chance of a change of scene. When Laura questioned the wisdom of calling on somebody who had only just lost her brother, Rosemary reminded her that she had been kind to Marie when her father had died. 'She's probably expecting you,' she added.

'She'll barely remember me,' worried Laura. 'I really don't think it would be very diplomatic of us.'

'Well, how about this? We'll drive slowly past and see if there's any sign of life. If it's true that the poor girl has no other relatives, she might be desperate for a friendly face. On the other hand, if the yard's full of cars, we'll know she's open for visitors, and we might as well join in. Either way, I'm sure it'll be OK.'

'Oh, you,' said Laura, half-irritated, half-amused. 'You'd talk anybody into anything, you would.'

'And you just dither and worry about silly little niggles,' Rosemary told her.

The plan worked reasonably well. Rosemary drove the Land Rover slowly past the farm gate, noticing that it was empty of cars. Coming to a stop, she then began to reverse and drive into the yard. Instantly, a yellow labrador charged towards them, his ears flattened with suspicion, his voice raised in loud defence of his property.

'Oh, there's Bobby!' said Laura happily. 'I'd forgotten about him.'

'Huh?' Rosemary was confused. 'He looks as if he's determined to kill us.'

'No, he's just doing his job. He's a lamb, really. I caught Malcolm Sutton kicking him in a field when I was here last year.'

'That Malcolm – everything I hear about him makes me think he got what he deserved. The dog must have turned psychotic as a result.'

Laura laughed. 'He's not psychotic.' She opened the door of the Land Rover, and leaned out. 'Here, Bobby. It's only us. Where's your Mummy then? Have you been a good boy?' The dog stopped barking, but kept a narrow eye on the intruders. Every few seconds his lip curled back in a semi-snarl. Laura continued to work on him. 'What a good dog! It's only us. You don't want to hurt nice Auntie Laura, now do you? Come on, Rosemary.'

'Are you sure he's not psychotic?'

Laura was slowly getting down from the Land Rover, still crooning nonsense at the dog. 'Don't be daft,' she said. She held out a hand, and Bobby sniffed it carefully, before finally deciding she was acceptable. She patted his head with a laugh and he wagged his tail.

Marie Sutton appeared at the door of the handsome red brick farmhouse, watching Laura with some concern. 'He never lets people do that,' she said.

'Don't worry,' Laura smiled. 'He did everything he should when we first got here. You must have heard him. I've had to work hard to get this far with him.'

'I was terrified,' Rosemary added.

'Don't I know you?' Marie said to Laura, her face looking stretched and blank. 'I'm afraid my mind isn't working very well. You've heard, I suppose…'

'Of course. You probably don't remember me – I'm Laura Thyme, the vicar's cousin. I was here last year when your father died. At the fête.'

'Oh, yes, how stupid of me. I remember you perfectly now. You were very kind.'

'It was us who found your brother's body this morning,' Rosemary said gently. 'And we're terribly sorry. We don't want to intrude at all, but the thing is, Mr Danvers suggested you might lend us your garden shredder. We're working flat out, you see, to get the churchyard tidied up before the Fayre. I'm sorry if it seems a strange time to call, but Mr Danvers —'

'Bother Mr Danvers,' Marie said irritably. 'He always thinks he knows what I want, or what's good for me. If I have got a shredder – and I honestly can't remember ever seeing one here – it must be in the barn over there. Help yourselves.'

'We are so sorry about your brother,' Laura echoed Rosemary's condolences. 'It must have come as a dreadful shock.'

Marie merely nodded, and folded her arms tightly across her midriff. She seemed cold and shaky.

'Look,' Laura said, 'we really didn't mean to intrude. You look tired. Go back in, and we'll just get the shredder and leave you in peace.'

Marie sighed. 'No, no. Come in and I'll make some tea. To be honest, I've had enough of my own company.'

'Hasn't anybody at all been to see you?' Rosemary demanded.

'Well —' Marie tilted her head like a young girl afraid of saying the wrong thing. 'Not really. There's nobody here now, at least.'

The equivocal nature of this answer was not lost on Laura or Rosemary. As they followed Marie into the farmhouse, Rosemary mouthed 'Linton?' to her friend.

Laura found herself revising the assessment she had formed at the archery lesson of Marie as rather a drippy creature. As the girl set about preparing tea she seemed confident and relaxed, despite the circumstances. She lifted a big old-fashioned kettle from a massive Aga, and poured the boiling water into an earthernware teapot that had to be over a century old. A plate of homemade shortbread was produced, and strong tea poured into good quality china mugs. Everything felt settled and unpretentious.

'You don't really want to move from here, do you?' Laura asked.

Marie looked at her. 'Of course not,' she said. 'But I can't see any option. There's hardly any money in farming these days, and the work's far too much for me on my own. I've muddled through since Daddy died, renting out most of the land, and consulting all sorts of people, but it doesn't look possible to keep going any longer.'

'But Franklin Danvers isn't altogether the white knight he claims to be?' Rosemary suggested.

Marie groaned. 'He means well, I don't doubt that. He certainly isn't planning to swindle me. But quite honestly, I think he's being very unrealistic. I mean – who's going to come out here to visit yet another museum of medieval life, or whatever he decides to call it?'

'So what about Redland Linton?' asked Rosemary boldly.

'Oh, he hasn't been so bad. He's a lot more subtle in his methods than Franklin is.'

Rosemary nodded eagerly. 'Yes, he is a nice man, isn't he. I felt sorry for him last night – he never got a chance to have his say about what Knussens want to do here. Your brother completely stole the show.'

Marie went pale at the mention of Malcolm. 'So I gather,' she said tightly. 'Typical of Malcolm.'

'You've heard the whole story then?' Laura was quick to ask.

Marie flushed. 'Village gossip,' she said vaguely. 'I know Malcolm spoke to Harriet afterwards, and she seemed to be in quite a state about it. And Franklin threw one of his fits.'

'I gather there was no love lost between Malcolm and Mr Danvers.' Laura said.

Marie gazed over the fields, apparently deep in thought. 'I don't think anybody really liked Malcolm. And I'm not sure that Franklin is particularly popular himself. But villages are strange places. People accept each other, even when they give the impression of being arch enemies.'

They drank their tea companionably for a few minutes, until Marie got up abruptly, as if remembering something she had to do. But once on her feet, she seemed at a loss as to what she'd meant to do. She pushed back her sleeves in the hot kitchen, revealing strong forearms. And we called her a wimp, thought Laura. How wrong can you get?

'The police think I killed Malcolm, you know,' Marie burst out suddenly. 'They sent three officers to tell me what had happened. Actually, only one stayed with me and the other two started searching the outbuildings. Don't you think that's a bit high-handed?'

'They must have asked your permission,' said Laura. 'Otherwise they'd have needed a warrant.'

'Of course I said they could. I haven't got anything to hide. And they still haven't told me exactly what happened to him. I suppose you know.' She looked from one to the other.

'I'm sure they don't suspect you,' Laura soothed her, avoiding a direct reply. 'They won't have formed any theories yet. It's all a matter of collecting evidence at this stage, and working out the relationships. Didn't they ask you to identify him?'

'No. Keith did that for me. I suppose almost anybody could have done it. They all knew Malcolm.'

'Hasn't he been back home at all since last summer?' Laura asked.

Marie shook her head. 'For a long time, I never wanted to see him again, but he is – was – my brother, after all. We were inseparable as children. But he would persist in provoking Daddy all the time. It was dreadful towards the end. They were constantly shouting at each other. Malcolm was getting into some very dubious business to do with antiques, which Daddy and I both thought probably wasn't legal. He wouldn't tell us about it properly, which just made it worse. But he started making quite a lot of money – which is how he got up the nerve to leave. He'd never have done it otherwise. He liked his comforts, did my brother. That's why he couldn't stand farming. Too much weather, he used to say.'

Laura and Rosemary listened as they sipped their tea, letting Marie unload her feelings about Malcolm. She went on, 'And poor Harriet! He treated her really badly. You couldn't blame Daddy for disinheriting him. The farm would never have been safe in his hands.'

'So you knew he wanted to sell the land for a housing estate?'

Marie groaned. 'Yes, he told me yesterday.'

'Did he come here?'

Marie nodded. 'He tried to, but Bobby went crazy before he got through the gate. I had to go and talk to him in the road. He talked about meeting the Planning Officer and selling two hundred acres for some incredible sum of money. He said I should let him handle the public meeting. I wish I hadn't now.'

Laura frowned, trying to piece the story together. 'But it's your land, isn't it? Your father left it to you outright.'

'Yes, he did. But if Malcolm wanted a share, I couldn't for shame refuse him. He was my brother. And if his plan was realistic, there'd be plenty of money for both of us – and I could have stayed on here, with the remaining hundred acres.'

'Sounds a bit too good to be true.'

'I know,' nodded Marie sadly. 'It's amazing what the prospect of sudden wealth does to a person. Even though I couldn't really believe that Malcolm knew what he was talking about, I couldn't help starting to dream. New carpets, proper heating, get the roof insulated...the list was a mile long.'

'But you'd have been in dreadful trouble with the village,' Laura said.

Marie forced a smile. 'Thanks to Malcolm, Sutton's already a dirty word around here. I doubt if it could get much worse.'

Rosemary reached out and patted the girl's hand. 'Chin up,' she said. 'It'll all be all right – you'll see. Now, we'd better be getting along, if we can find that shredder.' Her concern for Marie increased, and she added, 'Isn't there somebody who could come and stay with you, keep you company?'

Marie flushed, and pulled her hand away. 'Please – don't worry about me. I'm used to being here on my own. Besides, I've got Bobby. He'll watch out for me.'

Rosemary's eye fell on a sick-looking yucca plant standing on a sideboard. 'The poor thing,' she burst out, without thinking. 'It's too dark for it there, you know.'

Marie looked at her with absolute incomprehension until Rosemary went over and picked up the plant. 'Oh!' she said. 'Is that what's wrong with it? Daddy gave it to me, the Christmas before he died. It was fine for a while.'

'Would you like me to take it away and give it some first aid? After all, it's what I do – and I think I can save it. Repotting, cutting back, feeding,' she muttered the treatment to herself.

Marie smiled wanly. 'Would you?' she said. 'That would be very kind.'

'A pleasure,' said Rosemary, without lifting her gaze from the unhappy yucca.

Laura and Rosemary loaded the shredder into the back of the Land Rover, and drove out of the farmyard.

'Lovely place,' said Laura again, looking back.

'Glorious,' Rosemary agreed. 'And who do we think her

mystery visitor was, then?'

'She does sound rather fond of your Mr Linton,' Laura said. 'I'd put him at the top of the list.'

'Mm,' said Rosemary, trying to suppress the niggling flutter of jealousy that was suddenly afflicting her.

Chapter Eight

Redland Linton received an urgent phone call from his MD, shortly before the end of the day. 'What's all this about a murder?' demanded Ms Sophia Stansfield. 'I hear it involves the Brocketts people.'

Linton did his best to explain the sequence of events.

'Why didn't you call me the moment you heard about it?'

'I've been rather busy,' he said, trying not to sound too subservient. The thing he hated most about his job was having a woman in charge. She always made him feel he was being chastised by his mother, every time she spoke to him.

'So, tell me now – how does this affect Knussens?'

'It's too soon to say. The farm belongs to Marie outright, so the death of her brother ought not to change anything. But it's sure to cause some delay. I can't go bothering her about selling the farm when she's in the middle of all this.'

'Yes you can. Offer her a shoulder to cry on. Tell her you can take a weight off her back, set her on a whole new start in life. She'll listen now, better than ever. Honestly, Redland, I sometimes think you've got no grasp of how women work.'

He gritted his teeth. 'I know Marie,' he said. 'She's not going to fall for the soft soap approach. If I make one false move, she'll cancel the sale altogether.'

'So don't make a false move.' Sophia's voice was dangerously smooth. 'You know how crucial this purchase is for the business. Don't let it slip through our fingers now. Just do what you have to, or you know what the consequences are going to be.'

Laura found the shredding oddly soothing, for the last hour of the day. The police had finished their forensic examinations, but the yellow tape was still stretched across the area where Malcolm's body had been found. As far as she and Rosemary could tell, the atmosphere of the village had changed only subtly, despite the fact of a brutal murder in its midst. A few passers-by paused to look over the wall into the churchyard before hurrying on their way – but not many people walked up and down the village street. There was no shop or post office, no school or doctor's surgery, to bring people into Baffington. Laura tried to imagine an influx of another forty or fifty people, if Malcolm's proposed new houses were ever to be built, and could not see it as anything positive. There would be additional cars rushing past the green, as their drivers commuted to jobs in a town or city far away, as well as extra school buses, and mothers taking children to clubs and sports. Whilst it could be argued that a modicum of extra life in the place wouldn't be a bad thing, a near-doubling of the population, with people who knew nothing about the history or traditions of the area, could only be destructive.

The car that drew up with a jerk outside the churchyard, just as Rosemary was putting her tools away and flexing her hands after so many hours of slashing and pruning, was familiar to Laura. She moved to the lych-gate to meet its occupant.

'All right?' she asked her cousin-once-removed. 'You seem a bit stressed.'

'Stressed!' His tone was bordering on hysterical, rather to Laura's concern. 'You have no idea.'

'I suppose you'll be in the thick of it, one way or another,' she said, trying to sound sympathetic. 'Seeing as how the murder happened in one of your churchyards.'

'It's not so much the murder,' he snapped. 'It's all the consequences and implications. Did you know they asked me to identify the body? Wouldn't you think they'd go to Marie for that? Or Franklin. I only knew the man for a few weeks, this time last year.'

Laura adopted a thoughtful expression. 'Yes, we heard you'd had to do that. I presume nobody else had seen him since last year, either. And they like it to be a person of – responsibility, I suppose. Not very nice, though. How's Harriet?'

'I don't know. I haven't seen her since this morning. I expect she's still very upset.' His shoulders sagged. 'That man has given her nothing but trouble from the start. And then, just when she thought he'd gone away for ever, back he comes, and tries to take up where he left off.'

'I thought she seemed quite pleased to see him again.'

'So did I,' put in Rosemary, who had joined them. 'Phew, I'm whacked. Come and see what we've done, Keith,' she invited. 'At this rate, we'll be ready in plenty of time, provided the police get out of the way. Do you know when they'll take that silly tape down?'

'No idea,' said the vicar. 'I'll come and have a quick look at your progress. It's good to know that something's going ahead more or less as normal.' He glanced at his watch, plainly implying that he could give them only a few minutes of his over-stretched time.

Rosemary waved towards the far corner of the churchyard, where a great many brambles, nettles and docks had been massacred, and a few feet of straggly hedge trimmed back. 'I've left that buddleia,' she said. 'I'm sure it's self-seeded originally, but it should look quite good if I give it a better shape, and clear all round it. Is that all right with you?'

Keith didn't answer. He was inspecting the area with close attention. He took a few steps into the long grass at the edge of the cleared section, swinging his legs sideways to bend the grass out of the way. 'Are you looking for something?' Rosemary asked him.

He gave her a startled glance. 'Nothing special,' he said. 'But all kinds of things get thrown over the wall, and it's become a habit to me to do a bit of a sweep every now and then.'

'We haven't come across anything so far,' Rosemary said. 'So what about this buddleia?'

Keith shrugged helplessly. 'I don't see why it shouldn't stay.' He smiled crookedly. 'To be honest, I don't feel that my opinion counts for very much any more. It's Franklin who calls the shots.'

'Only until the Fayre, surely?' Rosemary said. 'You're the vicar, after all.'

Keith shuddered suddenly. 'Are you all right?' Laura asked. 'You look as if somebody's just walked over your grave.'

'I feel a bit like that,' he muttered. 'I don't mind telling you this is all rather a struggle. Everybody seems to want something from me. I've got three more visits today, that I really have to do before I can go home. And then the phone won't stop all evening.' He gave the churchyard another unhappy look. 'And this isn't at all normal, is it? Not even here. It's never going to be the same again.'

Laura made a surprised sound. 'You mean you'd rather it was left as a jungle? Are you saying you didn't want us to tidy it up?'

Keith heaved a painfully long sigh. 'Not really. It's just that with everything else turned on its head, it might have been nice to keep this little oasis of calm – something unchanging. It's silly, I know. It'll look much better when you've given it your treatment.'

'Poor old you,' Rosemary sympathised. 'You sound as if you've gone off the whole human race. After all, this Malcolm bloke – he wasn't very nice, was he? After last night, it wouldn't surprise me if more people were rejoicing today than are sorry he's dead. After all, it looked as if it was a quick and painless death.'

'Yes,' Keith agreed, gazing over their heads at the church tower behind them. 'It's not simple is it? The morality of it all, I mean. Although, of course, it's a wicked thing to kill somebody, whatever they're like.' He said the last words flatly, as if there was no real feeling behind them. 'Now, if you don't need me, I should get on. If you see Harriet, tell her —' he tailed off.

'Tell her what?' Laura prompted him.

'Oh, nothing. That I'm sorry. That I hope she'll come to me if she thinks I can help at all.' He sighed. 'But I expect she'll find somebody else to console her, rather than me.'

Aware of his impatience to be off, Rosemary checked him. 'One more thing,' she said. 'Will it be all right if we use the church vestry for storing our tools? There doesn't seem to be anywhere else.'

'Of course,' he said shortly. 'Do whatever you like.'

He drove off, sweeping round the village green rather too fast for comfort.

Rosemary nudged Laura with her elbow. 'No points for guessing what's wrong with him,' she said.

'What?'

'He's fallen for Harriet Luke, the same as all the other men around here.'

Laura groaned. 'Well, if he has, it doesn't seem to be making him very happy, poor fellow.'

'Obviously not. How could it, when she's been carrying a torch for Malcolm Sutton all this time? She made that pretty clear after the meeting last night. If you ask me, that little fact came as a very nasty shock to Keith last night – as well as one or two other people.'

'Possibly to Harriet herself,' Laura said. 'She might have thought she was altogether over him, only to realise otherwise when she saw him again.'

Rosemary considered this. 'And there I was, fondly hoping they'd get it back together, when I was watching them last night. He'd never have been any good for her, would he?'

'Absolutely not. And perhaps she understood that herself, when she found a minute to think about it.'

'And now he's dead, she can really get on with her life.'

'Something like that,' Laura nodded, with a solemn expression.

According to their habitual system, they gathered up all the tools they'd used during the day, Rosemary wading through long grass at the far side of the churchyard.

Suddenly she bent down to retrieve something. 'Hey! Look at this!' she called.

Laura turned to see her friend holding something that looked like a stick, with red and blue feathers attached to one end. 'What is it?' she asked, foolishly.

'One of Danvers' arrows,' Rosemary said. 'The point's all cracked. It must have been fired into the wall.'

Laura shrugged. 'I suppose they'll be all over the village, with everybody practising for the Battle.'

Rosemary examined it more carefully. 'You don't think this might be what Keith was looking for, just now?' she said. 'Do you?'

Laura blinked. 'What do you mean?'

'Nothing, really. It's just – it looks quite new. It hasn't been here very long. And given the circumstances, you have to admit it might be important.'

'For heaven's sake,' Laura protested, 'you're not suggesting Keith killed Malcolm, after a failed shot that hit the wall? That's bonkers.'

Rosemary smiled. 'Of course it is,' she said. 'Now let's go and have a drink.'

They took the drinks outside and sat at one of the tables on the pavement in front of the pub. Their muscles gradually relaxed after the strenuous work they'd done, and their minds slowed down. The sky was clear, the whole village bathed in the sharp light that the last hours of the day could sometimes produce.

'Is it just me, or is there something sinister at work in this village?' Laura said. 'I'm not usually sensitive to atmospheres, but I really feel spooked by this place.'

Rosemary shook her head. 'I think it's you,' she judged. 'Apart from the minor detail of a murder, it feels perfectly normal to me.'

Laura swept the place with an all-embracing glance. 'Look at it!' she insisted. 'Not a soul to be seen. It's as if the Black Death had returned, or all the men had been taken to fight the Battle of Poitiers or something. It's like a time warp. I keep expecting to see a procession of monks, or an army of bowmen come over the hill. That's what it is – I realise now. It's Danvers and his obsession with the Middle Ages. It's contagious.'

Rosemary giggled. 'I don't envy you your imagination. Just wait till the evening drinkers get going. You'll see which century this place is in then.'

'Ignore me,' Laura gave herself a shake. But despite her best efforts, she could not entirely escape her strange imaginings, even in the bar later on, enjoying a last drink after dinner. Rosemary prattled on about tree pruning and the need to create proper pathways between the graves, with several new hedges to break up the stark expanse of ground, while Laura's head remained full of medieval images.

The next morning was cool and drizzly. 'We can't use the shredder in this,' said Laura.

'Then I suggest we go and search for statuary,' said Rosemary. 'I could fancy some shopping for a change.'

'There's a place not far away, I think. One of those massive garden centres that sells plants only as an afterthought. But shouldn't we ask Mr Danvers first? After all, it's his money we're spending.'

'Maybe.' Rosemary was doubtful for a moment, and then she brightened. 'Let's drive up to his place, and go straight on from there. It'll be quicker.'

The gravel in front of Highview House crunched luxuriantly under the Land Rover. 'Shouldn't we go round the back?' Laura asked.

'Of course not. He invited us in through the front last time, didn't he?'

'Yes, but,' Laura stared up at the imposing façade, 'somehow it makes me feel inferior.'

'You're still in the Middles Ages, like him,' Rosemary laughed. 'Just because he's paying us doesn't make us his serfs.'

There was no answer when they rang the doorbell ('That's not from the Middle Ages, anyway,' muttered Rosemary), so they started to get back into the Land Rover. Then, 'Hello?' came a voice.

Gordon Lyall, the estate manager, appeared from the side of the house, pushing a wheelbarrow full of logs towards a pick-up truck parked beside a large garage.

'Oh, hello,' said Rosemary. 'Is Mr Danvers out?'

'He is.'

'Do you know where?'

'He went to see Marie, Marie Sutton, that is. He wants to see if there's anything she needs. I told him I'd go, but he wouldn't let me.'

'Oh. We were there yesterday,' said Rosemary, just for something to say. 'Marie appears to be managing quite well, in the circumstances.'

'Mmm,' was all the reply she got.

'Perhaps you can help us,' Laura said, explaining their intention to go and buy statues for the churchyard.

'Go ahead,' Lyall advised them. 'Charge it up to the estate. Mr Danvers won't mind.'

Before turning to leave, Laura tried again to thaw the frostiness that pervaded Lyall's manner. 'When's the next archery lesson?' she asked, before realising that this might not be the most sensitive question, under the circumstances.

As an ice-breaker, it was a total failure. Lyall scowled. 'No idea,' he said.

'Right. Well, we'll be off, then,' said Rosemary. 'Sorry to have bothered you. We'll catch Mr Danvers another time.'

The garden centre was even better than they'd expected. It boasted a large area of garden ornamentation, including an inventive collection of statues. Angels, Greek goddesses, cupids and a variety of animals all jostling for attention.

Laura and Rosemary spent half an hour examining everything in stock, comparing them with Franklin Danvers' print of the churchyard.

Laura worried about the Victorianism of their selection, given that the theme of the Fayre was the Middle Ages. 'It really isn't very authentic,' she said, more than once.

'Come on!' Rosemary chided her. 'We're just doing what we're told. These things never get the history completely right, after all.'

'Even when the chief organiser is a famous expert?'

'Evidently not, since he gave us that nineteenth-century print to follow.'

'True. And you know they have things in America called Renaissance Fairs?'

'Do they?'

'So I hear. Marvellously good fun, I'm sure, but about as accurate historically as most Hollywood blockbusters.'

'Like *Braveheart*.'

'And *Troy* and *Antony and Cleopatra* and a hundred others.'

'So the history doesn't matter. Is that what we're saying?'

'Not entirely. I'm sure Danvers will get everything else as accurate as he possibly can. Costume, food, weaponry, all that sort of thing. It might even be that he's getting us to tidy the churchyard as some sort of gesture, to keep Keith happy. Not really to do with the Fayre at all, or not directly.'

'Oh, look at her!' Laura suddenly darted off to admire a life-sized statue of a Roman goddess, with skimpy drapery not quite covering part of her bosom, and her arms full of flowers. 'Isn't she gorgeous!'

'Lovely,' agreed Rosemary breathlessly. She was hauling a trolley loaded with stonework.

'Wouldn't she liven up the churchyard, though,' Laura went on. 'Who is she?' There was a card attached to the statue's wrist. 'Persifone,' she read.

'Persephone, you idiot,' Rosemary corrected her. 'Flower-gathering Goddess of Agriculture. I thought everybody knew that.'

'I forgot,' said Laura. 'If I ever knew. Perhaps I was away that day.'

'Come on, we'll have to get on. I hope we haven't spent too much.'

'Slave driver,' grumbled Laura.

The back of the Land Rover was crammed with their purchases, and they drove carefully back to Baffington. The sky had cleared completely, and the sun was making up for lost time.

They were almost back in the village, when Laura noticed a man standing near The Holly Tree, talking to her cousin Keith. 'Must be almost lunchtime,' she said, in a low voice.

'What?' Rosemary looked at her watch. 'Barely. Are you hungry already?'

'I could be. Stop here, will you.'

'But – what about unloading all these angels and cherubs? I can get a lot closer than this. Oh! I see.' She quickly drew to a halt, and let Laura leave the vehicle before her.

Laura patted her hair, and brushed a few invisible specks off her shirt, and moved towards the pub as casually as she could. Both the men watched her. 'Keith,' she nodded. 'All right?'

Keith gave a feeble smile, which Laura hardly noticed. 'Mrs Thyme,' said Detective Inspector Flannery, with a much more enthusiastic expression. 'I was wondering why you weren't in the graveyard.'

'We had to go and buy some – well, statues,' Laura explained. 'It was rather damp for hedge-trimming first thing.'

'Well, it's very nice to see you,' he beamed. 'And you, Miss Boxer,' he acknowledged politely. By an unspoken agreement, Flannery and Laura walked slowly along the street together. She began by asking him if she and Rosemary could start work on the yew tree and the area surrounding it. The Detective Inspector nodded. 'We think we've found everything we're going to, now.'

'Which isn't much, from the sound of it. No incriminating footprints?'

He shook his head. 'It was always a forlorn hope, with so much undergrowth. And we're wondering now whether the victim somehow spun round as he was hit. That could mean the killer was out here in the village street.'

'Unlikely,' Laura commented. 'Where could you get a decent sight line from out here? There's a massive great yew tree to contend with, for a start. Malcolm was behind the tree from here.'

She had got to the corner of the churchyard wall, looking over it at the tree with the church beyond. The wall made a right angle, continuing a short way before becoming incorporated into the side of a house. Beyond that again, the wilder area of the graveyard extended towards a field.

Flannery looked over the wall for some seconds. 'You're right, more or less. Although from the corner here, you might get a clear shot.' He waved an arm towards the long grass to the left of the tree, where Malcolm had been found.

'But it's right outside this house. Much too public, surely?'

'I know. It just seems unpalatable to think a person could commit a deliberate murder in the grounds of a church. Foolish of me, I suppose.'

Laura gave him a look that combined surprise with compassion. 'People will do all kinds of unpalatable things, though – won't they?'

He gave a short huff of agreement, and they stood together for a moment, contemplating the wicked ways of the world. Back at the lych-gate, Rosemary and Keith were talking idly, casting frequent glances at the others.

'I suppose you'll never know exactly where the bowman was standing,' said Laura, wondering whether it really mattered, in any case.

'Quite,' the detective agreed. 'Which is why we're moving on to other areas of investigation, and letting people get on with their usual activities.' He squared his shoulders. 'Your friend seems to be waiting for you.'

'She's hungry,' said Laura, glad that Rosemary couldn't hear this parody of the truth.

He considered for a moment. 'Well, let's go and have lunch, then,' he said easily. 'I expect we're all hungry.'

Keith Briggs excused himself when they suggested he join them, leaving the threesome to make their way into the dining room of The Holly Tree. The police detective led his little group to a far corner and after a quick word with the landlord, the two nearest tables were quickly secured with 'Reserved' notices, to ensure adequate privacy. Rosemary and Laura exchanged glances, half impressed, half amused.

'There's something we forgot to tell you about Malcolm,' Rosemary began. 'When we said he was on the phone here, after the meeting, he called the person he was speaking to "Sunshine". He was arranging to meet the person in the churchyard later that evening.'

Flannery did not appear to find this information very thrilling. 'Sunshine,' he repeated. 'Isn't that just a general term, used by members of the criminal community? Sort of cockney.'

'That's what I thought,' Laura agreed. 'After all, it hardly seems to apply to anybody around here.'

'Unless it's meant ironically,' said Rosemary. 'Right little rays of sunshine, the lot of them. Even before the murder, there weren't a lot of laughs.'

'But we thought we should tell you, just the same,' Laura said virtuously.

'Oh, yes. I'm very glad you did,' he agreed, meeting Laura's gaze for several seconds longer than necessary. 'Would you like another lager?'

'Better not. We've got to work this afternoon. So have you, I imagine.'

'We're looking into Malcolm Sutton's past, especially the last year. It's proving very difficult to establish precisely where he was.'

'I saw him rush off,' said Laura pensively. 'After he'd dumped poor Harriet last summer.'

'Pardon?'

Laura blinked at him. 'Surely somebody must have told you about that?'

'You told me she was very pleased to see him when he reappeared, and that they'd had a relationship in the past. You didn't specify that he'd dumped her.'

'It makes a difference, I suppose,' Rosemary put in. 'We're not very good witnesses, are we? Leaving out all the most important bits.'

Flannery sighed. 'You and the rest of the population. Don't worry. I'm used to it.'

Laura sat up straighter. 'Well, we know he acquired a gun, for some reason – assuming the one lying beside him was his – and that he kept up with developments here, since he knew Marie was planning to sell Brockett's Farm. So he probably didn't leave the country. Given his character, it seems more than likely that he was mixing with shady company, living off his wits, and plotting how he could come back here and make some serious money.'

Flannery listened patiently, but it was obvious that he'd worked this much out for himself some time ago. Laura continued undaunted. 'And that suggests his killer wasn't anybody from Baffington at all. It must have been one of his criminal chums, hoping for a share, or something, and getting very angry with him.'

'Except, my dear Mrs Thyme, angry people don't hide in overgrown churchyards with a longbow, awaiting their moment and killing with a single very accurate shot.'

'They might,' Laura argued. 'If it was a slow burn sort of anger.'

'And maybe the shot wasn't the first go,' said Rosemary, remembering the arrow she'd found. She told Flannery about it. He pursed his lips briefly, and asked her to produce it, but seemed less than excited by the discovery.

Laura offered one or two more theories concerning the murder, and the Detective Inspector did his best not to be patronising. He inclined his head slowly, and devoted a minute or two to his steak pie, before replying. When he did, it was a non-committal, 'You could be right, of course.'

The lunch was over too quickly for Laura. She had done her best to provoke the man, as a sort of perverse female test, and he had passed beautifully. He seemed to her to be intelligent, conscientious and open-minded. And he showed every sign of liking her as much as she liked him. What more could anyone ask?

'What happens now?' she wanted to know.

'Oh, the usual,' he said, with a little wave of his hand. 'Checking, questioning, forensics – you know.'

'Well, it's all a bit different from my time,' she said humbly. 'We didn't have DNA testing, for one thing.'

Flannery merely nodded. As they got up to leave, a slight commotion could be heard in the adjacent bar. All three moved to the door for a better view.

Harriet Luke was facing Gordon Lyall across one of the bar tables. 'Yes!' she said loudly. 'All right. I've said I'll find it.'

Lyall made a pacifying motion with both hands. 'It's no good shouting at me about it,' he said. 'I'm just doing what I'm told. The police want all the longbows collected up and accounted for. It's a perfectly reasonable request, surely.'

'Yes, yes.' Harriet ran a hand through her hair, her face strained. 'It's just one more thing, that's all. It'll be in the cottage somewhere.'

Lyall raised his eyebrows. 'I hope so,' he said. 'Apart from anything else, those bows are worth quite a lot of money.'

Flannery led Rosemary and Laura out of the pub, without

saying anything more. Nobody was in any doubt that the monetary value of the longbows was the least important consideration at that moment.

Chapter Nine

Franklin Danvers was feeling swamped. No fewer than five villagers had telephoned him in the last hour, expressing concern that the Fayre could not possibly proceed with a murder investigation in their midst. Joyce Weaverspoon had said the whole horrible business was making her ill, and she couldn't promise to be available for the Banquet, as promised. Since Joyce was the only person capable of organising the team of serving wenches, this had come as a severe blow. Franklin had spent a ghastly five minutes assuring Joyce that it was a sacred duty to keep the Fayre on track, as a way of holding Baffington together. His language became more and more military as he talked of fighting spirit and esprit de corps and the need to keep Baffington's image shining. Eventually he felt he had convinced her, and she reluctantly agreed to carry on.

The final phone call came from Redland Linton, the man from Knussens. Speaking in obscurely vague terms, he only partially held Danvers' attention. Once he realised that the conversation had nothing to do with the Fayre, Danvers switched off mentally and merely gave monosyllabic responses. Afterwards, he wondered what in the world it was that he'd agreed to.

The church smelled musty, with dust motes floating in the sunbeams that filtered through the high windows. 'Somebody's going to have to give this place a good once-over,' said Rosemary. 'Otherwise it'll detract from the fabulous churchyard we're going to create.'

'Not us, I hope,' said Laura. 'I've never been very keen on polishing.'

'Certainly not us,' Rosemary agreed.

They were shifting the newly acquired statues closer together, in an attempt to leave enough space for Keith to use the vestry for its intended purpose. 'He'll manage,' said Rosemary optimistically. 'It won't be for very long, after all.'

'Excuse me?' came a female voice, interrupting them. 'What's going on?'

Laura peered round the curtain. 'Oh, Harriet. Keith said it would be all right to store things in here. Don't worry – it isn't as bad as it looks.'

Harriet Luke shrugged. 'Not my business,' she said. 'I've just come with some flowers. Work doesn't stop just because – just because somebody's been mur– mur–' she broke down, her face screwed up in an effort not to cry.

'Oh, dear,' said Rosemary. 'There, there.'

'You were fond of him, weren't you?' Laura said gently. 'This must be terribly difficult for you.'

'I'm being a fool,' Harriet said angrily. 'I know he would never have started up with me again. But we were really close, you know, at one time. I adored him. And I thought he felt the same about me. And when we spoke, after the meeting, he was being so sweet. At least at first. I thought, just for a minute, that…well, you know.'

'But you realised it wasn't going to happen?' Rosemary prompted.

'Not then. Later, yes. I quite quickly came to the conclusion that I should forget all about him, because he was never going to be trustworthy. I think I went a little bit giddy, seeing him again out of the blue like that – but all the time I knew there was never going to be any chance of picking up where we left off. I had my self-respect to consider, after all. He never did anybody any good in his life.' She spoke breathlessly, her face flushed with emotion. 'I know I'm not making much sense,' she finished miserably.

'I'm sure you've got lots of good friends here, who'll help you work through it all,' Rosemary suggested.

Harriet smiled bitterly. 'Not that you'd notice. So far, two people have made it clear that they believe they know who killed Malcolm, and another two have been giving me extremely peculiar looks. I won't name any names, but there are all sorts of whispering campaigns going on, some of them against me, some targeting Lyall, and perhaps the majority claiming Redland Linton is the obvious killer. It's all based on guesswork and personal prejudices. And it all makes me sick.'

Laura raised her eyebrows. 'Heavens!' she said. 'We haven't

noticed anything like that going on. How horrible.'

'It's human nature, though, isn't it,' said Rosemary. 'Wanting to have it all settled, and the culprit shut away. But fancy suspecting Redland. Just because he's a stranger in the village, I suppose.'

Harriet sagged exhaustedly onto a pew, letting some of the flowers fall from her grasp. 'I don't know,' she sighed. 'I can't even think properly.'

'Come on,' Laura tried to be bracing. 'It's not that bad. If you weren't involved in the crime, then you've got nothing to fear, have you?'

Harriet made an effort to regain her composure. 'It's not as simple as that,' she said. 'In a small village, it takes a long time before people forget things that have been said. Trust is lost, you see.'

'It seems to me that your Malcolm Sutton is responsible for a great deal of damage,' said Laura. 'And it isn't over with yet.'

'He wasn't my Malcolm Sutton,' Harriet snapped. 'I just told you. '

'Sorry,' Laura muttered, feeling quite daunted by Harriet's volatile moods.

'Now I don't know what to do,' Harriet went on, sinking back into gloom and despair. 'Everything's got into such a mess.'

'So —' Rosemary began determinedly, having remained on the sidelines for long enough. 'Where were you that evening?'

Harriet stared at her as if she'd grown a second head. 'How dare you?' she demanded. 'What gives you the right to ask me that?'

Rosemary gulped before replying. 'The ordinary right of one human being to another, I suppose. Plus the small detail that Laura and I actually found the body. That in itself involves us. We wouldn't be normal if we didn't want the whole thing solved, and justice done.'

Harriet's temper subsided slightly. 'If you want to know where I was, just ask the vicar. He'll vouch for me. I've already said as much to the police.' She bent to pick up the fallen flowers, making sure not to meet the eye of either Rosemary or Laura.

Then she spent a hurried five minutes arranging the blooms in a vase beside the altar. Nobody spoke again until Harriet said calmly, 'There's a choir practice here at five. We'll need everything to be tidy for it – all right?'

With raised eyebrows, Rosemary and Laura assured her they would leave the church as they'd found it.

'Is she saying she and Keith were together late that evening?' said Rosemary, after Harriet had gone. 'I mean – it must have been really late if she's using it as an alibi. Does that seem odd to you?'

Laura fiddled with one of her earrings. 'I'm not sure,' she said. 'I did have a feeling that Keith was rather fond of her, even last year. I suppose things could easily have moved on somewhat since then.'

'If it's true, it makes a good alibi for both of them,' Rosemary observed.

'Very neat,' said Laura, wondering why the suggestion bothered her. 'Now, I'm going out there to see if the police have taken that tape away. If they have, we might make a start on the yew tree. I won't be happy until it's done. If we're not careful one of those dead branches is going to drop off and kill another of Baffington's finest.'

'I'll be out in a minute,' Rosemary said. 'I just want to have a quick search for a scrubbing brush or something. Most of those headstones could do with a bit of a clean.'

Laura looked dubious. 'Isn't that a specialist job?'

'I'm only going to get some of the moss off them. I'll be very gentle.'

Laura went outside and Rosemary started her quest, convinced that the church ladies would have a collection of buckets and mops tucked away somewhere. Her investigations led her to a curtained-off alcove, which turned out to have a lot of folding chairs stacked inside it. Between two of the stacks, she spotted a metal mop-bucket, complete with old-fashioned string mop propped against the wall. Moving the chairs, she noticed a narrow door which seemed to lead out into the churchyard. As she stared at it, she realised that the wood of the door frame, close to the handle, was splintered.

Grasping the handle, which was stiff and rusted, she found the door opened easily at a push. Somebody had forced it, by hacking away at the frame until the whole lock had come loose. As soon as the door swung outwards, she checked the frame from the other side, realising that it still looked quite normal. Outside, as she'd expected, there was a particularly jungly section of churchyard, with the yew tree in a direct line of sight. Laura was halfway between the door and the tree, only her upper body visible in the undergrowth.

At the sound of the opening door, Laura looked up. 'Oh, hello,' she said.

Rosemary giggled at the picture she presented. 'Doctor Livingstone, I presume,' she said.

Laura did a quick impression of an African explorer, before saying, 'I didn't know there was a door there. It's practically invisible from out here.'

'Come and see what somebody's done,' Rosemary invited. 'The whole lock has been torn away. Mind you, the wood of the door frame isn't very good. The screws must have come out fairly easily.'

Laura waded through the undergrowth, arms held high to avoid nettles and briars. 'Doesn't it show from the inside? Why hasn't somebody noticed?'

Rosemary explained about the alcove and the stack of chairs. Then they both turned to face the churchyard again.

'There's a direct line of fire to the spot where Malcolm was killed,' said Rosemary, stretching out an arm to represent the flight of the arrow. 'At night, he'd have had no idea there was somebody standing here.' She looked down at the ground, thinking she might find some footprints. Instead she saw a small object on the threshold of the doorway, which she bent to pick up. It was carefully made of horn, with a notch at one end and a cylindrical hole at the other. 'Look at this!' she exclaimed. 'Isn't it one of those arrow things? What did Lyall call it?'

'A nock,' said Laura, one hand resting on the stone of the church wall, the other held out palm upwards for Rosemary's discovery.

'We've found the spot Flannery was looking for,' she went on. 'This is where the killer stood and fired an arrow at Malcolm Sutton,' she said, eyes wide.

Lyall had almost accomplished his task of collecting together all the longbows. He had made phone calls and visits, and stopped people in the village street, and not only Harriet Luke had indicated that they had better things to do than fetch the bow from whatever safe place they'd put it in. Joyce Weaverspoon, in particular, had objected vigorously. 'But I need so much more practice,' she had wailed.

'Sorry,' Lyall was implacable. 'They all have to be gathered in.'

Eventually all but one had been returned and DI Flannery had personally followed up each one, testing for fingerprints, and poring over the list of villagers who had been issued with a bow. The fact that one was still missing was the single most useful fact in his investigations to date.

But it proved to be less useful than he had first hoped. 'But surely you know who has or hasn't returned their weapon?' he demanded, as Lyall failed to produce just such a list.

Lyall grimaced apologetically. 'The trouble is,' he said, 'that some people just dumped them back here, without reporting to me at the same time. Everybody I asked said they'd returned theirs, but – well —'

'Let's start again,' said Flannery heavily. 'You are quite certain that twelve were issued after the practice, I suppose?'

Lyall nodded. 'There were twelve taken to the Glebe field from the workshop, on Monday afternoon.'

'And there are twelve names on your list?'

Lyall recited the names rapidly. 'Keith Briggs, Marie Sutton, Joyce Weaverspoon, Franklin Danvers, the three Broadford brothers, Harriet Luke, Jim from the pub, myself, and Mr and Mrs Hopkinson.'

'You've included yourself and Mr Danvers? Isn't that slightly odd?'

Lyall shrugged. 'Only because we do actually each have a longbow. There are only twelve finished and fit to use. There are no more anywhere in the village. I'm hoping to complete another three or four by the time of the Fayre, but at this moment, that's it.'

Flannery sighed. 'Well, let's go through the list one more time,' he suggested. 'And then I'll get somebody to collect the fingerprints from everyone on that list.'

Keith Briggs was a worried man. The presence of his cousin Laura had reminded him of his early weeks in the incumbency, when the only thing that caused him sleepless nights was the feebleness of the village fête. A year on, there were far worse causes for concern. Everywhere he turned he seemed to meet hostility and suspicion. His role as comforter and counsellor had suddenly evaporated, leaving him feeling wretched and useless. Another consequence of Laura's presence was that he could not avoid thinking about his mother and her continued opposition to his choice of career. Although he struggled to maintain his certainty as to the rightness of his course, his mother's attitude inevitably led to self-doubts.

And now, with the village collapsing around him, he added shame to the list of painful emotions he carried with him on his daily rounds. Shame like a leech, draining away his confidence and his faith.

The daily rounds themselves were beginning to feel futile. He visited the elderly and the sick, he chaired parish meetings and tried to invigorate the Baffington church choir. And he told himself, for the tenth time that day, he really must go and see Marie Sutton.

Finally, with only an hour to spare before the choir practice, he directed his car towards Brockett's Farm. Speaking to Marie on the telephone was not enough. Despite her resistance, he knew his obligations. In any case, Malcolm would eventually have to have a funeral and he, the Reverend Keith Briggs, would expect to officiate.

But in the gateway to the farm, he found his way obstructed. Another vehicle was emerging, and the driver, on seeing Keith, waved for him to stop and then got out of his own car.

'Vicar!' said Redland Linton, extending a friendly hand, 'It's good to see you.'

'Oh – um – you too,' said Keith.

'Visiting Marie, are you?'

Keith merely nodded.

'Well, if you'll take my advice, you'll leave it for now. As you see, I've just come from there, and I'm afraid she's not in a very receptive mood.'

'If she's upset, then —'

'No, no. Not exactly upset. She's busy, to be honest. Otherwise engaged.'

Keith frowned. 'I'm sorry, but I'm not sure – I mean —'

'You mean you don't know whether you can take my word for it.' Linton laughed. 'Quite right. I don't blame you a bit. But it's true. I know what everybody around here thinks of me, and I can see it might look bad, bothering her so soon after her loss. But the fact is, Knussens are in a position to make life very much easier for poor Miss Sutton. I've just left her with a detailed proposal, and I'm hoping, you see, that she'll sit down and read it right away, and come to the best decision for all of us.'

Keith drew a deep breath. 'Mr Linton,' he said, rather loudly, 'I hope you haven't been bullying her?'

Linton looked genuinely hurt. 'Of course not. I'm extremely fond of the girl. Don't forget, she approached us, in the first instance. She knows the value of the yew woods on her land, and saw our appeal for just such woodlands, back last winter. There's no question of bullying.' His reproachful look made Keith hang his head and mumble, 'Sorry.'

'So, be a good chap,' Linton pressed on. 'Come back again later. Trust me – it's for the best.'

And Keith allowed himself to be turned away, with a sense of being reprieved once again.

Rosemary was trying to concentrate on the churchyard, despite the turbulence just beyond the wall, in the village beyond. 'Look at it,' she'd said, waving an arm at the large area of undisturbed undergrowth. 'We've got days of hard grind before it begins to look respectable.'

'Yes, I know,' Laura said. 'I've been doing it.' She pointed to the patch she'd been slashing at when Rosemary had appeared like a vision from the small side door. 'Most of that goes back to just a few big brambles. If we can dig them out, it'll make a huge difference.'

Rosemary's gaze had shifted to the large tomb just to the right of the church door. 'That ought to be made into a feature,' she said thoughtfully. 'If we cut everything back from around it, and cleaned it all up, and maybe added one or two shrubs to set it off, it would look magnificent.'

Laura moved closer. 'Sir Isaac Wimpey,' she read. 'Born 15th July 1824. Died 12th April eighteen ninety-something. Oh dear, a bit of the stone's come away. It's either a six or an eight, I think. It looks bad like this. Neglected. I wonder who he was.'

'There's a quote running all around the bottom,' Rosemary noted. 'See?' She read the inscription slowly. ' "To the memory of Sir Isaac, the finest horseman in five counties. Mourned by his many friends, who erected this monument to preserve his memory forever. May he enjoy the glorious pursuit perpetually."' She looked at Laura. '"Glorious pursuit" – doesn't that mean cricket?'

Laura pondered briefly. 'I think it's more likely to mean fox hunting in this context. Sounds as if he didn't have any family.'

Rosemary picked cautiously at the broken numeral. 'It would be nice to fix this, don't you think? If we knew the right date, we could do a quick repair job on it.'

'Somebody around here probably remembers what it was. If not, we can ask Danvers,' Laura advised. 'He'll know where the records are.'

They had closed the hidden door again, replacing the chairs as they'd been originally. Rosemary had noted that the bowman must have done the same, covering his – or her – tracks with considerable care. 'It might be sensible to keep quiet about it,' Laura said. 'At least until we manage to tell the police.'

The work occupied them until shortly before five, after which they straightened up painfully and surveyed their handiwork. 'How about that?' Rosemary breathed proudly.

'Unrecognisable,' Laura smiled. 'All we need now is an admiring audience.'

Instead they were approached by a glum-looking Lyall, who seemed oblivious to the churchyard improvement.

'I've just seen Harriet,' he said, his manner somewhat more assertive than previously. 'The poor girl seems very upset about everything.' He shook his head crossly. 'She even says she won't take part in the longbow contest, now. Says we ought not to hold it at all, after what happened.'

'She has a point,' said Rosemary. 'Don't you think? I mean, what's Marie going to feel every time an arrow thumps into that target?'

'Don't you worry about Marie. She isn't shedding any tears over that worthless brother of hers.'

'But Harriet is,' Laura observed.

'Aye,' he nodded. 'And it strikes me that you two must have made it all worse, from something she said.'

'What? How?' They stared at him.

'I don't know, do I? She wasn't making very much sense, but she seems to think you asked her some pretty insensitive questions. I hate to see any girl upset, but Harriet Luke hasn't asked for any of this. She just wants to find herself a good man and settle down.'

'We only asked her where she was on the evening that Malcolm was killed,' said Rosemary defensively. 'She said everybody in the village keeps asking each other that, anyway.'

'So what did she say?' Lyall's expression was intense, his thick black eyebrows pulled into a frown. The fact that he had been in the army was all too apparent in his upright bearing and slightly old-fashioned attitude towards women. He saw himself as their protector, it seemed, and very well fitted to the role he was too, Laura noted, realising how handsome and strong he was. He and Danvers made a good pair, both of them more comfortable with the values and habits of the Middle Ages than those of the present day.

'She told us to ask the vicar,' Rosemary answered his question a trifle reluctantly. Too late, it occurred to her that it might be unwise to reveal this detail to Lyall. Jealousy seemed to be in the air, as well as fierce passions concerning the future of Brockett's Farm.

Lyall gave this some thought. 'You mean, she said the vicar could account for where she was, from when Sutton was last seen until the time he was killed?' His face changed to an expression of disbelief. 'Not possible,' he concluded.

'Why not?' Laura wanted to know.

'What would the vicar and Harriet be doing together at that time of night?'

'Church business?' offered Rosemary.

Lyall shook his head. 'They've agreed to cover for each other, that's what it is.'

'I don't think Keith would tell direct lies to the police,' Laura objected. 'He is a vicar, after all.'

'Maybe they think they're helping – making things easier.'

'And maybe it's true,' Rosemary said.

Lyall's face darkened even further. 'The sooner all this is sorted, the better. Nobody feels safe, the way things are. That Sutton bloke deserved all he got, I don't care who hears me say it. But until the police catch the killer, this village is going to be a nasty place to be.'

'You've been collecting up the longbows, haven't you?' Laura remembered. 'Did you find them all?'

'I can't tell you,' he said stiffly. 'It's all in the hands of the police.'

They watched him march away. 'I don't know about you,' muttered Laura, 'but I still can't decide whether he's an old-fashioned gentleman, or – or –'

'I think you might have been closer to it when you compared him to Heathcliff,' said Rosemary. 'Something isn't right about him. He looks like a man with a secret to me.'

'Probably just another of the local men who's crazy about Harriet,' sighed Laura.

They took a short break on the village green, drinking lemonade they'd bought at the pub. They were sitting on a wooden bench dedicated to a local lady by the name of Audrey Winthrop, who had died ten years earlier. As they pondered the difficult questions about Malcolm's death, an elderly man, somewhat red in the face, approached them. 'Good afternoon, ladies,' he greeted them. 'Gerald Winthrop.' If he had been wearing a hat, he would have doffed it to them.

'Winthrop!' said Laura, turning to read the small plaque on the back of the seat. 'Is this...'

'My dear departed wife,' he nodded. 'It always gives me great pleasure to see somebody using the seat.'

Rosemary smiled up at him. 'Hello again,' she said. 'I remember we met on Tuesday – just after we found —'

'Yes, yes, I remember,' he said hurriedly. 'Terrible business. Upset the whole village quite dreadfully.'

'You've lived here a long time, then?' Laura remarked, after an awkward silence.

'Not so terribly long, as it happens. I retired early from the stock exchange and set up a little business of my own down here. It was a dream come true, until —' he sighed and glanced at Audrey's plaque, as if it were her gravestone. 'She only had three years here. It was a very cruel fate.'

'And are you still running your business?' Rosemary asked him gently. He did seem rather old to be working, but she knew all too well that self-employed people kept at it much longer than most.

'In a small way,' he nodded. 'Antiques, you know. Medieval artefacts, mostly.'

'Oh!' Laura said with enthusiasm. 'Like Mr Danvers. You must work together then?'

Mr Winthrop's face hardened slightly. 'You might say so,' he conceded. 'Although we sometimes find ourselves differing over definitions. I'm strictly a dealer, you see, and he's a collector. It can cause – well, differences.' He lapsed into a brooding silence for a few moments.

'And are you very much involved in the Fayre?' Rosemary said, to get him going again.

Mr Winthrop perked up. 'Oh yes. I think it's a splendid idea. Anything that increases local interest in the period has my approval. I'm very much with Franklin on that. I'm the church organist as well, for my sins. We're due for a practice in a few minutes. I was on my way there when I noticed you two ladies on The Seat.'

Laura had a sudden idea. 'Dreadful business with the murder,' she said. 'I suppose you must have known Malcolm quite well?' She remembered something Marie had mentioned. 'Didn't he have something to do with antiques as well?' she asked.

The man's face grew several shades redder. 'He should never have come back here,' he hissed. 'Causing all kinds of trouble within hours of his return. The man was a menace.' He didn't actually say *and he's better off dead*, but the words hung in the air.

'Bad news for the young ladies of the village, I gather,' said Rosemary.

'Bad news for everybody,' Mr Winthrop snarled. 'Do you know —' he leaned his face closer to theirs, 'I caught him trying to sell fake artefacts. Can you imagine what that would do to the market? People's trust is fragile enough at the best of times. The man was a shameless criminal.'

'When was this?' Laura asked.

'Oh, a year and a half ago, something like that. Well, I wasn't going to put up with it. I went to his father – who happened to be a good friend of mine – and put it to him straight. Either send that boy packing, or I'll set the police onto him.'

'Quite right too,' approved Rosemary.

'And he went,' Laura concluded.

'Yes, he went, but not for several more months. Not before he'd broken poor Miss Luke's heart and caused his father so much worry it finished the poor chap. Whoever it was that slaughtered the wretch did everybody a favour. He had it coming to him.'

'It wasn't you, was it?' asked Rosemary playfully. 'I bet you're pretty good with a longbow.'

Mr Winthrop laughed in genuine amusement. 'Not me. My aim's so bad that Franklin's man, Lyall, told me I needn't think I'd be required for the battle display. No, no, my place is at the church organ – and I've yet to discover a way you can kill anybody with that.'

Rosemary giggled, and Mr Winthrop savoured her amusement for a moment. Then, with an alarmed glance at his watch, and a polite 'Excuse me, the rehearsal starts in five minutes.' He hurried away.

'You might drive somebody to suicide if you played the organ badly enough,' Laura muttered to his retreating back.

'What a nice old man,' said Rosemary fondly.

'I doubt if Malcolm Sutton thought so – or Franklin Danvers, from the sound of it,' Laura said. 'From my limited experience of antique dealers, they can be pretty ruthless when they choose.'

Laura had placed the little horn nock in a plastic bag, in best police detective fashion, and kept it in her room at the pub. 'It's obviously one of Mr Danvers',' she said to Rosemary. 'Made the old-fashioned way.'

From the church came the sounds of the choir rehearsal, which seemed to be lasting a considerable time. Needing to straighten up in the vestry, Laura and Rosemary tiptoed to and fro, pausing frequently to listen to the music. Keith was conducting a motley collection of adults and youngsters, who were valiantly trying to tackle a complicated series of madrigals. Up to that point, the singing had been unaccompanied, but now Mr Winthrop was invited to join in on the organ.

'The basses need you to keep them true,' said the vicar. 'Could you give them the line at the top of page three?'

Mr Winthrop played most of the line, and then hit a note that was very far from true. It wheezed and groaned like a suffering bison. Keith winced. 'What on earth was that?' he demanded.

'I have no idea,' said Mr Winthrop, playing the note three or four more times, with the same result. 'It was all right on Sunday.'

'Can you play round it somehow?' Keith asked. 'We really do have to get on. Mr Danvers wants us to give a three-hour concert as part of the Fayre.'

'Yes, I know,' said Mr Winthrop, his patience strained. 'I'll do what I can. It might come right by itself.'

The rehearsal struggled on, with the bass parts still far from perfect. Rosemary and Laura stopped work and stood just outside the vestry, enjoying the whole thing. 'I hate to say it,' Rosemary whispered, 'but your cousin Keith isn't very good at this, is he?'

Laura grinned. 'I don't suppose it was in his job description. Hymns, perhaps, and Handel's *Messiah*, but five-part madrigals seem a bit beyond the call of duty.'

'If Danvers thinks it's so important, why doesn't he conduct them?'

'Because I get the impression he's a man who has mastered the art of delegation,' said Laura. 'Ouch!' This last came involuntarily from her lips as Mr Winthrop accidentally played the defective note again. 'There really is something wrong with that organ.'

'Damp got in,' suggested Rosemary carelessly. 'Or a stray bit of bramble from the churchyard.'

'Hmm,' said Laura. 'I think I'll just go and have a little look.'

Rosemary let her go, still enjoying the parts of the madrigal that the choir did best. Harriet Luke's soprano was clearly discernible, leading the others in a pure tuneful voice. Not just lovely to look at, but a talented singer as well, thought Rosemary. Some people have all the luck.

Earlier in the day Laura had found a stepladder in the vestry, and moved it to a small dark area beside the organ pipes, to make space for the statues. Now it was a simple matter to quietly set it up, and climb to the top of the organ, without anybody in the church noticing her. She spotted a dangling string protruding a few inches from one of the largest pipes, and slowly began to pull at it.

Almost immediately a smooth length of wood emerged, which she quickly identified as a longbow. Her surprise caused her to wobble on the steps, and clutch wildly at the nearest pipe. Uttering a stifled squeal of alarm, she kicked out, trying to regain her balance, making a loud thunk against an organ pipe. Fortunately the organ was robust enough to remain steady, and after a moment to get her nerve back, she reversed down the steps, carrying the bow. Only then did she realise that her antics had attracted the attentions of the entire choir.

There was another observer of Laura's discovery, standing unobtrusively just inside the main church door. DI Flannery had returned to Baffington a few minutes earlier, hoping to witness some of the more subtle interactions amongst the residents. It was a habit he had developed with some success over the years. On this occasion it paid off even more magnificently than he could have wished for.

At Laura's sudden disturbance, necks were craned and Mr

Winthrop got to his feet. Keith, still trying to conduct the choir, was the slowest to grasp that something odd was happening. Finally even he turned to see what had put the singers off.

'Laura!' he cried. 'What on earth are you doing?'

In some embarrassment, she held the longbow aloft. 'I think I've just found the cause of the trouble with the organ,' she said. With a nod to Mr Winthrop, she added, 'Try it now.'

Fumblingly, he pressed the key. It gave a clear ringing note.

But the vicar was staring at the bow in horror, his face drawn and deathly pale. 'You – you,' he stammered. 'How? Where?'

Laura moved towards him. 'It was stuffed down one of the organ pipes,' she said slowly. 'It must be the one used to kill Malcolm Sutton.'

It was the end of the choir practice. Loud mutterings filled the church as the singers discussed this latest twist. They looked from Laura to Keith to the longbow – and then, one by one, most of them turned to stare at Harriet Luke. Because Harriet was moaning, a hand clamped tightly across her mouth.

DI Flannery took careful note of these reactions before slipping quietly out of the church, a satisfied smile playing on his lips.

Half an hour later the Detective Inspector interviewed Keith and Harriet in the living room of Harriet's cottage. 'I just want to try to understand the importance of what happened here this afternoon,' he said. 'I've been speaking to Mr Lyall about the longbows, and need some help.'

'You ought to ask Franklin,' Harriet said. 'They're his bows.'

Flannery smiled. 'I will,' he assured her. 'But I believe you two can clarify one or two details for me.'

'Go on then,' said Keith tiredly.

'Firstly – am I right in thinking that the discovery of the longbow in the organ pipe a little while ago came as a considerable shock to you both? You'll perhaps be aware that I was present, and saw your reactions.'

'No – we were not aware of that,' said Keith, speaking for Harriet.

'No matter. The point is, it was a shock to you both,' continued the detective.

'Of course it was,' said Keith. 'A complete bolt from the blue.'

'Were you aware that a longbow was missing? That Mr Lyall had failed to locate the twelfth one, after being asked to collect them all in?'

They both shook their heads.

Flannery permitted a short silence before asking carefully, 'I'm sorry to ask this, but would you two kindly explain to me just what your relationship is.'

Keith tensed, as if about to leap to his feet. He avoided looking at Harriet, who was gazing fixedly at her own hands. 'Harriet works for me,' said Keith. 'That's all.'

'So when you both tell me you were together on Monday evening, at the approximate time of the murder, I'm to believe that you were merely discussing work matters? Is that right?'

'We were talking about the public meeting, and the Fayre,' said Keith.

'And exactly where were you?'

'We've already told you all this,' said Harriet. 'We were here in this house. We had coffee, and then Keith left at about midnight. Possibly a little bit later.'

'And this was a normal occurrence, was it? The two of you would often stay up late talking over coffee? On a purely businesslike basis?'

'Why not?' Keith burst out. 'What are you implying?'

Flannery said nothing, sitting back with a patient expression. Harriet broke the silence. 'It wasn't a normal occurrence,' she said. 'The evening had been very unusual, and we both needed to talk about it, and the implications.'

'And that's all?' They nodded. 'In that case, why the hysterics this afternoon, when the longbow was found?'

Harriet's face crumpled. 'Because,' she cried, 'I realised I was looking at the weapon that had killed Malcolm. And whatever else he might have been, he was at one time my boyfriend – my lover. Can't you understand what that felt like? It was as if I was seeing the arrow hitting him. I think it was at that moment that the real facts got through to me – that Malcolm is dead, and I'll never ever see him again.' She collapsed into helpless sobs. Keith patted her arm ineffectually, and the Detective Inspector closed his notebook.

The long summer evening seemed much too nice to waste indoors, debating the events of the day. 'Tell you what,' said Rosemary, 'why don't we go and see the yew woods at Brockett's? They're obviously important to Redland and Knussens. I'd be interested to try and work out why.'

'Isn't it private property?' Laura objected.

'There's sure to be a public footpath through it,' Rosemary said confidently. 'In this sort of area, there's always a footpath.'

'I'm sure you're right,' said Laura with a sceptical twitch of her eyebrow.

Rosemary was right. Parking the Land Rover beside a fingerpost pointing directly towards the woods, the two walked along the footpath, where long grasses swished against their legs, and evening shadows made flickering patterns through the trees. In spite of herself, Laura began to take an interest in the woods, once they got closer to them. Rosemary identified the trees as Irish yews, a more recent species to Britain than the one in the churchyard. 'They grow differently, see,' she pointed out. 'The branches are practically vertical.'

'And do you think the Knussens man's story about a cancer cure is credible?'

'Well, it is partly right. I know there's a substance called taxol obtained from yew trees that's used in chemotherapy, in combination with other things. There's probably a steady demand for it, but I got the impression he was talking about something new, as if it's still at the experimental stage.'

'What's wrong with that?'

'Probably nothing. I just had a funny feeling about it, for some reason. And look here —' she indicated a wound in the bark of one of the trees. 'Somebody's been collecting samples of bark, very recently.'

'That'll be Knussens, presumably. I wonder whether they had permission.'

Before Rosemary could answer, there was a flurry in the undergrowth close by, followed by a fast-moving bundle of yellow animal, making a considerable noise.

'Hey!' Laura shouted. 'Down, boy!'

The labrador took no notice, but leaped all round them barking his loudest. Laura tried the same crooning she'd used on him before, plus everything she knew from her police training to subdue him, with little success. Rosemary retreated nervously to the far side of the largest of the yew trees. 'What's come over him?' she quavered. 'He wasn't as bad as this on Tuesday.'

Greatly to their relief, a whistle sounded not far away, and the dog instantly went quiet. 'Bobby!' came a female voice. 'What's the matter?'

Within moments, Marie Sutton appeared, carrying a dog lead and whistle. 'Oh, it's you two again, is it? You're trespassing,' she said.

'Sorry – but there was a footpath sign,' Laura argued.

'The path goes over there. You've left it about fifty yards back. People often seem to do that, despite the clear fingerpost.' Marie sounded irritable and tired. Laura decided to make allowances for her behaviour, under the circumstances.

'We must have been too busy talking to see it,' she smiled. 'At least Bobby knows what's what.'

'He was like a different dog,' said Rosemary faintly, still keeping a respectful distance.

'I encourage him to protect this part of my land from intruders,' said Marie. She looked stronger and taller than she had the last time they'd met, as if she felt ready for a fight of some kind.

'Well, no harm done,' said Laura. 'He was only doing his job, after all.'

Marie gave her a look as if trying to work out how the tables got turned, putting her in the wrong.

'It was all my fault,' Rosemary added. 'I couldn't resist having a look at your yews.'

Marie said nothing, her expression tight and preoccupied. The dog stayed close beside her, looking up worriedly at her face. 'Oh, Bobby,' she sighed, after a few moments. 'What're we going to do?'

Laura took charge. 'You poor thing,' she sympathised. 'You must be feeling in a dreadful muddle, with everything that's happened. Not just your brother getting killed like that, but the worry over the farm, and everything. Why don't you go back to the house, and —' She had been about to suggest a cup of tea, but stopped herself just in time. Marie Sutton was in no mood for platitudes.

'Oh, yes, I suppose I should. I came out here to try and forget it all for a bit, but there's no getting away from the truth, is there?' Her eyes were large and tragic, as they had been the previous summer when her father had died. Laura remembered how sorry for the girl she had felt then, as well.

Marie turned and began to walk away, the dog at her heels. Then she stopped, as if remembering something. 'You could call in, if you like. I'm sorry if I was rude.'

'We can't stop now,' Rosemary said. 'But don't forget I've still got your yucca.'

'That's right,' said Marie absently.

Suddenly the dog began barking again, with a renewal of his aggressive keep-off-my-territory note – even more businesslike than before. All three women looked in the same direction as Bobby. There was a man approaching. 'Call him off, will you!' he demanded, his voice squeaky with apprehension.

'Oh – Redland!' said Marie, barely audible over the barking. 'Sorry about this. Bobby! Quiet now.'

The dog gradually subsided, grumbling throatily to himself. Marie spoke at a more normal pitch. 'I wasn't sure if you'd come.'

Laura and Rosemary watched Linton picking his way between the trees, seeming to know just where he was going. He looked at the women, rapidly assessing the situation. Laura thought he seemed rather proprietorial, considering how uncertain things were.

'I went to the house, but you weren't there,' he said. 'So I decided to come down here on the off chance of finding you.' He glanced round at the trees, as if to check that they were all present and correct. 'How are you? Hello, Rosemary. We must stop meeting like this.'

Rosemary giggled, and Marie seemed to relax. Even the dog quietened down. 'I'm surviving,' Marie said. 'It's kind of you to come.'

Rosemary could not resist the temptation to question him. 'These trees,' she began, 'are they the ones you think might provide a new cancer cure?'

'Um —' said Linton, glancing at Marie.

Rosemary carried on, without waiting for a reply. 'I see you've been taking some samples. I just wondered what you'd discovered. Is it all a deadly secret, or have you already publicised your findings?' She spoke lightly, more interested in keeping his attention than in cross-questioning him.

But Linton took it in a different vein. He shook his head impatiently. 'There's no secret. We're well known as pioneers of natural therapies for a whole range of diseases, of which the yew bark is just one. I mean – one of the therapies, not one of the diseases.' He forced a laugh. 'But it's all in Marie's hands.' He looked at the young owner of the farm with a smile. 'There's no hurry for a decision now, of course. With the tragic death of your brother, I wouldn't dream of hassling you.'

Marie sighed. 'I am sorry, Redland. I was so close to deciding, only a few days ago. I really like the idea of the yews providing help for sick people. But now —'

'I know,' he said.

'But I promise I won't keep you in suspense for too much longer. Once the police have caught Malcolm's killer, and we've had the funeral, I'll be in touch. Is that all right?'

Redland Linton moved closer to her, and took her hand. 'Thanks, Marie,' he said. 'You've been really good about everything, and I very much appreciate it.'

Bobby, who had been idly sniffing about in the undergrowth, suddenly growled and pushed himself between his mistress and her visitor. Rosemary could have hugged him. She decided to take things further. 'Actually,' she said, 'we wondered whether we could come and see you sometime? We thought you might show us around your premises.'

Linton looked at her. 'Oh?' he said, as if the idea was the wildest thing he'd ever heard.

'Yes. We'd like to pick your brains a little bit about yew trees,' she said. 'Because of the one in the churchyard, you see. We're supposed to be preserving it, and I thought you might have some ideas.'

'Well, if you really want to,' he said reluctantly. 'When were you thinking of?'

'Tomorrow afternoon?' Rosemary suggested. 'We've got heaps of work to do, but we could probably get away at about four.'

Linton shrugged. 'Sounds OK,' he said.

'And you'll show us round, will you?' Rosemary persisted.

'If you like,' he agreed. 'Anything to increase good relations with Baffington.' He spoke with only a hint of irony.

'Good. We'll see you tomorrow, then,' said Rosemary with a broad smile.

Once out of earshot, as they walked back to the road, they talked about Linton and his work. 'That business about a cure for cancer,' Laura said slowly. 'It's very emotive, isn't it? They must assume goodwill on all sides, because they're doing such a virtuous thing. It gives them huge moral credit.'

Rosemary cocked her head. 'So?' she challenged.

'So it feels like a kind of blackmail to me. It isn't fair. Marie must be under enormous pressure to sell to Knussens. And I just wonder whether in the long run, Franklin Danvers and his Medieval Museum might not be a much better option.'

'Pooh!' scoffed Rosemary. 'You must be joking. All that traffic and noise.'

Laura shook her head. 'Not necessarily. Remember Lyall's workshop, with those fabulous smells. Don't you think that sort of thing should be preserved?'

'Probably. But it doesn't have to be at the expense of Knussens. Their plans to make medicinal use of the Brockett yews would bring nothing but good to the world.'

'Are you sure about that? You didn't sound too certain a few days ago.'

Rosemary shook her head indecisively. 'Ask me again tomorrow,' was all she would say.

Almost before work began next morning, Franklin Danvers was in the churchyard, running an analytical eye over the progress achieved. 'Not much time for getting new hedges in,' he observed.

Rosemary paused halfway through putting on her leather gloves. 'Well, no,' she agreed. 'But we can at least plant some young shrubs, which would have a dramatic effect. We'll get started on marking out where they ought to go today, and prepare the ground for them.'

'And the yew tree still needs attention,' Danvers continued.

'Yes,' said Rosemary, with as much patience as she could muster. 'We'll try to do that today, as well.'

'Good,' he said heavily. 'But even so – I'm not sure —'

'You can rely on us,' Laura assured him. 'We've got all kinds of ideas for restoring the whole churchyard to its former splendour.'

'Which reminds me,' added Rosemary. 'That tomb.' She pointed to the large sarcophagus containing Sir Isaac Wimpey. 'I think it deserves to be given pride of place. But the lettering's been damaged. You don't happen to know where we can find out what year he died, do you?'

Danvers pursed his lips. 'That interloper,' he said, crossly. 'The man shouldn't even be here, let alone given such a prominent position. He came here from Devon, according to the stories, and quickly gathered around himself a crowd of local lads who should have known better. They had more money than sense, and devoted their time to sports, women and drink – probably not in that order. Wimpey died falling off a horse, and his cronies got together a subscription for this monstrosity.'

'His death must be in the church records, surely?' Laura said.

'As it happens, Keith had a look, a few months ago, and couldn't find it.'

'Or the local newspaper? It sounds as if he would have made a good story.'

'Possibly. But the local rag's archives burnt down in 1944. If copies exist at all, they'll be at the newspaper library in London.'

'Well, I think he sounds very romantic,' said Rosemary. 'And since his tomb is here to stay, we may as well make the most of it. If all else fails, I can look up his death certificate in St Catherine's House.'

Danvers shook his head. 'That's up to you,' he said. 'But I can't see how you'll find the time.'

Laura gave a soft sigh. Mr Danvers probably didn't realise that he had just thrown down a challenge that Rosemary would never be able to resist.

The new day also saw Harriet Luke striving to control her emotions. She presented herself at Highview House at ten, only to find her employer absent. This was not especially unusual, and she let herself into the office at the back of the house, automatically switching on the computer.

Ten minutes later, Franklin Danvers found her busily reviewing orders for costumes required for the Fayre. 'There won't be enough pairs of boots for the men,' she told him. 'I asked for two dozen, but they've emailed to say they can only send us eighteen.'

'Does it matter?' Danvers seemed jaded and preoccupied.

'It does really,' she said. 'If six of them have to wear something different, it'll look peculiar. Even if we have to use home-made ones, with felt or something, it would be better than letting them wear walking boots or Wellingtons, or whatever comes to hand.'

'Harriet,' sighed Danvers, 'I do appreciate you making the effort to attend to all this. I realise you're doing it for my benefit.' He smiled at her. 'This Fayre would never be taking place at all if it wasn't for you.'

'Yes, well,' she said briskly. 'It's too late to abandon it now. And if it's worth doing at all, it's worth doing properly. Listen, I think I should go to London tomorrow, and see if I can track down another six pairs of boots. I know one or two places I can try. But I need to see them, not just get a description on the phone. Besides, it'll be nice to get away from here for a bit.'

'As you like,' said Danvers. 'Though I can't see why everybody suddenly wants to go to London.'

Before Harriet could ask him who else had expressed the same intention, they heard a car door slam in the yard outside.

'Lyall,' said Danvers, peering through the window. 'Looks to be in a vile mood again.'

The estate manager came to the office door. 'Sorry I'm late,' he said gruffly. 'The police wanted to speak to me.'

'Again?' said Danvers.

'Right. About those longbows. They've been making me go through the list of people who had one, about a million times. My head's spinning with it.'

'And were you helpful?'

'Eventually,' Lyall nodded, looking at Harriet. 'I'm sorry,' he said, 'but I had to tell them the truth.'

'What do you mean?' she demanded, her eyes very wide.

'Harriet – you're the only person I can't be sure about. You said at first that you couldn't remember where your bow was. And even though you assured me you found it, I didn't actually see you returning it. The police have fingerprinted all of them, and your prints aren't there. So they think that must have been your bow in the organ pipe. I'm sorry,' he repeated, 'but it looks as if you're going to have to answer a whole lot more questions.'

Harriet looked wildly from Lyall to Danvers and back. Her employer seemed almost as stunned as she was by this bombshell. 'Good Lord!' he spluttered. 'That's impossible. The police can't be such fools as to think –' He smacked his hand on the desk in an explosion of frustration. 'How can they suspect Harriet of all people,' he asked Lyall, who merely shook his head wordlessly.

Chapter Eleven

Keith saw the police collect Harriet, early that afternoon. He had been hoping to catch her for a discreet chat, away from inquisitive village eyes, and had therefore gone through the churchyard and out of the gate at the back. Before he could cross the narrow lane to Harriet's cottage, he realised she was walking away from him, down towards the village street, accompanied by a young policewoman. Without thinking, he began to run after them.

'Harriet!' he called. 'What's happening?'

The two women stopped and turned. Harriet gave a bleak smile. 'I think it's called "helping with enquiries",' she said.

'You're being arrested?' he gasped. 'My God!'

'No, sir,' said the policewoman. 'Miss Luke is not technically under arrest. We'd just like to ask her a few more questions. If she can give us a satisfactory account, then she'll be free to leave any time she likes.'

'But why not question her here, like you did before?'

'Much more convenient at the station, sir,' said the woman.

'Not for Harriet, it isn't,' he objected.

'Keith,' Harriet pleaded. 'Don't get in a state. It'll be all right.'

He directed a look of pure anguish at her, which made her flush and drop her gaze. 'But —' he began. 'It isn't right.'

'Please don't get upset, sir,' clucked the policewoman. 'All being well, she'll be back before you know it.'

'Will you bring her home again, or does she have to call a taxi?'

'We'll bring her, sir. Don't you worry about that. There's a fair bit of traffic in and out of Baffington just now, as you'll appreciate.'

Keith watched helplessly as Harriet was ushered into the back seat of a police car. Then he walked along the street, past the front of the pub, and hung about by the lych-gate into the churchyard, hoping to find his cousin.

Rosemary and Laura emerged from The Holly Tree two minutes later. 'Oh, hello, Keith,' Laura said cheerfully. 'Checking up on our time-keeping, are you? Well, we were rather late going for lunch today, which is why we're only just getting started on our afternoon shift.'

Keith ignored her explanation. 'They've taken Harriet for questioning!' he blurted. 'I don't know what to do.'

'What!' Rosemary went up to him, on the other side from Laura. 'Why?'

'I have no idea. They questioned us together, yesterday, after the choir practice – you know, about the longbow you found – and everything seemed to be all right then. At least, that's what I thought.' He frowned miserably at his feet. 'I don't think I can cope with much more of this,' he mumbled. 'It just seems to get worse and worse.'

'Don't despair,' Laura urged him. 'Did they say they'd arrested Harriet?'

He shook his head. 'They'll bring her back when they've done with her.'

'Oh, well then,' she said, 'there's nothing to worry about. Just a few questions. After all,' she added superfluously, 'this is a murder enquiry.'

'Yes!' Keith shouted. 'I know that. What I don't know is what I'm meant to be doing about it, when nobody wants me to speak to them, nobody cares what I'm going through.'

'Hey,' said Laura, as if to a small boy. 'Calm down. It's difficult for everybody. Just hang on, until the police catch the killer. After that, everything will straighten itself out and the village can get back to normal. Besides, you can't give up now – you're needed for the Medieval Fayre, remember.'

This was not the best thing to have said. Keith gave a strangled moan, clutching handfuls of his own hair, and began to walk unsteadily across the green to where he'd left his car.

'Oh, dear,' said Rosemary.

'We missed seeing them taking Harriet,' said Laura. 'That's a pity.'

'Why? So you could have another glimpse of your dishy detective? How do you know it was him, anyway? He probably sent a junior.'

'Of course he wouldn't have come personally,' said Laura. 'I know that.' But her tone was wistful. 'I just mean we could have reassured Keith better if we'd heard what was said.'

Rosemary let it go at that, mindful that Laura wasn't the only one to harbour feelings towards one of the men they'd met recently. Her appointment with Redland Linton later that afternoon was causing flutters of anticipation, and made the time seem to drag.

'Come on,' she said. 'Back to work. Danvers is going to want to see progress on those hedges by this time tomorrow.' The afternoon had turned out hot, forcing Laura and Rosemary to find less exposed tasks than the clearance work. Laura had been cutting back some of the lower sections of the yew tree, putting the trimmings into a black bin liner. Rosemary carelessly stripped the needles from a low branch and tore them into bits between her fingers. When Laura's bag was full, she took it into the vestry. Rosemary followed her.

Laura went over to a bucket containing the young trees they had acquired for the new hedges. 'I need to give them my special treatment first,' she said now. 'Give me an hour or so, will you?'

'I would, but I've just remembered that wretched yucca of Marie's. If I don't see to it soon, it'll die on me, and I'll never be able to face her if that happens.'

Ten minutes later, the yucca had been stripped of its dead leaves, and Rosemary was starting to extract it from its confining pot, preparatory to giving it a new home with fresh compost and a good feed. 'Hey!' she breathed, glancing at Laura, who was adding some sort of liquid to the pail containing the young trees. 'What's this?'

'Hmm?' Laura said, without looking up.

Rosemary went over to her. 'What are you doing with those saplings?' she asked.

'Never you mind. Just a traditional remedy I thought I'd try.'

Rosemary shrugged. 'Some silly old wives' tale, I suppose.'

Laura continued with what she was doing. 'So?' she said. 'I am an old wife.'

Rosemary snorted, and thrust her hand under Laura's nose. 'Look at this,' she ordered. 'It was tied around the stem of

Marie's yucca.'

In her hand was a cardboard label, that must have come with the yucca when it had been first bought. 'The writing's gone very faint, but you can still see some of it,' she said. 'Just shows the poor thing's never been properly watered, for a bit of card not to have rotted away.'

'What does it say?'

Rosemary deciphered the faded writing with difficulty. '"Happy 'stmas, Sunshine. Lo' 'm Daddy."' That must be "love from", I suppose. She said her father gave her the plant the Christmas before he died.'

'"Sunshine!"' Laura yelped. 'Did you say "Sunshine"?'

'Marie Sutton,' Rosemary stared at the card. 'Malcolm was meeting his sister in the churchyard, when he got himself killed.'

They argued about the wisdom of confronting Marie with their discovery. Laura favoured going straight to the police, but Rosemary insisted they ought to hear what the girl had to say first. 'We might have got it all wrong,' she worried. 'Jumping to conclusions.'

'I don't see how,' Laura said.

'Come on,' Rosemary started towards the Land Rover. 'Nothing like the present.'

'Malcolm had a gun, remember,' Laura said, holding onto the side door handle as Rosemary took a bend on two wheels. 'Does that mean he planned to shoot Marie? So he could have the farm all to himself? Slow down, will you? We'll be in the ditch at this rate. And – do you think she – Marie, I mean – saw him there, with the gun, and tiptoed through the church with a bow and arrow, and she killed him?'

'Sounds a bit improbable,' said Rosemary, slowing very slightly. 'I mean – she was useless at archery. We saw her.'

Laura tried to concentrate. 'We didn't see her even try. Maybe it was all a clever act to make everybody think she was useless. After all, she knew Malcolm had come back that day, which is more than anybody else did. What if she stole one of Danvers' bows, for the purpose of deliberately killing her brother? Maybe we were right about her and Redland Linton, that they are intending to live at Brockett's together, with his pharmaceutical business to keep them going very nicely. Malcolm would have been in the way.'

'We'll soon find out,' said Rosemary, steering the Land Rover into the yard of Brockett's Farm.

Marie's labrador barked in a frenzy when Rosemary rang the front doorbell. When nobody came to the door, the dog became increasingly hysterical until Laura decided they should retreat and give the poor thing some peace.

'But what if Marie's in there?' Rosemary protested. 'Her car's in the yard, look.'

'If she is, she's unconscious,' said Laura, before slapping a hand across her mouth. 'Oh! You don't think…?'

'Of course not,' said Rosemary robustly.

Anxiously, Laura tried to peer through the window next to the door, relieved that it belonged to a room the dog couldn't enter. She wouldn't have been surprised if he'd come smashing through the glass, lacerating himself in the process.

'I can't see…' she began, before a voice behind her cut her short.

'Hello?' came Marie's clear country tones. 'What's all the noise about?'

'Your dog,' said Rosemary, superfluously.

'You've got him all worked up,' Marie reproached them, stepping past to open the front door and let the animal free. As soon as he saw his mistress, his temper cooled and he danced around the three of them, tail wagging.

'I was right across the first field,' Marie panted.

Rosemary was reminded of Harriet's state of high emotion the previous day, and wondered whether there might be a link. Or were Malcolm Sutton's two women – sister and former girlfriend – both so distraught by his death that they just weren't functioning properly?

'Sorry,' said Rosemary. 'I'll just go and get your yucca, and then we'll leave you in peace.'

Rosemary went to the Land Rover to fetch the plant. 'I've

repotted it, and removed the straggly bits, and polished it up,' she said. 'It's amazing what a bit of basic kindness can achieve.'

Marie took it, but then seemed unsure what she ought to do with it. 'Thanks,' she muttered. 'It's very kind of you.'

'This was tied to it,' Rosemary said, producing the tattered label. 'You might want it, even though it's so damaged. Your father called you "Sunshine", did he?'

Marie nodded. 'Ever since I was little.'

'What about Malcolm?'

'What do you mean?'

'Did he call you "Sunshine" as well?'

'Now and then, when he wanted something from me. It was usually meant sarcastically when he said it.'

Rosemary spoke gently. 'Marie, we heard your brother on the phone to somebody, an hour or so before he died. He used the word "Sunshine" to that person, and he was arranging to meet them in the churchyard. We decided we ought to tell you, before we go to the police.'

'Go to the police?' Marie seemed bewildered. 'Why would you do that?'

'Because if we didn't, we'd be obstructing them in their enquiries,' said Laura, pompously. 'Surely you understand that.'

'Did you meet Malcolm that evening?' Rosemary prompted.

Marie sat down on the edge of a stone trough which was full of summer flowers. 'I went there, as we'd arranged,' she said, her shoulders slumped. 'But Malcolm was already dead. I saw him under that great tree, with the gun beside him on the grass, and I assumed he'd been planning to shoot me. He'd lured me there, saying he wanted to talk about the farm, somewhere quiet and neutral, in the light of what had happened at the meeting. Actually, I think it was because Bobby hated him so much, he hardly dared come here. Anyway, I wanted to know how the meeting had gone, so I was quite happy to do as he asked. It never occurred to me I'd be in any danger.'

'So when you saw him dead, why didn't you call the police?'

Marie looked up, meeting Rosemary's eye with a faint smile. 'For one very simple reason,' she said. 'I was glad he was dead, and I was grateful to whoever did it. After all, it seems obvious that he was planning to threaten me in some way, using that gun. Whoever killed him quite possibly saved my life. That's why I wanted to give them time to hide the evidence, or get away, or whatever they needed to do.'

'And get yourself right out of the picture as well,' Laura suggested.

Marie nodded. 'That, too.'

'So who do you think killed him?' Rosemary asked.

'Oh, I know who did it,' said Marie flatly. 'But I really don't think I should tell you that. You'll just go straight to the police and tell them, won't you?'

'Hearsay evidence – it wouldn't count,' said Laura briskly.

Marie frowned. 'Really?'

'It would be different if you confessed to us that you did it. But all you're doing is passing on a suspicion. For goodness' sake – the whole village is doing that anyway. If you actually saw the murder being committed, then I'd very strongly advise you to go to the police of your own accord, as soon as possible. But I don't think that is what you're saying, is it?'

Marie seemed to yield to Laura's authority with some relief. 'You really know what you're talking about, don't you?' she said. 'I've been dreadfully worried about it all. Everything seems so horribly complicated. There's Linton on at me all the time, and Mr Danvers trying to get me on his side, being so sweet and kind all of a sudden. I don't want to be ungrateful, but honestly – it's all a bit much.'

'Now will you tell us who you believe killed Malcolm?' Rosemary said, in a near whisper. 'You'll feel better if you share it. And Laura can advise you on what to do next.'

'Harriet,' said Marie. 'Harriet and the vicar. They were both in the churchyard, as my brother was lying dead amongst the graves outside. I saw them going out through the little gate behind the church, that leads to the lane where Harriet's cottage is.'

Into the sudden silence that followed this revelation came a yelp from Bobby, accompanied by a slow wag of his tail. 'Oh – it's Lyall,' said Marie, her face flushing.

'Don't worry – he didn't hear what you said just now,' Rosemary assured her. 'We'd better be going.'

Laura was standing frozen to the spot by the implications of what Marie had said. 'You must have got it wrong,' she muttered, quickly. 'You can't have seen what you think you did.'

Rosemary gave her a little push. 'Hush,' she said. Then, more loudly, she addressed Marie. 'We'll need to talk a bit more about this. But for now, it was good of you to be so straight with us.'

Lyall was approaching, and heard these last words. His eyebrows raised, as he looked enquiringly at Marie. She took a deep breath. 'Hello,' she said. 'More bounty from Mr Danvers, I suppose?'

Lyall gave a quick nod. 'A load of logs for your Rayburn,' he said.

In the Land Rover, Rosemary went over what they had just learned. 'I'll say one thing,' she commented, 'your Detective Flannery is more on the ball than I thought. He's had his eye on Harriet from the start.'

But Laura wasn't listening. She had her hands clasped together and pressed to her chest, in an attitude of anguish. 'Not Keith,' she whispered. 'Surely not Keith. What on earth is his mother going to say?'

Their appointment with Redland Linton was imminent, as Rosemary suddenly remembered. 'We'd better go straight there,' she said. 'If you feel up to it.'

Laura squared her shoulders. 'I suppose so,' she muttered. 'Not that I can see much point to it now. All I want to do is find Keith and ask him what was going on that evening.'

'Maybe it would be better to leave that until later, anyway,' Rosemary advised. 'When you've had time to consider all the angles.'

'Angles?'

'Implications. Besides – what can you do?'

'I don't want to do anything. I want him to tell me it's all a mistake, and of course he wasn't involved in the murder.'

'Plenty of time for that this evening,' Rosemary said. 'Meanwhile, I for one am looking forward to meeting Redland again. He was very friendly yesterday, don't you think?'

With an effort, Laura gave the matter her attention. 'Smarmy, I thought. Trying too hard to be charming. I can't bring myself to trust him, to be honest.'

'You've got him all wrong,' Rosemary protested.

'I don't think so. You're obviously sloppy about him – though I can't see what the attraction is. He's just a self-serving suit, trying to get on the right side of Marie Sutton and everybody else. You've been much too influenced by his boyish good looks. You ought to take my word for it that he isn't on the side of the angels, whatever he tries to make people think.'

'Curing cancer seems rather a benevolent enterprise to me,' said Rosemary crossly.

'Surely you don't think he's doing it out of the goodness of his heart? If it works, it'll earn him and his company a fortune.'

'Laura! Such cynicism shouldn't be allowed. Redland's a perfectly decent chap. Marie herself said he hadn't been hassling her nearly as much as Danvers had.'

Laura stared at the passing hedgerows, muttering about childishness and misplaced affections. 'What?' Rosemary demanded. 'What are you saying?'

'You don't want to know. But you'll see that I'm right. I'm a very good judge of character, and I can tell you for certain that Mr Redland Linton is not showing his hand. There is more to him than we've yet seen, and it isn't good or decent.'

'Ohh,' Rosemary growled. 'You think you're so clever. It'll great when you have to eat your words.'

Laura was unwilling to let Rosemary have the last word. The more she thought about it, the more she found reasons to doubt the integrity of the man under discussion. The claims for the yew trees had struck even Rosemary as unconvincing, when she'd first heard them. If Marie's brother had investigated and questioned Knussens's intentions, what might he have unearthed?

'I wonder if he's any good with a longbow?' she said aloud, knowing she was being provocative.

'Of course he isn't,' snapped Rosemary.

'How do you know?'

'Because we talked about our interests and hobbies over dinner last weekend, and he never mentioned it.'

'Oh, I see. That clinches it, then.'

On the final minutes of the journey, they tried to stick to neutral topics of conversation, which wasn't easy. Inevitably, they returned to the topic of Keith, with Laura describing how his mother had never made any secret of the fact that Keith repeatedly disappointed her.

'The final straw was when he decided to go into the Church,' she said. 'Sandy was beside herself. She said some awful things.'

'Such as?'

'How about "It's as if he had deliberately gone against us, doing what he's done," and "After everything I tried to teach him, he has to waste his life on that outdated rubbish."'

'Nasty,' Rosemary agreed. 'Poor old Keith.'

Laura went on to explain how she had struggled to put Keith's side of the story, to suggest that going into the church was far too big a commitment to be done from the sort of motives Sandy suspected. 'And he's good at it,' she had insisted. 'It suits him really well.' But Sandy wouldn't listen. All her expectations for her son had crumbled to ashes when he enrolled for ordination. She had wanted him to go travelling with her, to work near to home and bring up a family which Sandy could enjoy at close quarters. Instead, not only was he a hundred miles away but he showed no sign at all of marrying and providing her with grandchildren. 'The whole thing is a ghastly disappointment to me,' she had wailed.

'What a mess,' Rosemary sympathised, as Laura recounted the whole sad story. 'Poor old Keith. You'd think any mother would be proud of him.'

'He was never going to be the son she wanted,' Laura said. 'He was always too quiet and bookish for her. I remember she took him skiing one year and he was terrified. When she forced him onto the slopes, he broke his ankle.'

'Heavens! She must have felt guilty.'

'She might have done, but she wrapped it up in such a way as to make it Keith's fault, not hers. She didn't give up, either. He had to go to all sorts of dreadful energetic after-school clubs. Gymnastics and horse-riding. He hated all of it.'

'And what about his father?'

'Oh, Digby was on Sandy's side, which makes it all so much worse. He used to tell Keith he ought to listen to his mother, she knew what was best for him. He never gave the boy any support.'

'Do you think he's really theirs, or was there a mix-up at the hospital when he was born?'

Laura chuckled. 'You may well ask,' she said.

Then the conversation switched to the tomb in the churchyard, and the romantic story behind it. This proved to be more fertile ground, and they enjoyed a few minutes of fantasy, imagining the dashing Sir Isaac in his hunting pink. 'Pity Mr Danvers isn't more interested in him,' said Rosemary.

'Not his period,' said Laura. 'The man should have been a crusader instead.'

But there was no avoiding the subject of Redland Linton and his employers for long. 'Promise me you'll at least keep an open mind about him,' Laura pleaded.

'Of course,' Rosemary said lightly. 'I'll even try and find out exactly what's going on at this research place of his – how's that for objectivity? But I still say he's a perfectly nice chap, doing a fine job.'

'I suppose I'll have to settle for that, then,' said Laura. 'Oh, look – I think we're there.'

A large sign beside a double gate announced 'Knussens – Nature's Way'. Rosemary drove in, and parked beside a handsome Elizabethan mansion which had evidently been taken over for offices. On all sides were newer buildings, glasshouses and polytunnels.

'Is this their headquarters, then?' Laura asked.

'No, I don't think so. They're based somewhere near Leicester, as far as I know. But they've been steadily expanding over the past few years, and this is one of the more recent developments. Looks as if they do a lot of the practical stuff here.'

'The house must have cost them a packet,' Laura marvelled, admiring the creeper growing up the western half of the building.

'Very good for corporate meetings, courses, presentations – all that kind of thing,' Rosemary said knowingly. 'Well worth the outlay for the image it conveys – especially to foreign visitors.'

'And this is where Linton works, is it?'

'I'm not sure,' admitted Rosemary. 'I get the impression he moves around quite a lot.'

'So, what do we do now? March up to the front door and ring the bell?'

'Why not?'

But before they had a chance to do any such thing, a familiar figure appeared from one of the glasshouses.

'Good timing,' he smiled. 'I got out of a meeting five minutes ago – just long enough to get my breath back.'

He held out an arm to each of them, shepherding them towards a low wooden building across the gravel from where they stood. 'I thought you'd like to see some of our literature,' he said.

'Actually, I'm more interested in your plants,' said Rosemary. 'Particularly the work you've been doing with yews.'

'It really isn't at a stage where I can show you very much.' Linton spoke easily, charm billowing from him like expensive aftershave. 'We've been trying to establish a new generation of young yews, so all there is to see is a lot of baby trees. Rather dull, really.'

'You know I won't think that,' she insisted. 'It all sounds tremendously exciting, to judge from what you said at the meeting on Monday.'

'I didn't get a chance to say anything much,' he chuckled, as if the whole drama of that evening had been nothing more than a minor amusement.

Laura decided to shift the conversation. 'You were very kind to Marie yesterday,' she observed. 'She must appreciate that.'

'The poor girl has had a lot to put up with,' he said. 'And I probably don't need to remind you that she willingly put the farm on the market. It was of her own accord. Knussens hasn't put any pressure on her at all.'

'So you didn't have an eye on those yews until recently?' Laura asked.

'Well —' he hesitated. 'We knew they were there. We commissioned a survey of all woodland species, a year or so ago. Cost a fortune, I might add. It's the nature of our business, you see – we harvest ordinary materials such as leaves, bark, seeds, roots, for our remedies. We had intended to apply to the Sutton family for permission to use their trees, without needing to buy the land. But we suddenly realised we could make excellent use of the land as well, growing on the new young trees, once they're out of the nursery. And then, before we got around to making our approach, Miss Sutton herself contacted us, when she heard about our interest.'

'And now you're after the whole place, lock, stock and barrel.'

Linton faced Laura squarely. 'You've seen Brockett's Farm,' he said. 'Three hundred acres of excellent agricultural land, including a small lake, good diversity of species, highly desirable buildings – we'd have been daft not to consider purchasing it when it became available, if only to be sure of protecting the trees.'

'That makes sense,' said Rosemary. 'Now, if it isn't too late in the day, we'd really love a quick guided tour of this place. I've always been fascinated by Knussens, and the way they manage to stay so pure amidst all the commercial pressures there must be to introduce – well, impurities, I suppose.'

Linton shifted his weight from one leg to the other. 'You do understand that most of what goes on here is original research, don't you? That is, we have to be quite circumspect about who sees it. We have competitors, after all.'

'But not us,' Rosemary protested. 'We're not going to steal any of your secrets.'

'No, of course not,' he said uncomfortably. 'But I can't ignore the fact that you're not just an untutored layman. You do actually know about plant chemistry and what its implications might be. Just one careless word in the wrong place, and we could lose our edge completely.'

'You sound awfully paranoid,' Laura remarked. 'Surely we

couldn't learn anything just from a little look round?'

'It's your work on yews that really interests me,' Rosemary explained. 'And that isn't really a secret, is it? Everybody knows about taxol and its therapeutic properties.'

Linton did not relax on hearing this, but aware of their persistence, he seemed to come to a decision. 'Right,' he said briskly. 'Fine. Come this way.'

He led them into a building which appeared to have been erected very recently. Gleaming aluminium benches lined both sides, laden with pots in which grew young yew trees of every size from an inch to three or four feet high. Light poured in through the glass roof and sides, and the temperature was a few degrees higher than that outside.

'The nursery,' announced Linton.

Laura tried to catch Rosemary's eye, to gauge her reaction, but in vain. 'Amazing!' she gasped, more to buy time than in genuine astonishment. The truth was that she found little to excite her in the ranks of baby trees.

Rosemary was slowly drifting down the central aisle, peering at the plants, saying nothing. Linton hurried after her, abandoning Laura.

'Are they English yews?' Rosemary asked, her brow creased slightly.

'Mostly, yes,' said Linton. 'Some are Italian. Some are hybrids.'

'Hybrids?'

'That's right.'

Laura came up behind. 'What a lot of work it must be,' she said. 'How many people do you employ here?'

'Twenty-two, including the admin and sales people.'

'You sell from here, do you?' Laura wasn't sure, but she suspected that Rosemary would like a moment free from Linton's scrutiny. Eventually, common politeness would force him to turn and face Laura directly if she kept asking questions.

It worked after two more attempts, and Laura glimpsed, over Linton's shoulder, Rosemary rapidly snatching foliage from some of the larger saplings, and stuffing it into her jeans pockets. Good work, thought Laura approvingly.

'It must be very rewarding, what you're doing,' Laura babbled, trying to hold the man's attention. 'Hard to think of anything more so, in fact.'

Linton made a sound of modest agreement, with a smile that struck Laura as slightly sickly.

They were not offered tea or a tour of the offices. When they emerged from the glasshouse, cars were leaving the gravelled parking area in ones and twos. Home time, Laura realised.

Rosemary gave effusive thanks, gazing into Linton's face with a look that was almost hunger. 'I hope I'll see you again soon,' she said. 'If you're in Baffington, come and have a chat in the churchyard. We'll be working in there for another week or so yet.'

'Right,' he said, with a quick glance at his watch. 'I might just do that.'

Back in the village, Rosemary went up to their room to change for the evening meal, leaving Laura sitting outside in the last hour of sunshine, under strict instructions to relax and clear her mind of everything but the next day's work in the churchyard. But instead of getting out of her T-shirt and into a long-sleeved cotton top, Rosemary found herself watching the timeless village scene from the window.

The green was well tended, she noted, unlike the churchyard. Dogs were not permitted to run loose on it, and children had evidently been dissuaded from playing football. Instead, adult villagers strolled across, making their way to the pub, or the postbox in the churchyard wall. For two or three summer months each year, Rosemary guessed that there was a more relaxed social interaction than in the colder, darker seasons. The obligations incurred by the Fayre probably made this year even more convivial than usual. People would have a lot to discuss, with ideas and preparations and worries flying about.

She saw Franklin Danvers walking down the hill from his house, looking fit and summery in short sleeves and lightweight slacks. He walked briskly, but still managed to run a sharp eye over everything he passed. Rosemary watched him turning his head from side to side, inspecting the cottages bordering the green, gazing intently at the church, before pausing in front of the pub. Drawing back slightly, to avoid detection, she heard but did not see him meet with Lyall, just below her window.

'All right?' Danvers asked.

'Fine, sir, thank you.'

'Have you seen Harriet?'

'No, sir. I thought I should try to keep my distance, after this morning.'

Danvers grunted. 'Very sensible. The poor girl must be in a dreadful state.'

'Not my fault, though,' said Lyall mutinously. 'I had to tell the truth when they asked me outright.'

'But no real harm done,' Danvers said, in a tone that Rosemary considered strangely complacent. 'They can't possibly think she was the one who shot Sutton.'

Lyall gave no response to that, but from Danvers' next remark, it was clear he had refrained from any sort of agreement. 'You don't think she could have done it, do you?' Danvers persisted.

'Not for me to comment, sir,' said Lyall.

'Damn it, man, surely you know her better than that!'

'I know her well enough. She's a fine young woman. Talented, attractive, genuine. She lights up the village for all of us. But I mean it, sir. It's a matter for the police. If there's evidence, they'll find it. I've done my duty, answered their questions. But, sir – I've seen people do things you'd never have believed them capable of. There's darkness in us all, and I wouldn't care to swear that a single person here in Baffington could not have shot that arrow into Malcolm Sutton's heart.'

'Well,' Danvers floundered for a moment. 'Well, say what you like, I won't have poor Harriet upset any more. I've told her to go off to London for the day tomorrow, looking at boots for the soldiers in the Fayre. She can enjoy herself, as well. Go to a film or an art gallery or something.'

Lyall murmured some faint response to this, and Rosemary went down for an early meal with Laura.

Laura's attention had returned exclusively to the revelation they'd had from Marie Sutton. She had tried three times to phone the vicarage, but each attempt only produced his answerphone. 'I wonder where he can be,' she worried.

'Maybe he's having an early night,' Rosemary suggested, her own thoughts more on Linton and his tree nursery.

'I think we should go over there anyway.' Laura looked at her watch. 'It's only half- past eight.'

'Absolutely not,' Rosemary said firmly. 'He probably isn't at home. He might be at the bedside of a dying parishioner, or summoned to an audience with the Bishop – or anything.'

'I won't sleep a wink for worrying about him,' Laura threatened.

'Well just make sure you worry quietly,' begged Rosemary.

Keith was in fact not in the vicarage that evening. The big house felt even more unfriendly than usual, forcing him outside, where the fine evening brought some small comfort. His thoughts were full of Harriet Luke, and her treatment at the hands of the police. If only he could find the courage to go to her now, to talk things through with her, and offer himself as counsellor and comforter. Instead, she would be weeping on the shoulder of Gordon Lyall, if Keith was any judge. He had long been aware of a bond between the two, working together as they did for Franklin Danvers. Since the preparations for the Fayre got under way, Lyall and Harriet had spent hours together, discussing logistics, costumes, catering. How could they fail to become intimate – both so attractive, such an obvious couple?

It seemed to Keith that only the disapproving scrutiny from Mr Danvers had prevented a more public demonstration of mutual affection by this time. Lyall had been striding around with a spring in his step for some weeks past, and until the reappearance of Malcolm Sutton, Harriet too had seemed buoyant and bright-eyed. She had laughed easily, throwing herself into her parish work, as well as assisting Danvers. She had been excellent company, Keith mused gloomily. Until Malcolm Sutton turned up.

He found himself rambling down a country lane, leading away from the vicarage and its neighbours. It was a quiet, warm evening, the hedgerows full of wild flowers, the views across open fields to a large stretch of woodland in the distance. But Keith Briggs could appreciate none of the natural beauties around him. All he could think about was Harriet, and murderous arrows, and the endless questions from the police.

Chapter Twelve

Rosemary awoke full of determination to check the date on the Wimpey tomb. She roused Laura, saying she'd catch an early train, and be back by midday. Laura could run her to the station, and then get on with her hedge planting.

'But what about Keith?' Laura said. 'I must see him today.'

'Your best hope is to catch him at lunchtime,' Rosemary said. 'Then I'll be able to come with you.'

Laura pouted for a few minutes. 'Who says I wouldn't like a morning in London as well?' she wanted to know.

'Next time it'll be your turn,' said Rosemary gaily.

Laura dropped her friend at the station, with ten minutes to spare. As she turned the Land Rover round, and waited to rejoin the main road, a familiar red Discovery turned in. She saw that Gordon Lyall was driving, and Harriet Luke was in the passenger seat. 'Drat!' Laura thought. 'If we'd known they were coming, Rosemary could have begged a lift from them, instead of using me as a chauffeur.'

On the train, Rosemary's natural instinct was to move to the seat opposite Harriet, as soon as she recognised the woman getting into the next carriage. She could see that Harriet had found an empty set of four seats, with a table between the two facing pairs. Rosemary had started to get to her feet before it occurred to her that Harriet might prefer to be left alone. The journey would take about an hour and a half – a long time to be saddled with an unwanted companion. She decided to wait for a while, and watch for clues as to Harriet's state of mind.

It wasn't long before their eyes met, through the glass doors connecting the two carriages. Harriet's instant reaction was a smile and a wave, which Rosemary took as unambiguous encouragement. Gathering up her bag and jacket, she quickly moved seats.

'I wasn't sure whether you might prefer to be left alone,' she said.

Harriet grimaced. 'I wasn't sure you'd want to be seen with

me,' she replied. 'I imagine I've already got a reputation as a murderer, after what happened yesterday.'

'I doubt if many people know what happened,' Rosemary comforted her. 'Laura and I certainly haven't told anybody.'

'I ought to be annoyed with you and your friend,' Harriet went on. 'Finding that longbow in the church really got things going. The police aren't going to rest until they've worked out who put it there.'

'And it wasn't you,' said Rosemary, trying not to make it sound like a question.

'No,' Harriet confirmed, in a low voice. 'I went to my cottage and found mine, and left it in Lyall's workshop. Stupidly, I didn't make sure he'd seen me doing it. I assumed he would take my word for it. Besides, I wasn't the only one who just dumped their bow without saying anything.'

'So why did the police pick on you?'

'Because the others had fingerprints on. Marie Sutton handed hers to Lyall right away. The Broadford brothers were all in the clear.'

Rosemary raised her eyebrows in a silent question. Harriet explained that there were three brothers in the Broadford family, all keen archers. 'Descended from longbowmen in the 1500s, I expect,' she added with a rueful smile.

'Of course, it's making an assumption to think the hidden bow was the one used to kill Malcolm,' Rosemary realised.

Harriet blinked. 'Why else would anybody shove it down an organ pipe?' she demanded.

Rosemary giggled. 'I really can't imagine,' she admitted.

They discussed their reasons for going to London, Harriet seeming interested in the story of Sir Isaac Wimpey. 'That date has been broken for ages,' she remembered. 'As a child, I used to chip away at the moss, hoping it would come clearer. I probably added to the damage, without meaning to. How will you ever be able to repair it?'

'It won't be possible to do a proper job. It would all have to be refaced and started again, ideally. I don't see anybody wanting to cough up the cash for that. I thought I'd try and fill the gap with some sort of composite. It won't be easy, but it's worth a try.'

'You should get Lyall to help. He's handy at that sort of thing.'

'Which train are you going home on?' Rosemary wondered. 'Are you making a day of it?'

'I might,' said Harriet, with no sign of enthusiasm. 'I couldn't wait to escape from Baffington for a bit. But now, all I can think of is what's going on there, and all the million things we still have to do for the Fayre. I'll probably get a train back at about three this afternoon. Do you want to go together?'

Rosemary shook her head. 'I'll have to get back sooner than that. Laura's cross as it is at me dashing off on something she doesn't think is at all important.'

They parted at the London station with smiles, and Rosemary took the underground to the Aldwych, and the collection of registers for births, marriages and deaths at St Catherine's House.

It took her less than ten minutes to establish that a certain Isaac Wimpey had died in the month of April, 1898, in the parish of Baffington. The large volumes of chronological indexes were so easily accessed that she wished she had other lines of enquiry to pursue. But she could think of nothing else she could usefully check, and so left the building and stood on the pavement, wondering whether she could justify a quick exploration of Covent Garden and its colourful market.

The temptation proved too great, and she spent almost an hour amongst the stalls before buying a cup of coffee and sitting at an open-air table to drink it. An entertainer was treating a crowd of tourists to a performance of comic juggling that she could barely see from where she sat. Judging by the howls of laughter, it was an excellent show.

Finally, she got up and wended her way through the small streets towards Leicester Square and the tube station there. Except, she realised, standing beneath the huge Odeon cinema, she had walked too far, missing the underground completely. Tutting in exasperation, she turned back, taking a right fork into a short pedestrianised area.

It took her several seconds to recognise two familiar faces, sitting at a table outside a pub. When she did, she quickly turned her back, instinctively hoping not to be seen. Later, when examining these instincts, she understood that there had been something clandestine in the way the two huddled together, talking earnestly.

Franklin Danvers should not have had anything to discuss with Redland Linton, to Rosemary's way of thinking. They were rivals for Brockett's Farm, and both presumably under police scrutiny as possible murderers, unlikely as they might both seem to have committed the crime. She ducked away, taking a more circuitous route to the underground station.

On the way back to Baffington, having just caught the 11.15 train, she gave the matter her concentrated attention. Was it possible that Danvers and Linton had somehow conspired to kill Malcolm Sutton, because of the farm? Were they stitching Marie up in some way? Or did they have some other mutual interest entirely? Whatever the explanation, they had certainly looked shifty. By meeting in Soho, they clearly intended to be well away from anybody who might know them.

Rosemary sighed impatiently. The sooner she could share her discovery with Laura, the better she'd be pleased.

Laura had finally managed to catch Keith on the phone, a little before nine that morning. 'I'd like to talk to you,' she said. 'Are you free at lunchtime?'

He sighed. 'I've got a funeral at eleven,' he told her. 'In fact, I'm leaving shortly, because the widow wants a private blessing beforehand. Unusual, these days,' he added.

Laura was briefly distracted. 'You mean a blessing of the body?'

Keith explained that the deceased was lying in an open coffin at his home, as was the usual practice many decades earlier. 'They still like the old-fashioned ways in some of these villages,' he said.

'Nice,' approved Laura. 'But Keith —'

'I'll try to come over to Baffington afterwards,' he promised. 'But I can't say what time it'll be. They'll expect me to go to the lunch after the funeral.'

Forced to settle for that, Laura worked steadily through the morning, finally achieving her goal of climbing halfway up the huge yew tree and sawing through the dead branches with a sharp bow saw. Once into the rhythm of it, she found it satisfying in several ways. 'Here I am,' she muttered, 'a woman in her middle years, not afraid to go up a ladder and tackle a job that most people would think only a man could do. And a man would insist on using a chain saw, instead of doing it the good old-fashioned way.' The branches thundered to the ground, one after another, leaving the tree considerably more healthy and less overbearing. Her animosity towards it remained unabated, fuelling her with energy for the sawing. She was tempted to remove healthy wood as well as dead, to reduce the tree to something much more modest. Maybe, she thought, Lyall could make more longbows out of some of the straighter branches.

When Rosemary arrived at the lych-gate in a taxi, shortly before one-thirty, Laura was valiantly dragging the dead wood into a stack behind the church. Proudly, she waited for awed admiration for what she had accomplished. Instead, all she got was a hasty, 'Oh, you shouldn't have tackled it by yourself,' and a rapid breathless account of what Rosemary had seen in London.

'I had to wait ages for a taxi,' she grumbled, bringing the story to a close. 'They said they'd already had to come out to Baffington today, and their drivers were starting to wonder what was going on here.'

Laura leaned wearily against the churchyard wall. 'What a morning!' she exclaimed.

But Rosemary's attention had been diverted. 'I think we've got a visitor,' she said.

Mr Winthrop paused warily at the lych-gate, seeing the pile of yew branches on the ground. 'Goodness me,' he said. 'You have been busy.'

'High time this tree had a seeing-to,' said Laura, dropping the saw carefully on top of the dead wood. 'It should never have been allowed to get so big.'

The organist inspected the tree. 'I expect you're right,' he said. 'But I must say I've always been very fond of the old thing. I hope it won't be upset by what you've done to it.'

'Not at all,' said Rosemary. 'It's going to feel much better without all that rotten stuff clogging it up. And look how much lighter it is down here. Light,' she repeated, 'is what plants need above everything else. We can really get on with the new hedges now, and get some good healthy grass to grow instead of all the rubbish that was here. That tree has a lot to answer for.'

Laura rubbed one knee, which had taken most of her weight as she'd cut through the branches. 'I must say, it's a job well done,' she boasted.

'I'm most impressed,' said Mr Winthrop. 'I don't think I ever quite envisaged either of you ladies actually climbing the tree.'

'Oh, well – if a job's worth doing —' said Laura, swiping her hands together. 'And I had a superb view up there. I could see the whole village. There's even a glimpse of Brockett's Farm in the distance.'

'Really?' The elderly man was evidently not interested in the view. 'Well, things to do…' he took a few steps towards the pub, nodding as he went.

The Holly Tree had set tables on the pavement at the front, as well as in the garden area at the back, and the sight of people drinking long cold beers and eating ploughman's lunches made Laura and Rosemary feel all the more thirsty. 'I think we've earned a break,' said Laura.

'Definitely,' Rosemary nodded. 'This is turning out to be a very long day.' They walked through the lych-gate, intending to spend a few minutes in the pub.

A noise drew them to stare towards the upper end of the village street, and Laura quick-wittedly laid a restraining hand on Rosemary's arm. 'Keep back!' she said.

A large red four-wheel drive vehicle was approaching much too rapidly for comfort. The steep street sent it careering downhill at close to forty miles an hour. 'Get away!' Laura shouted at the people lunching outside the pub. As far as she could judge, they were in the direct line of approach, with potentially ghastly consequences. But the people didn't move. They froze in horror, perhaps realising that the impact was only seconds away, and they couldn't hope to climb out of the all-in-one picnic tables in time.

The driver of the oncoming vehicle was, however, conscious –

and heroic. The steering evidently still worked, even if the brakes did not, and the whole monstrous machine was slewed at the final second into the big holly tree that gave the pub its name.

The crunch was loud, metallic and sickening. The four-wheel-drive did not bounce, or roll over. It simply thudded into the tree with appalling force. Glass shattered from the headlamps, and the front tyres hissed. All around was the silence of horrified shock.

Laura was the first to recover. She ran round the vehicle to see who was driving, and whether the people at the tables had escaped unhurt. 'My God! It's Harriet!' she cried.

Rosemary was right behind her. 'Is she —?'

'No, no, I don't think so. But she's not moving.'

Laura sounded worried, and her concern spread through the gathering crowd. Somebody phoned for an ambulance and Laura was momentarily reminded of the death of Mr Sutton the previous year, only a few yards across the village green. Harriet was obviously unconscious, although breathing regularly, as far as Laura could tell. 'Please keep back,' she said, several times, as onlookers edged forward for a closer look.

Keith Briggs joined them, almost green with horror, but talking enough for ten. 'But what happened to her? Why was she driving the Discovery? Where's Lyall? Oh, Harriet! Where's the ambulance?' He babbled on, not addressing anybody in particular, getting in Laura's way as she tried to release Harriet's seatbelt, and ensure that she had no injuries that hadn't been visible at first.

'Keith, I'm sure she'll be all right,' she told him, hoping her words were true. 'At least she's a good colour – better than you, come to that.'

'But what if the car explodes?' Keith wailed. 'It might catch fire, and she'll be burnt alive. We need to get her out.'

'It won't explode,' Laura assured him. 'That only happens in films.'

Rosemary's small sceptical *tch* at this went unheard by everybody but Laura. 'It's safer to leave her where she is, just in case there's spinal damage,' she added loudly.

The siren of the ambulance in the distance brought general

relief. Laura stood aside while the paramedics carefully levered Harriet out of the vehicle and into the ambulance.

The paramedics scanned the crowd. 'Is anybody here related?' one of them asked.

'No,' said Keith, in a choked voice. 'But I'm her employer. I think I should go with her.'

Before he got into the ambulance, he turned to Laura. 'Will you follow us?' he asked. 'I'll need a lift home later on.'

Laura nodded. 'We'll give you a little while, and then come for you,' she said. 'Now don't worry. She's in good hands now.'

The mood relaxed somewhat with the removal of the casualty, but there was still quite a state of excitement. A renewed flurry of interest was caused by the appearance of Franklin Danvers, striding down the hill, his gaze fixed on the vehicle embedded in the holly tree. Rosemary glanced at her watch in some surprise. He must have caught a train only an hour or so after she'd seen him in London, to be back so soon.

Between them, the onlookers managed to explain what had happened. Danvers seemed to be struck dumb with shock. 'That's my car,' he gasped wonderingly. Then he put his hands to his face, 'Harriet!' he moaned, two or three times. 'Oh, Harriet.'

'Yours?' Laura echoed. 'I thought it was Lyall's.'

'He uses it,' Danvers said carelessly. 'It's the estate vehicle.' Finally, he seemed to master himself, and eyed his wrecked Discovery with a sort of loathing. 'I'll have to get it towed away, I suppose,' he mumbled.

'Actually, the police will want to examine it first,' Laura told him. 'I imagine they'll be here at any moment.'

Danvers took a few jerky steps up and down the street. 'Poor Harriet!' he cried again. 'Poor girl. What a thing to happen.' He stared blankly at the vehicle. 'But why was she driving it? She was supposed to be in London. Lyall took her to the train this morning.'

Rosemary clamped her lips together, fearful of revealing too much if she said anything. Her head was full of images of people flying back and forth to London, by train, car and even plane. Perhaps, she thought wildly, Danvers had his own private helicopter. But whatever nefarious business he might have been up to with Linton, there was no concealing his consternation at Harriet's accident. Where Keith Briggs had looked green, Danvers was a deathly grey, and his hands were shaking.

'She'll be all right,' Laura was repeating. 'Now you just go home, and have a rest.' Eventually, Danvers obeyed, stumbling up the hill to his house like a man twice his age.

Rosemary insisted they had some tea before fetching Keith from the hospital. 'After all, it's been a shock for us as well. If Harriet had pulled any harder on the steering wheel, she'd have hit the lych-gate instead of the tree, and we'd have gone under those wheels ourselves. I don't know about you, but it makes me shaky to think of it.'

'The brakes failed,' Laura said slowly. 'Brakes don't just fail on almost-new Discoveries.'

Then DI Flannery arrived, with a pair of uniformed officers, and the questions began. Laura stepped forward, and gave him a brief but lucid account of events. The officers strung the familiar yellow tape around the smashed vehicle, and took some photographs. They then walked up the street to the top of the hill where they surmised that Harriet first lost control.

'She was very brave,' Rosemary said. 'Veering into the tree, the way she did, to avoid hitting the people at the tables.'

'Hmm,' said Flannery.

'What?' Laura demanded. 'What are you thinking?'

He met her eyes, smiling slightly, mixing the personal with the professional in a way she had always been taught was not allowed. 'I'm keeping an open mind,' he said. 'Although I don't think anybody believes that this is a coincidence. What happened here today is most definitely connected to the murder of Malcolm Sutton. Wouldn't you agree?'

'Oh yes,' Laura nodded vigorously. 'Yes, I certainly would.'

All thoughts of work abandoned for the day, Laura and Rosemary set off in the Land Rover to collect Keith from the hospital. Rosemary could not stop talking, pursuing her disjointed thoughts round and round in circles.

'It doesn't make any sense,' she repeated for the third time. 'I can't fit any of it together. It's all just a long string of "Why?" questions.'

'Danvers and Keith both seemed to feel the same,' Laura observed. 'All they could do was ask a lot of questions. Nobody's got any answers, as far as I can see.'

'But there must be an explanation. There's a key to all this that we haven't grasped. Some secret motive somewhere that nobody's guessed.'

'Money,' said Laura. 'It must be about money. And that points to Brockett's Farm.'

'I don't see where you get that idea from,' Rosemary demurred. 'I think it's more likely to be matters of the heart.'

'Well, as far as we know, neither one explains the facts. Besides, in a small village you get all kinds of other things going on. People needing to save face, old resentments bubbling to the surface, and, in this case, there's the threat of a new housing development. I still wonder if that explains it somehow.'

'You think Danvers might have been conspiring with Linton to stop Malcolm's plans?' Rosemary gave her own suggestion a bit more thought. 'Yes, that might work. But now this business of Harriet's accident throws all that into confusion, as well.'

'We have to assume it was a deliberate attempt to kill her,' said Laura. 'And that means it can't have been Harriet who shot Sutton.'

'Not necessarily,' Rosemary argued. 'Although it's a good point.'

'I'm sure it does mean that,' Laura repeated. 'After all, nobody seems to have cared enough about Malcolm to want to avenge his murder. Much more likely that Harriet noticed or discovered something important, and the killer had to stop her from speaking out.'

'Then it has to be Marie Sutton,' said Rosemary. 'She's the only one who fits.'

'No she's not – there's Lyall,' Laura said.

'Or even poor old Keith, I suppose,' Rosemary added, making Laura groan loudly.

A short silence was broken by Laura suddenly uttering a cry which caused Rosemary to stare at her in alarm. 'What?' she said. 'What's the matter?'

'I've had a thought,' Laura said excitedly.

'Well, don't. Not when I'm driving. You almost made me go into the ditch.'

'Sorry – but I think we've jumped to a completely wrong conclusion.'

'Oh?'

'What if whoever tampered with those brakes expected Danvers to be driving it, not Harriet at all? After all, it's his car, not hers.'

Rosemary gave this a few moments' consideration. 'Or Lyall,' she suggested. 'It was more the estate vehicle, really. I've only ever seen him driving it.'

'True. He took Harriet to the station in it this morning.'

'And probably intended to meet her again this afternoon. She must have come back much earlier than the original plan.' Rosemary smacked the steering wheel. 'I bet it was her who got a taxi back to Baffington. They said somebody had. She must have got the 10.15 train from London. That means she was only in town for about an hour. How peculiar.'

'Never mind that now. What if somebody was trying to kill Lyall, assuming he'd be the next person to drive the Discovery? Does that mean he knows who the murderer is?'

Rosemary sighed. 'It's all too much for me. The only thing that does seem clear is that it wasn't Redland Linton. What possible reason, or opportunity, could he have to sabotage Mr Danvers' vehicle?'

'And it wasn't Harriet, either,' said Laura. 'The police are going to have to think again about her.'

The vicar looked much happier when they collected him from the hospital. 'She's sitting up, talking quite lucidly,' he reported. 'They don't think there's any serious damage. They'll keep her in overnight, just to be sure.'

'Thank goodness for that,' Laura said. 'You must be feeling relieved.'

'Relieved!' he said. 'That doesn't come close to describing how I feel. I was so frightened she might…' He rubbed a hand across his face, and said nothing more, until they reached the Land Rover in the car park.

'Oh,' he remembered. 'Would one of you be kind enough to pop back and see Harriet? She wants some things brought from her house. You know…clothes, and toiletries and so forth. I don't think I'm quite the right person…'

Rosemary hardly hesitated before volunteering. 'Will you two wait here for me?' she asked. 'I'll try not to be long.'

Laura and Keith looked at each other. Then Keith spoke to Rosemary. 'Take your time. I think Harriet might be glad of another woman to talk to. I got the impression she needed to unburden herself of something.'

Sensing something slightly odd, Rosemary went off to find Harriet's ward. When she eventually reached it, the injured woman was lying back, eyes closed, with a dressing covering one side of her forehead. Rosemary cleared her throat tentatively, and Harriet's eyes flew open.

'Oh!' she said. 'I didn't think anybody would come.'

'Keith asked me to.'

'Oh, Keith,' Harriet sighed. Rosemary raised her eyebrows, but said nothing. Harriet seemed woozy, her thoughts in disarray. She went on, 'He's being very sweet, of course, but really…'

'What?'

'He's the final straw, to be honest. I don't know what it is, these past months, but I can't seem to move for men making advances. As soon as Malcolm left, it was as if I was fair game for practically all the single men – and one or two of the married ones – in the place. I even started to wonder whether I was imagining it, whether it was me and not them at all. But I'm sure it was real.'

'I'm not surprised,' Rosemary smiled. 'You're very attractive, single, clever. What did you expect?'

'I don't know,' Harriet moaned. 'Not for them to start fighting over me, anyway. Not for Keith to join in. I mean, for heaven's sake, he's the vicar.'

Rosemary smiled. 'I think you'll find that even vicars are human,' she said quietly. 'Now, tell me what you want me to fetch from your house, and I'll bring it all back for you this evening. How long are they keeping you in here?'

'Probably just overnight, for observation. I suppose the police will want to speak to me yet again.'

Rosemary blinked, before saying, 'Oh, yes, perhaps they will. What happened, anyway?'

'The brakes didn't work. I'd come back early from London, and got a taxi from the station. Franklin said he'd ask Lyall to fetch me, and he would have done, if I'd come at the time I said – I was meant to get back on the four-fifty train. But I didn't want to disturb him in the middle of the day. I was just getting on with the job. Franklin needed some special linen for the pennants, as well as staffs to attach them to, so I was going to get some. I sometimes borrow the Discovery if there's a lot to carry. I needed to keep busy, to make myself stop thinking about Malcolm.'

'Why not stay in London all day, then? Surely that would have been the perfect displacement activity?'

'I couldn't concentrate. I just had an overwhelming urge to come home again.'

Rosemary looked at her closely. 'Did you get the job done – with the boots?'

'Sort of. I went to one place, and they seemed all right. To be honest, I didn't really care about the boots. I didn't care about the Fayre at all.'

'But when you got back, you set off straight away to see to the pennants.'

Harriet frowned, pulling at the wound on her head and squeaking with pain. 'You sound just like the police,' she accused

Rosemary. 'Everybody forever asking questions.'

'Sorry,' said Rosemary. 'It's just —'

'Oh, I know. It all seems to revolve around me. Malcolm, Keith, Lyall…the only one who isn't bothering me these days is Franklin. And that's because he can't think about anything but his blessed Fayre.'

'But the brakes,' Rosemary returned to the crux of recent events. 'Didn't they work at all?'

'No,' Harriet repeated, careful not to shake her sore head. 'Nothing happened when I pushed the pedal.'

Rosemary knew something about car mechanics. 'Then somebody must have done some serious sabotage,' she said firmly. 'Brakes don't just fail these days.'

'I might have been killed,' Harriet said faintly. 'Somebody tried to kill me. Lyall. It must have been Lyall. But why?'

Rosemary thought about this. 'Except,' she said slowly, 'the plan was for Lyall to be driving the car this afternoon, not you. What if it was somebody who wanted to get him out of the way?'

Harriet closed her eyes. 'I can't think,' she moaned. 'It was a dreadful, wicked thing to do.' Her eyes flew open again. 'And Franklin's going to be furious. He's very proud of that car.'

Laura's walk with Keith was much more difficult. Making every effort to be circumspect and diplomatic, she asked him whether he was aware of any village gossip concerning himself and Harriet. He stopped in his tracks, and stared at her, his expression a mixture of anger and embarrassment.

'No!' he said loudly. 'What have you heard?'

She brushed the question aside. 'It isn't so surprising,' she said calmly. 'Harriet's extremely attractive, and you're an eligible bachelor. You and she work together. What makes you so cross about it?'

'It isn't fair to Harriet,' he said. 'They've had her paired up with just about every man in the village, ever since Malcolm Sutton left. I hate gossip, Laura. It's malevolent and destructive. I don't mind admitting that since I arrived here, I've found it all extremely shocking, and very difficult to cope with.'

'I don't think people mean it unkindly. In my experience – which I admit isn't very extensive – village people are strangely non-judgmental. They might talk about each other a lot, but it's amazing what they'll accept. They even quite like eccentrics like your Mr Danvers.'

'They don't like Lyall, poor chap,' said Keith. 'He's another one they've matched up with Harriet, the idiots.'

'That's probably just because of his manner. He doesn't do himself any favours, being so short with people.'

'But he isn't interested in Harriet. I'm sure he isn't.'

Laura suddenly remembered Bobby's affectionate greeting when Lyall had appeared at Brockett's, and a powerful realisation hit her. Saying nothing, she stored it away as an important new factor to consider properly when she had less to distract her. Meanwhile, she tried to get back to the more central issue. 'So there's nothing in the stories about you and Harriet? That's rather a shame.'

Keith flushed a deep red, and avoided her gaze. 'What do you mean?' he mumbled.

'Only that she's a nice girl. Under normal circumstances, there'd be nothing at all sinister in the idea – but the fact that there was a brutal murder a few days ago changes all that. Nobody can escape scrutiny, and every single word or act is treated with suspicion. So, when people talk about seeing you and Harriet together near the church on that very evening, well…' she looked at him almost pleadingly, 'Well, Keith, it starts to look serious. Do you understand?'

He frowned. 'Not entirely. Nobody saw us near the church, I'm sure.'

'But you were there, Keith. Somebody did see you,' she insisted. 'That person believes that you and Harriet killed Malcolm together.'

The look he gave her was full of torment. 'Who?' he choked. 'Who saw us?'

'That doesn't matter, does it. Tell me the truth, Keith. Was Harriet with you?'

He closed his eyes for a second, as if expecting his cousin to have vanished when he opened them again. 'Yes,' he said tiredly.

'Ah,' Laura breathed. 'I see. Actually, Harriet told us that you would vouch for her whereabouts on Monday evening. You don't have to be coy about it, for heaven's sake. If you and she are —'

'We're not,' he said. 'We were together, yes, but we weren't – I mean –'

'Take it slowly,' said Laura, her heart thumping painfully. 'I'm sure it isn't as bad as it sounds.'

He gazed beseechingly at her. 'I can't tell you. I promised Harriet. I promised,' he repeated.

'I think I understand,' Laura said gently. 'Harriet's put you in rather a spot, by the sound of it.'

'She's frightened,' he said again. 'I have to do what I can to make her feel better.'

'Do you know what she's afraid of?' Laura asked.

Keith looked cornered. 'She realises how it must have looked between her and Malcolm on Monday, and what the police are likely to think, when they're told about it.'

'So you've agreed to vouch for her,' Laura summarised. 'Just as she told us you would.'

He nodded dumbly. Despite his pallor and tension, there was a light of conviction in his eyes. Laura nodded her acceptance of what he'd told her, but could not avoid a growing concern for him. 'Are you going to be all right?' she asked. 'You seem to be under a lot of strain.'

He smiled crookedly. 'It isn't just Harriet. I was thinking about this time last year. Remember that awful fête, which made a grand total of sixty-six pounds? I thought then that nothing could get worse, that I'd started at a low point here and would build it up to a real community. I saw Franklin as a true benefactor, committed to the people, an asset to the village. I even supported his plans for the Medieval Museum at Brockett's. Now it's all turned to ashes, the villagers are at each other's throats. There's no trust, no goodwill.' He put his hands over his face in a gesture of despair. 'I can't go on, Laura,' he mumbled through his fingers. 'I've reached the end of the line.'

'Come on,' she said, half soothing, half bracing. 'It isn't as bad as all that. You're just upset about Harriet.'

He uncovered his face, showing eyes large with misery. 'What if somebody did that deliberately?' he moaned. 'If somebody in this village tried to kill Harriet? How is that possible? What on earth were they thinking of? And —' he shuddered, '— what might happen next?'

Laura just shook her head, relieved to see Rosemary approaching in the distance. She led Keith to the Land Rover, wondering how best to boost his spirits.

'I can see it's awful for you,' she said. 'After all, in your position, you must have rather a lot to lose.'

'We've all got a lot to lose,' he said, with quiet dignity. 'And we have to face up to reality, however morally ambiguous that might make our actions.'

Laura was thinking about her cousin Sandy. 'There's more of your mother in you than either of you realise,' she observed. 'I remember a time when she would have taken a very similar line to the one I think you've just taken. And I get the impression that you've instinctively cast the police in the role of villains in all this – just as your mother would do, with her rebellious ways.'

Keith laughed humourlessly at this. 'Trust you, Laura, to see it like that. I challenge you to go and tell Mum what you've just told me.'

Laura squared her shoulders. 'Well, I will then,' she said. 'I'll go and see them on Sunday. They can give me lunch.'

Keith shook his head helplessly. 'Be sure to give them my love,' he said, with no hint of irony.

Rosemary approached them warily, casting an enquiring glance at Laura. 'Problems?' she said, just a shade too chirpily.

'Keith's still suffering from the shock of Harriet's…accident,' she said.

'Oh! Well, not to worry,' Rosemary breezed, unhelpfully. 'She's going to be absolutely fine. You saw that for yourself.'

Keith just shook his head helplessly, as they all climbed into the front seat of the Land Rover.

Having dropped Keith off at his vicarage, they arrived back in Baffington, just before seven o'clock, expecting the usual evening routine to begin. But when they walked into The Holly Tree, Laura was handed a note by the landlord.

'Hey,' laughed Rosemary. 'Is that a love letter?'

Laura gave her a haughty look. 'I think you've been dreaming a bit too much about a certain Mr Linton,' she said, before opening the note. Her intake of breath was more than a little embarrassed, as she read: 'Dear Mrs Thyme. I wondered whether you could spare an hour or two this evening to come with me for a meal? I apologise for the short notice, but in this job, it's best to seize the moment. If I don't hear from you, I'll collect you at seven-thirty. Paul Flannery.'

'What?' demanded Rosemary, jumping from side to side, trying to read it for herself.

'Um, it looks as if I'll be out this evening,' Laura said, with a flush. 'That police inspector wants to talk to me.'

'Talk to you? By yourself? What about me?'

'I suppose he thinks it only needs one of us. Or perhaps he thinks I'd make a better witness, or something,' she tailed away weakly.

Rosemary adopted a mulish expression. 'I think that's very unfair. Am I meant to twiddle my thumbs here all evening while you go off dallying with the DI?'

'You could go and visit Mr Danvers,' Laura suggested lightly. 'Ask him to explain the intricacies of medieval herb gardens, or something.'

'I already know all there is to know about herb gardens,' Rosemary sniffed. 'If I'd realised this was going to happen, I might have managed to persuade Redland to go for a drink.' She fiddled with the crushed yew needles in her pocket. 'I can set my microscope up in the vestry, I suppose,' she said grudgingly. 'And make some slides from these samples.'

'There then!' said Laura with relief. 'I knew you were going to be busy.'

She wore a longer pair of earrings than the usual daytime ones, and a clean jumper over cotton trousers, hedging her bets as to whether the meal was to be mainly social, or a routine part of

Flannery's murder investigation. Perhaps he always invited the first person at the scene of a murder out for dinner – although if that were so, Rosemary would have been asked along as well.

He took her to a bistro in the nearest town, where he was apparently completely unrecognised. The place felt oddly old-fashioned to Laura, reminding her of meals with her former husband in the seventies where the menu was on blackboards and candles melted into exotic shapes on the check-clothed tables. The smells were all of rich red meat and garlicky sauces. When Flannery ordered a bottle of red wine, it looked like blood in the heavy glasses.

She had decided from the start to let him take the lead. He could even order for her if he wanted to. She was just going to wallow in the experience of being out with a man again, whatever his motives might turn out to be. And they turned out to have a lot less to do with his work as a police detective than she had feared.

He asked her about her work, her family and her ideas for the future. He told her his own story, which mirrored hers very closely. His wife, tired of disrupted plans and broken promises, had gone off with an estate agent, and was living in a late Victorian villa on the south coast. His two daughters kept dutifully in touch with him, but he seldom saw them. His manner, as he disclosed all this, was resigned, almost passive. He smiled ruefully at himself, shrugging at intervals.

'But aren't you angry?' Laura asked. 'I was absolutely furious when it happened to me.'

'No point in getting angry,' he said.

'Maybe – but I didn't feel I had much choice. You feel what you feel, whether there's a point to it or not.'

'No, no,' he disagreed. 'You have to keep your feelings under control.'

Something about this struck Laura as risky territory. It would be very unfortunate if they discovered unbridgeable differences so early in the evening, when she was so determined to enjoy herself. She diverted the conversation deftly into other channels, asking him whether he enjoyed films, or books, or sport.

They discovered a shared liking for Ealing comedies and Alfred Hitchcock, which tided them over very pleasantly right through to the dessert. Then Flannery appeared to have a pang of conscience, or something of the sort, and his brows crept closer together.

'I should ask you about Baffington,' he said, with a hint of regret. 'Whether you've got any sort of hunches about the murder.'

'Hunches?' she repeated. 'I thought you'd be more interested in evidence.'

'Evidence is my department,' he said, with a hint of loftiness. 'I wouldn't expect you to produce any. But the undercurrents, the subtle interactions – that's much more difficult for me and my team to discover, and much easier for you and Miss Boxer.'

Laura paused to think, before shaking her head. 'I'd hate to inadvertently point you in the direction of someone who's completely innocent,' she demurred.

'Off the record,' he invited, with a twinkle in his eye. 'Just between the two of us.'

'I suppose your most obvious suspect is Gordon Lyall,' she began tentatively, fishing for confirmation. 'At least, it looks as if he had the best opportunity to wreck the Discovery's brakes. Except —' she paused, wondering whether it would be wise to reveal the theory about Lyall being the intended victim, rather than the perpetrator.

'Except things might well not be as they seem,' he smiled. 'Don't worry, we fully realise that.'

'So —?'

'Lyall is certainly very interesting,' Flannery continued. 'We're not sure where his affections lie, but he seems to be fond of Harriet Luke.'

'Oh, no!' Laura corrected him. 'I'm convinced he's involved with Marie Sutton.' And she explained about the dog and its obvious preference for the estate manager.

Flannery obviously found this an important new avenue of enquiry. 'I see,' he said, sitting up straighter, his eyes flickering from side to side, as he assessed the implications. 'That does throw a new light on things. Lyall could have been trying to protect his beloved – Marie, not Harriet – from Malcolm. After all, Sutton had a gun, which he might well have intended to use on his sister. If Lyall somehow got wind of that...' Flannery frowned, thinking hard. 'On the other hand, he might even have been defending his boss's interests. He probably likes the idea of a Medieval Museum at Brockett's Farm, seeing a big career opportunity for himself there. When Sutton appeared to be putting the kybosh on that whole idea, that'd be enough to make him grab a longbow and do the dirty deed.'

'Yes,' Laura agreed. 'That's all perfectly plausible. Lyall seems almost as potty about the Middle Ages as Danvers is.'

'And Harriet Luke?' the detective continued, after a few moments.

'What about her? Surely she's out of the picture since the accident. Somebody tried to kill her. It must have been the same person who killed Sutton.'

'Let's just think about that,' he said, somewhat ponderously. 'She was jilted by Sutton last year. She can use a longbow. She has a great deal invested in the welfare of the village, working for the vicar and Mr Danvers as she does, so that Sutton's announcement at that meeting would have seemed outrageous to her. She appears to be a strong assertive young woman, with a suggestion of a quick temper.'

'Yes,' said Laura, 'but none of that counts any more, since the accident this afternoon – does it?' An image came into her head of the tormented young vicar, only a few hours previously, tying himself in knots to protect Harriet, to keep a promise he had made to her, and she quailed. However much Flannery might persuade her to reveal, she could never say anything to implicate Keith.

He seemed to read her mind. 'So how about the vicar?' was his next question.

Laura swallowed nervously. 'Keith? What about him?'

'Has he got the same strong commitment to the village as Miss Luke? After all, he hasn't been there very long, has he?'

Laura shook her head, thinking quickly. 'He's plainly very

upset indeed by the murder,' she began. 'I think he's terrified by it, quite frankly.'

'You make him sound rather weak.'

'I didn't mean to. After all, I am related to him.'

'Would you remind me just how you two are related?'

Laura explained, at some length, reminiscing about Keith as a young boy, and Sandy as a tearaway who had not made a very good job of mothering the lad. 'It's a little bit like me and my daughter,' she added.

Flannery seemed more than happy to hear this story, regardless of its irrelevance to the case in hand. 'So you don't think he's weak?' he summarised.

'Maybe that is how he seems, but it's not really true. He's struggling to believe in the people he's chosen to work with. He's their minister, their shepherd, you might say. He has to be able to believe in them. And where Harriet is concerned, I imagine he needs to believe more in her than anybody.'

Flannery gave her a severe look. 'Mrs Thyme, I don't think you're being entirely straightforward with me, are you? I feel sure that you're aware that Reverend Briggs and Miss Luke were seen together close to the church on Monday evening.'

Laura floundered. What was he trying to make her say? 'Ummm,' was all she could manage.

The police detective sat back in his chair. 'It's all right,' he said. 'I just wanted to gauge your reaction. It was unfair of me, I admit.' His direct gaze seemed to pin her to her seat. 'I might need your help over the next day or two,' he added, mysteriously. 'If so, I'll telephone you.'

They had finished their coffee, as well as the After Eight mint that came with it. There seemed little option but to acknowledge that the meal was over, and it was time they left.

Chapter Fourteen

Rosemary had only been in the vestry for two minutes, when she became aware of voices in the church. 'I simply can't understand the sort of mentality that would do such a thing,' came a plaintive elderly male voice. 'Ramming a longbow into an organ pipe is the act of a deranged mind.'

Mr Winthrop really isn't keeping up, thought Rosemary. Who cared any more about the concealed longbow, after everything that had happened subsequently?

The other man's response was a short laugh with very little mirth in it. 'I expect you're right,' it said. 'But you must admit it made a good hiding place. If it hadn't been for that meddlesome woman…'

At this, Rosemary thought she should make a move, before she heard any more embarrassing criticism of herself or Laura. Making a deliberate clatter amongst the statues and other equipment, she emerged through the curtain into the body of the church.

'Hello,' she said.

The two men stared at her as if a ghost had suddenly materialised before them. Then Franklin Danvers overcame his shock, greeting her with a jovial smile. 'Miss Boxer!' he exclaimed. 'Fancy you being here at this time of night.'

Rosemary looked at her watch. 'It's only ten to eight,' she said. 'Hardly the witching hour just yet.'

'And broad daylight still,' added Mr Winthrop. 'I do like these long summer evenings. You can get so much done.'

'I suppose you've commandeered the vestry for your work,' Danvers went on. 'I should have realised you wouldn't have a proper place for storage.' A thought seemed to strike him. 'How would it be if you transferred up to my place? I'm sure you'd find that more convenient, and the vicar would be glad to get his vestry back.'

Rosemary made a show of considering this suggestion. 'Actually,' she began, 'it would be easier to stay here, thanks all the same. On the spot, you see. It's only for the things that might get wet, or stolen, or need to be kept out of the way until we've completed the clearance work. If we had to keep popping back and forth to your house, it would take up much more time.' The strangeness of Danvers' one-track concentration on the Baffington Fayre, in the midst of violence, accident and wholesale mayhem made her speak carefully to him.

He looked at her sternly, as if unaccustomed to being thwarted. Belatedly, Rosemary understood that his suggestion had in fact been more like an instruction. 'I think when I show you what I'm offering, you'll change your mind,' he said. 'Why don't you come along now, and see?'

'Oh! But I haven't had dinner,' she exclaimed. 'I was going back to The Holly Tree in a few minutes.'

'Have it with me,' he invited graciously.

Somehow Rosemary found the prospect of a meal with Franklin Danvers in his grand mansion, presumably cooked and served by an employee she had not yet met, less than appealing. 'That's really kind of you, but I couldn't,' she said. 'Not at such short notice. Besides, The Holly Tree are keeping a table for me. And I'm expecting Laura back at any time,' she lied desperately.

Danvers seemed to be holding in his frustration with difficulty. 'That's a pity,' he said tightly.

Mr Winthrop, antique dealer and organist, witnessed this exchange with considerable interest, showing no sign of feeling in the way or having anything else to do. He appeared to be waiting patiently for Danvers to remember his existence.

Finally, he cleared his throat, and said, 'Franklin, have you forgotten…?'

Danvers turned to him, his face glowing with irritation. 'What?' he barked.

'You wanted to consult me on how we could add some medieval touches to the church. I told you about that carved chest I found last month. It could be fifteenth century. It could sit over there, I thought, with perhaps a display of local coats of arms on the wall above it.'

'Yes, yes, very good,' said Danvers.

'And tapestries. If we could find a contemporary wall tapestry, or even a good replica…'

'An authentic one would be priceless. We couldn't risk putting it in a public place,' Danvers told him, his attention returning to the subject in spite of himself. 'I'm not sure they ever put them in churches, anyway, did they?'

Mr Winthrop pursed his lips. 'I think it's quite likely they did, to keep the place warm, the same as in the large houses and castles.'

'We could think about it,' Danvers conceded. 'If the vicar had any knowledge of history, we might have consulted him. As it is…' he sighed impatiently.

'You expect too much,' Mr Winthrop said. 'Vicars aren't like they used to be – experts on church interiors, architecture, folklore, history, and heaven knows what else. They haven't been like that since the late nineteenth century.'

'And now we have lightweight individuals who talk in incomprehensible jargon and have no time for the things that really matter.' Danvers' frustration was all too evident, and Rosemary took a step backwards, hoping she wouldn't be noticed. After a few more steps, she murmured, 'Well, if you'll excuse me,' and made her escape before Danvers could stop her and make any more suggestions about her work. The microscope was left in its box in the vestry, all thought of doing some scientific analysis forgotten.

Rosemary found herself feeling hungry and rather agitated, her head whirling from all the goings on. Where was Laura when she needed her? Why couldn't she, Rosemary, have been asked to dinner by a nice available man, she asked herself, before remembering that she had just turned down an invitation to do exactly that.

So Franklin Danvers was not her idea of congenial male company – wasn't he better than nothing? There was nothing actually wrong with him, and he had plenty of topics he could have talked about. Shouldn't she have accepted in the spirit of the job? If she'd offended him, he might send them away before they'd completed the churchyard commission. With a deep sigh, she admitted to herself that it was a case of sour grapes. If she couldn't go out with Redland Linton, she didn't want to go out with anybody.

* * *

By ten o'clock, Laura had returned and Rosemary had bought them a nightcap in the bar, where they could compare notes on their evenings. Laura tried hard to avoid seeming girlish or coy about her date with Inspector Flannery, and Rosemary tried not to feel jealous. But neither was entirely successful.

'He likes Ealing comedies,' Laura said, with a fond smile.

'Laura, everybody likes Ealing comedies. What did he say about the murder? Who does he think did it?'

Laura's chin lifted in a gesture of 'I-know-more-than-you-about-police-procedure' and said calmly, 'He'd hardly disclose something like that, now would he?'

'I don't see why not. I thought that's what he wanted to talk to you about.'

'Actually, he just wanted a pleasant evening in congenial company. We barely discussed his work at all.'

'Well – I call that a wicked waste of an opportunity,' Rosemary complained.

Laura considered this. 'On his part or mine?' she asked.

'Both, of course. Didn't he ask you anything? Did you tell him about Marie being Sunshine?'

Laura shook her head. 'I think that's best left to Marie herself.'

Rosemary pushed out her lips at this in a doubtful expression. 'What if Marie killed Malcolm, all along? What if she somehow interfered with Danvers' car? What if she goes berserk and shoots somebody else in the night? Wouldn't that make you feel dreadful?'

'She won't,' said Laura with complete confidence. 'Why would she?'

Rosemary held up a hand with two fingers firmly crossed. 'If this was a story, you'd just have consigned some wretch to certain death,' she said. 'You really shouldn't say things like that.'

Laura ignored her, lost in a long yawn. 'I'm ready for bed,' she said. 'It's been a long day.'

Franklin Danvers did something that evening which he almost never did. He walked the half-mile to the small stone house which he had acquired some years previously, and made available to his estate manager. Lyall had erected a sturdy wooden fence around the property, and made it clear that he preferred not to be disturbed. Not particularly sociable himself, Danvers had had no difficulty in honouring this preference.

But now he urgently needed to speak to the man, and having waited in vain all day for Lyall to show himself at Highview House, he decided there was no option but to break the unspoken taboo.

There was no sign of life as he let himself in through the garden gate. No flickering television screen glimpsed through the lounge window, no cooking smells or music playing. Glancing from side to side, it seemed to Danvers that the garden had been neglected, weeds growing in the flowerbeds, and long grass sprouting through the flagstones of the path. Lyall's rather elderly Vauxhall was parked on a gravelled area beside the house, but Danvers knew better than to take this as a promising sign that Lyall might be in. His manager rarely used the car, taking the Discovery for estate work, and walking across fields or down country lanes on local matters.

Vigorous knocking at the front door yielded no response. Trying the back, he found the same air of abandonment. Frowning, he tried to recall when he had last paid Lyall a visit, and concluded it was at least six months previously. Not only was the man not at home this evening – Danvers began to wonder if his employee had effectively moved elsewhere a considerable time ago.

But if that was the case, then where had he been spending his time? And why such secrecy about it?

A surge of rage and frustration flooded through him. Nothing was straightforward any more. As soon as one problem was resolved, something else popped up in its place. The Fayre was barely a week away, and still the archers were in chaos, the choir unrehearsed, the costumes incomplete. With Harriet in hospital, and Lyall mysteriously vanished, the whole enterprise felt doomed. And it was all his estate manager's fault.

There was, he decided, only one course of action open to him. Regardless of the late hour, he hurried back home, and went straight to the telephone. As soon as it was answered, he said curtly, 'Yes, I wish to report a suspicious development in the Sutton murder at Baffington. Mr Gordon Lyall has gone missing – which seems to indicate to me that he's the guilty party. I suggest you waste no time in prosecuting a search for him.'

It seemed strange to Rosemary and Laura to awake to another clear sky and a new day working in the churchyard. So much had happened the day before that they half expected to find the village full of armed response teams, or the villagers assembled to demand satisfactory action. Instead, everything appeared to be eerily normal.

Laura began by putting some of her yew tree trimmings through the shredder, and making a tidy stack of the larger branches. It was a pity, she thought, that the timber would be no good for carving or turning. Already it was cracked and dry and hollow at the core. Firewood, she decided – and then only in a closed wood burner, because of the way it would spit. Staring up at the tree, she felt a surprising flicker of affection for it, a hope that it would survive another few centuries, watching over the comings and goings of the people of Baffington. Whatever it might have symbolised in the past, it had now become a fixture, without which Baffington would lose much of its identity.

A short while later, she suggested to Rosemary that they might venture to bring one or two of the smaller statues outside, to try them in various positions around the churchyard. Rosemary agreed with enthusiasm. 'That would really feel like progress,' she said.

Standing back to admire the pair of cherubs, Rosemary began to plan some of the finishing touches they would have to make before the work could be considered complete.

'I wonder if Danvers would mind us planting some traditional churchyard plants,' she said.

'Providing they're medieval, I imagine he'd be delighted.'

'Churchyards have been very important, through the centuries, you know – as a way of preserving rare plants. With agriculture destroying so many wild flowers, you could say the church has actually saved some of them.'

'Oh? For example?'

'Meadow saxifrage,' said Rosemary, promptly. 'Lovely thing. One of my favourites.'

'Oh yes!' Laura enthused. 'I had some in my garden. Sweet little pink flowers.'

'No, that's a totally different version. The one I mean has white flowers. You've probably never seen it. It's rare now.'

'And you'd like to plant some in Baffington churchyard?'

'I'd love to, if I could find some. It would take a bit of tracking down, but there's sure to be a nursery somewhere that has it.'

'I can't see Danvers objecting,' Laura said.

'What does he do all day, I wonder? Have you noticed how we hardly ever see him? He must be beavering away with his books, swotting up on the details of medieval life. It could send a person peculiar after a while.'

'He seems fairly sane to me. A bit bossy, I suppose. But his employees seem to like him most of the time.'

'I can't help feeling something's about to happen,' Laura said, after a few minutes spent digging out some buttercups which had escaped notice. 'Don't you think it's horribly quiet for a Saturday?'

'They've all gone to the supermarket, I expect,' panted Rosemary, who was attacking a large dock. 'Oh, I hate docks!' she burst out.

'Well you know what they say about them.'

'What?' Rosemary straightened up, with a puzzled expression.

'Their roots go down to hell and the devil keeps a hold of them.'

'Surely not in a churchyard?'

Their peals of near-hysterical laughter echoed around the silent village, and still nobody came near them.

In the middle of the morning, Rosemary suddenly smacked herself on the head. 'I completely forgot!' she exclaimed.

'What?' Laura straightened from digging a trench for the new hedgerow.

'The microscope! I never did look at those bits of yew I got from Knussens. I'll have to do it today or they'll dry up and die.'

'How long will it take?'

'An hour or so. It'll be a bit rough and ready, but I only want to have a look at the cell structure, down the microscope.'

'I bet what you really want is an excuse to go back for another chat with dishy Redland Linton,' Laura teased her. When Rosemary made no reply, she went on, 'I honestly don't know what you see in him. He strikes me as shifty. His eyes are too close together, and he isn't being straight with Marie.'

'Well I like him. He's deep, that's all, and has business worries. I'm convinced he's a perfectly decent person underneath.'

'Come off it! You would never have taken those samples if you thought it was all above board.'

'I took the samples purely out of scientific interest, not because I think Redland is doing anything sneaky. After all – what on earth could he be doing? All I expect to find is some interesting new hybrid, at best. That would explain the secrecy. But since when has breeding trees been a crime?'

Laura sniffed sceptically. 'That depends,' she said, with irritating vagueness.

Without further argument, Rosemary disappeared into the vestry, leaving Laura doggedly working on her new hedges. After a few minutes, Laura found herself lost in thought, as she worked.

She thought mainly about her cousin Keith and the state he was in. He was worryingly distressed by the events of the past days, seeming to doubt his own abilities, and even his own morality, if his strange hints were anything to go by. She was troubled, too, by her own failure to heal the rift between Keith and his mother. The rigours of the churchyard job, the distraction of the murder and the demands of the Fayre had all obscured this project almost to the point of oblivion.

'Laura!' came Rosemary's voice. 'Are you there?'

'Yes,' she replied. 'Can I come in now?'

'Come and see!' came the excited response.

Laura found her friend holding two glass slides, one in each hand. Deftly, Rosemary slid one of them under the lens and stood back, inviting Laura to examine it. 'This one's from the tree outside – see the way the cells are formed? The shape, and the way they connect together?'

Peering down microscopes was not something Laura often did, and she could make little sense of what Rosemary was trying to show her.

'Sorry,' she gave up. 'Can you just explain it to me?'

But Rosemary persevered. 'Look again,' she ordered. 'Remember the patterns.'

OK,' Laura muttered, trying again. 'But honestly, I'll take your word for it.'

Rosemary then whipped out the slide and inserted the second one. 'Now this one,' she said.

Laura obeyed, and did indeed observe a different pattern. 'Beautiful!' she breathed, admiring the colours and the clear sharp detail revealed of the hidden world of cellular structures.

'Not beautiful at all,' Rosemary snapped. 'Extremely sinister.'

'Why?'

'Well, I won't go into too much detail, but these cells here —' she flicked the offending slide, causing it to shift slightly, 'are all wrong. They would never appear naturally in an ordinary yew tree, whether it's Irish, Spanish or English. There's foreign material that's been introduced.'

'Er…?' said Laura.

'I can't say what it is – where it's come from – but it very much looks to me as if there's been some genetic engineering going on here,' said Rosemary. 'Knussens must have been using GM on those saplings in their glasshouses. I think they must have found a way to force the plants to produce much higher levels of taxol than could ever occur naturally. I might have it wrong, but something very strange has been going on, and these slides prove it.'

'Amazing!' Laura said. 'You are clever.'

'You don't understand,' Rosemary punched the table, making the microscope wobble. 'Not only is it illegal in this country, at this point in time, but it's outrageous for Knussens, who make such a big thing of being natural. "Nature's Way" remember. It would destroy them if word got out. I'm stunned that they should ever imagine they could get away with it.'

'I see,' said Laura. 'You mean you've just given Redland Linton a very strong motive for murder. Combined with your sighting of him with Danvers in London, it's beginning to look rather bad for your chum, isn't it.'

'I suppose it is,' nodded Rosemary miserably. 'Especially if he thought Malcolm Sutton suspected something about this GM thing.' Then she brightened. 'But we don't know that it's Redland who's doing the modifying,' she added. 'It might be some sinister scientist who's infiltrated Knussens incognito. Redland might not know anything about it.'

'Oh, Rosemary,' sighed Laura. 'You and your flights of fancy.'

Chapter Fifteen

'I think we deserve an afternoon off, seeing as it's Saturday,' Laura said, standing back to admire the results of her morning's work. 'And tomorrow I'm going to visit Sandy. I can get the train.'

Rosemary was crouching over the tomb of Sir Isaac Wimpey once more, tracing onto paper the exact shape of the broken figure 8. 'All right,' she mumbled. 'I'll have plenty to occupy me here. The hard part will be to make the filler stick properly.'

'You could try pinning it,' Laura suggested. 'Just a little metal peg to hold it straight.'

'That might work,' Rosemary said. 'But it would mean drilling into the actual sarcophagus. What if the whole thing cracks open?'

Laura shuddered. 'Don't even think about it,' she said. 'If you ask me, you've taken on something a lot bigger than you thought.'

'Maybe I have,' said Rosemary absently. Something in her tone made Laura wonder if she was only talking about Sir Isaac's tomb.

The police had removed the Discovery early that morning, leaving the damaged holly tree open to public gaze. Rosemary inspected it, hands on hips. 'It's unsafe like that,' she decided. 'It'll have to come down.'

'So it's an ill wind,' said Laura, with a smirk. 'Keith will be pleased. It wasn't doing his churchyard any favours at all. Without it, there'll be a lovely light corner. It'll look much better.'

'It's a shame, though. They'll have to rename the pub.'

'They could call it The Empty Space,' Laura joked feebly.

A voice came from behind them. 'It's not a joking matter,' it said reprovingly.

'Goodness, you keep doing that!' Rosemary complained to Franklin Danvers. 'I've never known a man so light on his feet.'

'I doubt if you'd have heard a carthorse, the way you were so intent on that tree,' he responded crossly.

'Have you heard anything about your car?' Rosemary asked. 'It looked pretty badly hurt to me.'

'I never want to set eyes on the thing again, after what happened.'

'I wouldn't think you could blame the vehicle,' Laura said. 'It probably wasn't its fault.'

Danvers threw back his head. 'What do you mean? You surely don't think Harriet would deliberately…?'

'No, no, of course not.' Laura hurried to put him straight. 'More likely, somebody tampered with it.'

Danvers showed no sign of surprise at this remark, and Laura wondered whether he had merely been testing her, to see if she'd reached the same conclusion as he had himself.

'Well, it must have been Lyall,' Danvers said heavily. 'He probably saw her come back from London, and assumed she'd be taking the car to make some collections. She might even have told him that's what she planned.'

'Have you asked him?'

'No,' said Danvers, his annoyance returning. 'I can't find him. He's gone missing. I don't mind telling you, I've reported it to the police. As far as I'm concerned, running away like this is an admission of guilt.'

Laura and Rosemary were momentarily silenced by this latest turn of events. Eventually Laura said, 'Well, I think we should just leave everything to the police. If Lyall was responsible for Harriet's accident, they'll be sure to find him.'

Danvers shook his head. 'I wish I shared your confidence,' he said.

At that moment, Gordon Lyall was speaking to Marie Sutton, as they walked together in the yew wood. 'I'll have to go back,' he was saying. 'Danvers will have missed me by now, and be raising all sorts of alarm. And if it's true that the Discovery was tampered with, the police will have me in the frame for that, as well. Attempted murder. I should give myself up, and convince them that I was the intended victim, not Harriet.'

'No!' Marie objected firmly. 'If somebody tried to kill you, they might try again. It's all too uncertain as things are. You don't know who's behind all this, or what really happened with the car. It isn't safe, darling. I won't let you.'

Lyall bent to fondle Bobby's warm head, as the dog pressed affectionately against his legs. 'I can't stay hidden forever,' he said. 'When they really start to think about it, the police will come looking for me here, anyway.'

'Just another night or two – until it's clearer what's going on. I tell you,' she repeated, her voice rising, 'it isn't safe.'

'All right,' he conceded, putting an arm around her shoulders. 'I won't go against your wishes for now. But I wish I knew what was going on down there.' He nodded his head towards the village. 'Is Harriet all right? What's the vicar doing? I won't be able to bear the uncertainty for much longer.'

Marie pulled his head down to hers, and kissed him. 'It'll all be all right,' she murmured. 'As long as I have you here with me.'

Laura's anxiety about Keith did not lessen as the day wore on. 'And what about Harriet?' she said. 'Isn't she supposed to be coming home today?'

Rosemary had brought her microscope up to their room at the pub, away from prying eyes. 'Far too sensitive to leave in the vestry,' she said.

Laura had scoffed. 'Who around here would have any idea what they were seeing, even if they bothered to look?'

'You never know,' said Rosemary, with narrowed eyes. 'There's a lot going on around here that we aren't aware of.'

'Oh, well, not long to go now,' said Laura, ambiguously.

'Do you mean until the Fayre, or until your Flannery fellow catches the murderer?'

'Both,' said Laura. 'I hope.' She sighed. 'And I do feel bad about Keith. Here I am, meant to be helping to heal the breach with his mother, and all I can think about is how oddly he's behaving over the Malcolm Sutton business.'

'Well, you'll be able to put it all right tomorrow,' Rosemary consoled her. 'I can't see what else you could have done, anyway.

There's been far too much going on for much constructive family therapy.'

'True,' Laura agreed.

Keith insisted on driving Harriet home from the hospital, despite some opposition from Danvers. 'After all,' said the vicar, 'you haven't really got a suitable vehicle, have you? Not with the Discovery out of action, and Lyall missing. You can hardly collect her in the pick-up.'

Danvers had to concede that this was true. Apart from the Discovery, the only other transport on the estate was a battered Volkswagen Caddy, used for carrying logs and plants and the assorted materials needed for Lyall's workshop.

Harriet had telephoned Keith early in the morning, to say her discharge had been postponed until the registrar could examine her. 'And he's always later on a Saturday,' she'd sighed. 'I expect it'll be early afternoon before they let me go.'

'I'll be there,' Keith had promised, 'I can come between the two weddings I've got today.' Then he phoned Danvers as Harriet had asked.

She seemed very pale to Keith, as he drove them through the country lanes. 'I can't stop thinking about what happened,' he said. 'You could have been killed. Somebody tried to kill you.'

'Well, I'm alive,' she assured him. 'No lasting damage done. Although if you don't slow down, that could change. I keep telling you, you drive too fast.'

'Sorry.' He slowed minimally. 'I'm in a hurry to get you home, where you'll be safe.' He gave her a concerned look. 'When I saw you, unconscious, with that lump on your head – oh, Harriet – I thought you were dead.'

Harriet took a deep breath, and looked out of the car window. 'Calm down, Keith,' she pleaded. 'Forget about it. It's all over now.'

'But it isn't,' he almost shouted. 'What about everything that was happening before your accident? None of that is resolved. The police are still hunting for a murderer, still asking their questions and hanging about the village. And I still feel so ashamed,' he blurted.

She looked at him in amazement. 'Ashamed? You? But why?'

'You know why. I can't just pretend it was an aberration, on the spur of the moment. I can't live with myself, knowing what we've done.'

'Keith —' she laid a gentle hand on his arm. 'Don't.'

'But you must feel the same?' He flashed her a quick look. 'Surely you must.'

'No,' she shook her head. 'No, Keith. I don't feel the least bit guilty or ashamed. And I don't think you should, either. It's all over and done with now, and we just have to get on with our lives.'

'Well, I'm not sure I can do that,' he whispered.

Franklin Danvers had been a whirlwind of activity throughout the day, with the entire population apparently at his disposal. His whole attention went into the Fayre, and with the continuing absence of Lyall, he personally undertook to instruct and rehearse the villagers in all aspects of medieval life.

Rosemary and Laura had a hurried encounter with him at midday, at one of the tables outside the pub – which Jim had robustly refused to move, despite the previous day's accident. 'Lightning won't strike twice,' he said, when Laura made a comment.

Rosemary had hoped to show Danvers their progress in the churchyard, but he shook his head and said he hadn't got time. 'I'm coaching all these people from scratch,' he claimed. 'They need to know everything – from weaponry to music, via cooking, costume and creed.'

'Creed?' Rosemary echoed.

'Oh yes. You must never forget how central religion was to the people of those times. It coloured every single thought. They prayed before making any decisions, they monitored each other for any signs of heresy, they saw the hand of God in everything that happened. It's crucially important to remember how significant the Black Death was at the time, as well. Records are not by any means comprehensive, of course, but the impact was beyond anything we've known in our lifetimes. For example, almost a quarter of the clergy in Dorset and Somerset were wiped out over a period of a few months. That meant all the vital rituals of daily life were conducted by rapidly appointed replacements, or sometimes not at all. As for Wiltshire and Gloucestershire, well —'

Laura held up a hand, in laughing protest. 'Fascinating,' she said. 'You obviously live and breathe all this. But surely we can't hope to replicate what it was like, in the twenty-first century? It's like another world to us now.'

Danvers heaved a deep sigh. 'I had hoped that Keith would come to our assistance on that,' he said. 'But all he says is that times have changed and it isn't up to him to turn the clock back. He just doesn't seem to understand.'

'Perhaps he's worried that it would confuse people,' Laura suggested. 'I mean, there's a narrow line between all this play-acting, and real life, isn't there? Especially when it comes to spiritual matters.'

'Play-acting?' Danvers fixed her with a ferocious glare. 'Play-acting?'

'Sorry,' she said, trying to suppress a nervous laugh. 'But you know what I mean. We do have to keep a sense of proportion.'

'I'm not at all sure that I do know what you mean,' he said stiffly, getting to his feet. 'All I know is that this is a very big project, all staged, I might add, for the benefit of your cousin's church. The least he could do is to co-operate.'

Rosemary and Laura watched him stride off up the hill to the Glebe field, where four villagers were trying to get two horses to run towards each other. 'The man's obsessed,' said Rosemary. 'And just look at those poor horses. They'll never get the hang of jousting.'

'He seems to get a new idea every day,' Laura remarked. 'No wonder Keith is finding it all such a strain.'

'Danvers can be awfully aggressive,' Rosemary said. 'He rubs people up the wrong way and then shouts at them when they get obstinate. He has no idea how to handle them. I can't bear to watch him for more than a few minutes.'

'He gets results, though. They respect him for his expertise and enthusiasm. Everybody knows that without him, there'd just be endless dreary fêtes on the green. This business is really going to put Baffington on the map.'

Rosemary nibbled her lip thoughtfully. 'I wonder whether they'll like being on the map, once it's happened,' she said.

Rosemary and Laura ate their evening meal in a deserted dining room, in an atmosphere of impending crisis. 'It's like the eye of a hurricane,' said Rosemary, with a shiver. 'Waiting for something to happen.'

'Mmm,' Laura nodded. 'Very uncomfortable. I'll be glad to get out of here tomorrow. Perhaps it'll all look different when I get back.'

'I doubt it,' said Rosemary. Then she burst out, 'I feel so furious about Knussens and the genetic modifying they're doing. I just want to march over there and tackle him about it.'

'Not a wise move,' Laura observed. 'He'd probably sue you for defamation.'

'I have got evidence, remember. I could send it all to the media, I suppose – expose them for the hypocrites they are. It would put them out of business overnight.'

'And serve them right.'

'Well, yes...but I should give them a chance to explain first. I want to be fair.'

Laura cocked her head. 'Oh, I see,' she said. 'You've still got a thing about Linton, after all this.'

'I keep remembering what he said at the conference. It makes much more sense now. I think he probably believes that GM is the only solution to the world's problems. He was talking about global warming at the time, but he might well have the same attitude towards disease, and famine and – well, all the other evils of the world. He's a sort of born again biologist, seeing GM as the answer to everything.'

'Are you thinking he might be right?'

Rosemary clutched her hands together, wrestling with her

conflicting feelings and thoughts. 'If he is, it's still wrong to be using Knussens in such a way. It's blatantly dishonest. It's a betrayal of their customers. They should have the courage to come out with it, and tell everybody what they're doing.'

'Except that most people regard GM as the work of the devil,' Laura reminded her. 'They'd have an uphill struggle to persuade anyone that it was justified.'

'Precisely,' groaned Rosemary. 'That's why I feel so helpless.'

Laura could only make understanding noises, unable to come up with any further suggestions, until she remembered their initial reaction to Rosemary's discovery.

'We're forgetting something,' she said, with a dark look.

'Oh?'

'That all this gives Linton a motive for killing Malcolm. And that means we have to do something about it. If we don't, we're withholding vital information from the police, and that could get us into a lot of trouble.'

'Oh,' said Rosemary faintly. 'Oh, yes.'.

Laura had another thought. 'Do you suppose he might have been confiding in Danvers about it, when you saw them in London yesterday? Getting him to invest in Knussens, or something?'

Rosemary's eyes widened, as she considered the idea. Then she shook her head. 'Not really likely,' she concluded. 'Danvers isn't any sort of scientist. The only thing he ever thinks about is life in the Middle Ages.'

'Well, they must have been up to something,' Laura said.

As they prepared for bed, Laura asked, 'What'll you do tomorrow, while I'm at Sandy's?'

'Fix the tomb, dig out the last of the docks, pay a visit to Harriet – or even possibly Marie.'

'The forecast is for rain, according to Jim.' The landlord of The Holly Tree had been unusually talkative that evening, with few customers to occupy him. When Laura had asked him where everybody was, he'd reminded her that there was an international football match taking place, keeping everybody glued to their televisions. 'Oh,' she'd laughed. 'And there was me thinking they were all hiding indoors for fear of being murdered!'

Jim had smiled tightly. 'I'm going to have to fix up a telly in the bar,' he said glumly. 'There's nothing else for it.'

Laura had winced. 'That'd be a shame,' she said. 'It's nice as it is. Peaceful.' Jim didn't even smile that time.

'So I'll just have to see, won't I,' said Rosemary. At the time, Laura saw nothing ominous in these words.

In the train, Laura tried to rehearse what she would say to her cousin Sandy. Having seen Keith in his role as country vicar, over the past week, she felt she could present a stronger case in his defence than she had done previously. Despite his bewildering assertions concerning the killing of Malcolm Sutton, he was obviously a well-loved and effective clergyman. Surely, Laura thought, she could convince his mother that it was time she accepted his vocation.

Sandy's husband Digby met her at the station in his new Puma. With some surprise, Laura expressed her admiration for its sporty appearance and impressive turn of speed. Digby was sixty-two, a retired maths teacher, and the last person Laura would expect to drive such a machine.

'Glad you like her,' he smirked. 'It's something I've always wanted.'

Sandy, it seemed, was busy preparing lunch. This too was unusual – on previous visits, Digby had done all the cooking.

The house was a semi-detached Thirties red-brick villa close to the centre of town. There was garden front and back, both much neglected. As Digby ushered her in, she found the hallway littered with a familiar jumble of bags, coats, boxes, newspapers, shoes. Sandy's house had always looked as if recently ransacked by desperate burglars. For years the family had exchanged dark predictions that somehow Sandy would be punished for her sloppy ways, but so far she seemed to be getting away with it.

Unless, Laura thought suddenly, her estrangement from her son was a kind of retribution.

'This is a lovely surprise,' her cousin came quickly out of the kitchen, arms held wide for a hug. 'We don't see nearly enough of you.'

Gin and tonic was produced, and Laura found herself settled on a garden lounger beside a table on the patio already laid for lunch. The unkempt garden reminded her very much of the churchyard at Baffington, and she wondered whether Keith had made the same connection.

It was not until after the meal of chicken salad, heavy wholegrain bread and cold sparkling wine that Laura ventured onto the topic that was the purpose of her visit. Her heart was thumping painfully, as she tried to select the right words.

'I told you, didn't I, that I'm working at Baffington for a few weeks?' she began.

Sandy and Digby both nodded carelessly. Anyone knowing them less well might have been deceived.

'You haven't been to see Keith since he moved there, I gather. That's over a year now, and he's barely a hundred miles away. That's not much these days – especially for your lovely new car.'

'He's been here. Three times,' said Digby.

'It's not really the same thing. He'd love to show you his church, introduce you to his parishioners. Have you ever seen him conduct a service?'

Sandy shuddered exaggeratedly. 'It would freak me out,' she said. 'Hearing all that rubbish coming from my own son's lips.'

Laura almost gave up until she remembered the trouble that Keith had encountered in recent days. She began to describe the situation, assuming her cousin would have heard about the murder in Baffington. She was wrong.

'What are you talking about?' demanded Sandy. 'Somebody's been murdered? Is that what you mean?'

Laura sighed. 'You still don't read the papers, I see,' she accused.

'I listen to Radio Four,' Sandy defended. 'And there's been nothing on there about a murder in Baffington.'

'No, well, there wouldn't be,' said Laura. 'But poor Keith's in the thick of it. It's caused him a lot of distress.' She quickly gave the basic facts, emphasising Keith's close involvement. 'It was in his churchyard. He identified the body. And he is almost certainly on the police list of suspects,' she said, starkly.

'Ridiculous!' scoffed Digby. 'Our Keith'd never kill anybody.'

They made Laura repeat the whole story, including the names and personalities of all the prominent people concerned. It took her almost an hour, with all the interruptions and questions. At least, she thought wryly, Keith's parents have suddenly developed a much stronger interest in him than before.

'This Brockett's Farm,' Digby said slowly. 'That's surely where the key to the business lies. The GM bloke – he'll be the one, you mark my words.'

'My friend Amanda was given taxol for her cancer,' Sandy remembered. 'It's nasty stuff. Very powerful. They used it as a last resort. But they're getting good results from it for kidney tumours, apparently. It's funny how you start taking an interest in these things when somebody you know is affected.'

'What happened to Amanda?' Laura asked. 'I think I met her once. Wasn't she at your wedding?'

Sandy's eyes filmed over. 'We were friends for forty-five years. She died last month.'

'Oh, I'm sorry.'

'Actually, she gave me a talking to about Keith, just as you're doing. She always wanted to be his godmother, but I would never have him christened, of course.'

The conversation began to ramble back to the subject of Keith's vocation and Sandy's genuine inability to understand or support him, as a result. 'It's as if he ceased to be my son, don't you understand, the moment he said he was going into the church. People talk about conversions from one religion to another, but it's even worse when a person goes from active passionate atheism to active passionate Anglicanism,' she complained.

Laura tried to persuade herself that it was a hopeful sign that Sandy was at least willing to talk about how she felt. It made it easier for her to defend Keith and argue his point of view.

'He feels utterly abandoned by you,' she said, hoping she wasn't putting words into his mouth. 'It's not an easy job – he works seven days a week, well into the evening, always on call. He looks pale and thin, and not very happy.'

Sandy's eyebrows went up. 'And you think that's all my fault? Isn't it all down to this murder?'

Laura shook her head. 'He was much the same before the murder. Now it's just got a lot worse.' Instinctively Laura looked to Digby for support, and found, to her surprise, that she quickly got it.

'Poor lad,' he groaned. 'She's right, Sand. You know she is.'

But Sandy was not going to be a pushover. 'He knew how it would be. I gave him fair warning. I think you're just exaggerating this business with that man getting killed, to try to win me round.'

Laura lost her patience at that. 'You are such a selfish cow,' she raged. 'Everything has to be seen through your blinkered prejudices, doesn't it? You don't give a single thought to how your son might be feeling. How much he needs you. How you've turned it all sour for him, behaving the way you do. I remember how you would never let him give you anything for Mother's Day, because you said it was commercialised rubbish. You wouldn't let yourself see that people need to give something, sometimes. If you won't take a bit, you wreck the whole relationship.'

Sandy leaned back in her chair. 'Whew!' she breathed. 'Steady on. What's Mother's Day got to do with it?'

'It's you, that's what I mean. It's all on your terms. You don't try to see the other person's viewpoint.'

'I do. But I have to stick to my principles. I can't pretend to think something's all right when it isn't. That's hypocrisy.'

Laura had run out of accusations, and was fearful that if she said any more she would end up estranged from Sandy for ever. She didn't have enough relatives for that to be an option.

'All right,' she sighed. 'You win.'

'No she doesn't,' Digby objected. 'She doesn't at all. I've never been comfortable with all this, but – well, like most men, I went along with it for the sake of peace. But I've missed Keith. I would have liked seeing him at his ordination ceremony, and conducting an ordinary morning service in one of his villages.'

Both women looked at him with flickerings of contempt.

Laura bit back the 'it's-a-bit-late-now' remark. Sandy's more complicated expression displayed the frustration and self-dislike of the strong wife who dominates because her husband allows her to, but would sometimes prefer him to take control and hold the reins for a while.

The ringing of the telephone rescued them all. Digby went to answer it, his voice filling with concern and urgency as he listened. 'Yes, yes,' he said. 'We'll come.'

He turned to face the women. 'That was the police,' he said. 'They've arrested our Keith. He has just confessed to the murder of Mr Sutton.'

Rosemary had missed all the excitement of Keith's arrest in her pursuit of Redland Linton. On a bold whim, prompted in part by a steady drizzle from early morning, she had decided to track him down to his home, which she remembered he'd said was on the wharf at Bristol. Using a shameless piece of subterfuge, she had telephoned the conference hotel, convincing them that she had been a recent guest there, needing to contact Linton urgently. Would they be good enough to let her have his address? But they had flatly refused to divulge such a detail, offering instead his phone number, which she'd already found for herself. Thinking hard, she keyed the number into Google on the computer, and was amazed when the man's home address popped up, in the list of senior personnel on the Knussens website. Funny things, websites, she mused. They often seemed to assume that nobody would ever actually read them or use the information they contained.

Bristol was seventy miles away, and she got there in an hour and ten minutes, the Land Rover delighting in the clear motorway for much of the route.

Linton answered the door of his waterside apartment wearing a minimal singlet and very short shorts. 'Oh!' he gasped. 'It's you!'

'Sorry to bother you at a weekend, but I've got something important to talk to you about.'

With little sign of alarm, he stepped back to let her in. 'I was having a session on my multi-gym,' he explained. 'I'm glad you interrupted me, to be honest. It isn't much fun.'

'Why do it then?'

He looked as if this question had never occurred to him. 'To be fit,' he shrugged, as if that was the only and obvious reply.

Rosemary examined him with as much objectivity as she could muster. His face was open and friendly. His body glowed enticingly. He was affluent, and fit, and intelligent. And he was doing experiments in genetically modified trees which were not only illegal but immoral and probably dangerous.

They sat down in his open plan living space, facing each other across a low glass table. Rosemary started to describe what she had seen down her microscope, watching his face closely for changes in expression.

When she'd finished, he merely shook his head. 'You don't understand,' he said. 'You couldn't possibly grasp the implications from one quick look at the cell structure.'

'But it is GM,' she insisted. 'It can't be anything else.'

He put his hands behind his head, and leaned back in the leather chair. 'Rosemary, almost everything is GM, in one way or another. All we've been doing is expediting the process. It's not the least bit immoral or dangerous. We are genuinely driven by a desire to produce better cancer drugs. We don't claim to cure it. That's just tabloid language. Nothing will ever cure cancer, because it's not just one disease. It's a mistake the body makes in a host of different ways. All the medical profession aims to do is control it, render it harmless. But if we can develop a more effective variation of taxol, we'll have done a great deal to assist the process.'

'But you don't know what else you'll be changing, at the same time,' she insisted. 'There's been no proper research into what happens next. If you're changing yew trees now, what will it be tomorrow?'

He sighed. 'Yew trees have changed anyway. You know as well as I do that the Irish variety is dramatically different from the English. The quality of the timber in Italian and Spanish is different again. Why does it matter? Who's to say what's good and what isn't? There is no absolute standard of yewness. If it helps people to live longer lives, free from the pain and terror that ovarian and kidney tumours produce, that's as good as it gets, in my book.'

'OK,' said Rosemary slowly, finding herself yearning to agree with him, to restore her faith in him as a decent human being. 'So why don't you come out into the open with what you're doing? Why is it all such a secret?'

'Come on!' he said with exasperation. 'This is the real world we're talking about. Commercial, cut-throat, dog-eat-dog business. Knussens wants to make money from this, of course we do. If we didn't see a profit every year, we couldn't continue to operate. It's as simple as that. If we broadcast what's happening, somebody else will come along and collect the winnings.'

'But,' she made one last effort, 'Knussens is supposed to be natural. Your whole image is based on that. This isn't at all natural, what you're doing.'

'Oh yes it is,' he said with heavy emphasis.

A small glimmer of alarm happened in Rosemary's head. 'How?' she asked.

'It all depends on definitions. You could argue quite convincingly that everything is natural, because human beings are a part of nature, so whatever we do comes under that heading.'

'That's just playing with words. It isn't how the general public would see it.' Another thought hit her. 'And what were you doing meeting Franklin Danvers in London on Friday?'

The abrupt change of tack made Linton blink. 'Pardon?' he said.

'Near Leicester Square, sitting outside a pub. You looked very conspiratorial.'

He shook his head slowly. 'I was trying to buy him off, if you must know. Make it worth his while to drop the idea of buying Brockett's Farm.'

'Oh. And were you successful?'

'Sadly not. The man doesn't seem very interested in money,

funnily enough.'

'So what happens now? The people in the village aren't going to stand for Knussens having the farm, once they realise what you plan to do with it.'

'I'm afraid you're right,' he said, with a touch of regret. 'And that's why, Miss Rosemary Boxer, I'm going to have to keep you here, where you can't do any damage.'

'What?' The alarm burst into a floodlight of panic. 'What do you mean, keep me here? How long for?'

'Well, unfortunately, I'm afraid it might have to be for ever,' he said, getting out of his chair.

Chapter Sixteen

The reconciliation between Sandy and Keith did not go quite as hoped. It took nearly two hours to drive to the police station, Laura riding in the cramped back seat of the Puma, her eyes closed for much of the time as Digby overtook on blind bends and flashed his lights at anybody who impeded him. She was shaking by the time they finally arrived and even Sandy looked wobbly.

They were asked to wait in a room that smelt of disinfectant and had no windows, until somebody could be found to explain the situation to them.

Laura had been trying her best to think rationally, ever since the phone call. She had asked Digby and Sandy whether they had a competent family solicitor to represent Keith. 'Solicitor!' scoffed Sandy. 'Of course not.' Digby had explained more mildly that they preferred to handle routine legal matters for themselves, and Laura remembered how Sandy had always been suspicious of the legal profession – quite irrationally in her opinion.

'Well, he'll need somebody now,' she said. 'They'll provide whoever's on duty, if he doesn't nominate someone.'

'Let them,' said Sandy.

It quickly became evident that Sandy's contempt for the police force was even deeper than that for lawyers. She soon found her feet after the nerve-wracking journey, and started to make loud demands, opening the door and calling out into the corridor beyond.

'For heaven's sake!' Laura chastised her. 'We've only been here five minutes.'

'And they'll leave us here for five hours if we don't stick up for ourselves.'

'Sandy, precious, please listen to Laura. She knows what she's talking about,' Digby pleaded. Laura gave him a grateful look, despite the sloppy *precious*. Her ex-husband, whatever his faults, would never have called her 'precious' in a million years.

Much to their relief, only another minute passed before they were joined by a uniformed policewoman with a message. 'We're sorry to keep you waiting,' she smiled. 'We understand how distressing this must be for you. Please bear with us for literally three more minutes, and we'll brief you thoroughly at that time.'

Even Sandy was disarmed by this. She stared at the girl in astonishment. 'Brief us,' she murmured. 'Right. Thanks.' The girl left, closing the door behind her.

Despite the three minutes passing with immense slowness, the promise was kept, and a man came striding down the corridor, his heels loud on the floor.

Laura knew, before the door opened, who it would be. She almost threw herself into his arms, so great was her relief at seeing his familiar face. 'Hello,' he said, with a nod and a faint smile.

He introduced himself to Keith's parents, who appeared to be impressed at his seniority, although in Sandy's case it was a fleeting reaction. 'What have you done to him?' she shouted. 'Where's my boy?'

'Let's all sit down, shall we?' Flannery said. He took a moulded plastic chair from a row along one wall, and spun it round so he was sitting with its back against his stomach. He folded his arms over it and leaned his weight on them. It was the attitude of an old-fashioned schoolteacher, which struck Laura as either fantastically clever or a lucky accident.

Sandy sat rigidly on the edge of a chair directly facing him, with Laura and Digby on either side of her.

Carefully, with only occasional use of jargonised idiom, Flannery explained the situation. Keith had presented himself at the front desk, shortly before midday, having first conducted two church services in two of his parishes. In a state of suppressed agitation, he had made an unambiguous confession to the killing of Malcolm Sutton on the evening of Monday June 14th using a longbow and arrow belonging to Mr Franklin Danvers. When questioned about his reasons, he said Sutton had been a severe threat to the well-being of the village, upsetting numerous parishioners, and it had been a sudden impulse that he now desperately regretted.

'And of course you don't believe a word of it,' said Laura, the moment he paused for breath.

It came as a shock to her when nobody said anything. She turned to look at her cousin, expecting her to fly into attack mode and accuse Flannery of nameless iniquities which had somehow brought all this on their heads. Instead, she watched in horror as a tear trickled down Sandy's cheek.

'B – but —' Laura stammered, wanting to scream at them all: Of course Keith didn't do it, but the atmosphere in the room silenced her. Doubt was visible on the faces of both Keith's parents. The Detective Inspector was resolutely expressionless. He continued speaking as if Laura had said nothing.

'You must understand that we have to proceed on the assumption that the Reverend Briggs is telling the truth. We must assume for the moment that he is not delusional, and that he fully understands the implications of what he has told us. You will know that a plea of guilty counts for a lot when it comes to a trial. The matter is clearly very serious indeed, but —' he looked steadily at Sandy, 'it could be much worse.'

'Can we see him now?' Sandy asked in a voice that broke Laura's heart.

Keith was brought out to them, and whatever Laura might have been expecting to see, the reality was completely otherwise. The young clergyman was transfigured. His head was high, his eyes clear. 'Hello, Mother,' he said in a ringing voice, with a quick nod to his father and cousin before focusing all his attention on Sandy.

'Keith,' she choked. 'What have you done?'

'The right thing,' he told her, with a smile.

Laura struggled to keep up with the jumble of thoughts and impressions crowding in on her. Could it be that the vicar really had killed Malcolm Sutton, out of some misguided sense of self-sacrifice? Could he possibly have broken the Sixth Commandment and feel so good about it? On the other hand, could he have told such a huge lie (thereby breaking the Ninth Commandment, Laura realised) and equally feel he'd done the right thing? It was a moral puzzle that she felt unable to resolve, especially with the stunned parents to cope with as well.

Sandy floundered. 'You killed a man, and can stand there and claim it was right?' she demanded, in a stronger voice. 'What sort of man of God does that make you?'

Keith's expression began to assume a rigidity that suggested considerable tension below the surface. He gazed at some far-off invisible horizon, and said, 'There are times when God's will can seem to direct us down a sinful path,' he said.

'Come off it, old chap,' his father broke in. 'You can be a vicar without getting into all that sort of nonsense. This is your mum and dad speaking to you, not some class of theology students. Come down off that mountain and talk to us properly.'

'A man died,' Keith said, in a more normal voice. 'By violent means. Somebody must atone for that.'

'So you've offered yourself as a sacrificial lamb, have you?' Sandy was rapidly reverting to her usual sarcasm. 'We rushed here thinking you'd need us, that you'd had some sort of mental breakdown, and here you are preaching at us.'

Laura was diverted from the family scene by the entrance of DI Flannery again. She met his eye, and thought she detected an attempt on his part to reassure her. It's all right for you, she thought miserably. It isn't one of your family who's just confessed to murder.

'What happens now?' she asked.

'We've done most of the official business,' he told her. 'The Reverend has been formally charged, and apprised of his rights and duties. His solicitor has applied for bail, but we have no decision on that yet. I must tell you that it is very unlikely to be granted, given the severity of the crime.'

Digby seized on this detail, familiar to him from countless TV dramas. 'We can provide bail,' he said. 'How much?' He even started to reach into his inside pocket for his wallet.

'I don't think you heard me properly, sir. The decision won't be made for some time – and I must repeat that people confessing to murder are almost always remanded in custody.'

'So Keith can't leave here until that's been decided,' Laura summarised. 'And there's a risk he'll be kept on remand for ages. Months and months.'

'A guilty plea usually means a much shorter wait,' Flannery said, obviously trying to find some crumbs of comfort to offer them.

Sandy made a sound, half moan, half growl. 'Keith – did you really kill that man?' she asked, staring straight into her son's face.

Keith's face closed, as if a curtain had come down. 'I have said all I intend to say,' he replied.

'I'm afraid you'll have to go now,' Flannery told them. 'This visit wasn't part of the normal protocol in any case.'

'Thank you,' Laura said, sincerely. 'You've been very kind.'

'It's not easy for you, I know,' he said.

'Easy!' Sandy latched onto the word with contempt. 'You haven't the slightest idea.'

Laura persuaded Sandy and Digby back to the car, with no notion about what she ought to do next. Before leaving the building, she again met the gaze of DI Flannery and was grateful for the smile he gave her. 'You mustn't worry,' he said.

Laura suppressed a desire to snap at him, to point out that she had no choice but to worry. Instead, she just nodded at him, before following her cousin back to the car.

Sandy seemed to be stunned into silence, as they drove away. 'How could he?' she murmured, two or three times, but went no further than that. Digby smacked the steering wheel and whistled angrily, but said nothing. It was clear that they were both out of their depths.

'Will you stay in Baffington tonight?' Laura asked them. 'There's sure to be a room at the pub. Or you could stay at the vicarage, I suppose.' This last suggestion felt very dubious, considering that Keith's parents had never even seen his new home.

'We'll stay at the pub,' said Sandy. 'Although we didn't bring any night things with us.'

'I expect we can improvise,' said Laura, feeling suddenly exhausted.

At The Holly Tree, Laura was surprised to find no sign of Rosemary. This was a major disappointment, with so much to tell her. Her friend's opinion on the events of the afternoon would have been greatly valued at that moment.

Sandy and Digby were restless, their bewilderment growing as they continued to talk about what had happened. Laura had advised them to say nothing at all about Keith being in police custody, in the hope that the village could be kept in ignorance for a while longer. It felt to her as if the story was still not over by a long way, a feeling that had been strengthened by Keith's strange manner.

As the afternoon drew to a close, Rosemary still did not reappear. The Land Rover was absent, so Laura assumed that her friend had gone on some errand connected with the churchyard work. But when six o'clock came and went, and Digby invited her to eat with them at seven, she began to worry.

Rosemary's things, on her side of their shared room, were in no more disarray than usual, as far as Laura could see. She went down to the landlord and asked if he was sure Rosemary had left her no kind of message. 'Did you see her go?' she asked.

Yes, said Jim. Miss Boxer had set out in the middle of the morning – a little before eleven, he thought. And no, she had not left any message. Increasingly puzzled, Laura went back to the room, hoping for some kind of enlightenment.

The only possible source of information appeared to be the laptop, sitting tidily on the small table in the bedroom. Feeling quite furtive, Laura switched it on, and hoped she would remember how to operate it. Rosemary had not bothered with a password, which made things easier. Almost by accident, Laura soon blundered into the 'History' section, which gave the files accessed and websites visited in recent days. The last website that Rosemary had looked at was the one belonging to Knussens.

This was not surprising, and Laura could see no indication as to precisely which pages had been looked at on the screen. Frustrated, she sat down on the bed, and tried to think.

The last conversation they had had about Knussens involved the evidence Rosemary had found that they were genetically engineering yew trees, and that had seemed to them to give Redland Linton a motive for killing Malcolm Sutton.

'Oh, no,' breathed Laura, as the truth hit her. Of course, that's what Rosemary would do. She'd find where he lived, and confront him with her discovery. And she'd do it because she would want to believe well of him. She still liked him. She would be placatory, smiling and offering him an opportunity to explain himself. She would go to him at home because that would seem far less confrontational than a formal interview at work.

And Linton almost certainly would not like it. Even though he apparently hadn't killed Malcolm, because Keith said he did it.

And surely Rosemary would have the sense to tell Linton that people knew where she was, even if they didn't? More likely, Laura decided, that she had been asked out to dinner with him, and would show up in Baffington at midnight, happily vindicated in her faith in the man.

Which left Laura completely unsure as to what action, if any, she ought to take. Still sitting on the bed, with the laptop perched on her knees, she moved the cursor at random, finding nothing of any interest or use. Far from comfortable with computers, she had little idea how she might locate a phone number or address for Linton, anyway. In all probability, he had given Rosemary a contact number at the conference and her calling-up of the Knussens website was scarcely relevant. She switched the machine off, and got up to leave the room.

Halfway downstairs, she was met by the landlord, saying there was a call for her, on his private phone, which he was not too happy about. With humble apologies, Laura took the call in a small sitting room in an annex behind the main pub building. She knew already who it would be.

'How are you?' came Flannery's voice. 'And your cousin?'

'We're very upset,' Laura told him. 'As you might expect. Is this call going to make us feel better or worse?'

'Better, I hope.'

But Laura's mind was on somebody other than Keith Briggs, for the moment, and she needed to tell the police detective all about it. 'I think Rosemary's gone off to see the Linton man,' she burst out. 'The one from Knusssens. There's no sign of her here, and I can't think where else she might be.'

She more than half expected him to dismiss this as a red herring, irrelevant to the matter in hand. But she was wrong.

His voice came back sharp and alert.

'Where's that? Has she gone to his home?'

'I imagine so, on a Sunday. I have no idea where he lives.'

'And she's gone alone?'

'Must have done.'

'Stupid woman,' he said with intense feeling.

Laura's heart began to pound. 'Why?' she bleated. 'What's the matter?'

'With any luck, nothing. But Linton's an unknown quantity here.'

'You know about the GM material, do you?' Laura was struggling to follow his logic.

'What?' The word came down the phone like a bullet.

Laura did her best to explain, finishing with a demand for reassurance. 'Surely,' she wailed, 'now that Keith has confessed, Linton must be in the clear. The same as Harriet, and Lyall and —'

'Yes, yes, but the trouble is —' He interrupted himself. 'Never mind. Listen, we'd better try to find Linton's home address, and send somebody over to make sure everything's all right. Did she take her Land Rover with her?'

Laura confirmed this, giving him the registration number. She still couldn't believe that there was any serious need to worry about Rosemary. 'Be diplomatic, won't you,' she said to Flannery, who gave an exasperated sigh in response.

Then he changed the subject. 'Let me give you the good news,' he said. 'I told you I'd make you feel better.'

'Go on then,' she urged him.

'Reverend Briggs has been granted bail, after all. Or so we expect. Don't ask how, but it looks likely that he'll be free to leave sometime tomorrow. He'll have to stay in Baffington and report to us every day, but —'

Laura interrupted. 'That's a lot better than languishing in a prison cell,' she finished. 'I don't know how you managed it, but thank you. Sandy and Digby will be thrilled.'

'So go and tell them,' he said, and rang off.

* * *

Linton and Rosemary had, in a way, been dining together. Having checked her bag to ensure there was no mobile phone and concluded that she was not going to manage to call for rescue, he simply dead-locked his front door and removed the key, and told her they might as well both relax.

'You're joking,' she said. 'Relax for how long?'

'That is a problem, I admit. Ideally until I can convince you that what you think you saw down that microscope of yours was not at all what it seemed.'

She gave this some serious thought, although not before laughing sarcastically and reminding him that she did in fact know quite a lot about plant cell structure and what was and was not normal. 'Besides,' she reminded him, 'you more or less admitted it a little while ago.'

'I grant you that we have been conducting an intensive breeding programme, with an eye to working on the Brockett's Farm yews. They are extremely old specimens, you know. It's very rare to find so many together, dating back so far.'

'Except it's not possible to date them accurately, because the core rots away and you can't count rings as you would with other trees.' Even in the middle of a crisis, Rosemary could not resist a little lecture.

Which was when Linton suggested he prepare them a meal. He ordered her to remain in the living room, while he worked in the kitchen. Before leaving her, he unplugged the two phones in the main room and his bedroom. 'And don't try shouting out of the window,' he warned. 'Nobody would take any notice of you, and it will only make me cross.'

Instead, Rosemary paced backwards and forwards across the hardwood floor, trying to decide how much danger she was actually in. Linton had implied that he would have to kill her, but he did not behave like a man about to commit the ultimate crime. He would have to be clever about it if he wanted to escape detection, since Laura would soon guess where she was, and the police already had Linton in their sights. Was he perhaps waiting for darkness to fall, when he would do the deed and bundle her body outside and into the river only a few yards from his front door? Was he going to poison her, with the meal he was currently preparing? Somehow poisoning seemed to have gone out of fashion as a means of killing somebody – although Rosemary could think of a few plants she herself might use if it ever came to that.

She paced around the room again, trying to think what she should do. Shouting out of the window seemed a reasonable option, on reflection. The flat was on the third floor, which was too high to jump, but not too high to be heard by people outside. If she called in a sane-sounding tone, explaining that she was being held against her will, surely somebody would at least be worried enough to phone the police.

But there was a problem which she was embarrassed even to admit to herself. It was that she still liked the man, even after what he was doing. She liked his smile and his voice, and his air of youthful confidence. She rather feared that Laura would kill her, once she knew that she had become such a willing victim, even if Linton didn't.

As she dithered about her next move, eyeing the complicated window fastening that would probably not work without a key anyway, Linton came back into the room. 'Ready in five minutes,' he said. 'I hope you like trout?'

His easy conversational tone gave a bizarre ambiguity to the situation. However much she might want to demand her freedom, or threaten him with consequences, she couldn't bring herself to do anything more than smile weakly and confess to a liking for trout.

Which only left trickery. She tried hard to think of a subterfuge that would fool him into letting her go. Everything that came to mind only led to more danger, when she thought it through. She could tell him that Laura knew exactly where she was, and would come looking for her if she wasn't back by bedtime. She could even add that her friend would be sure to tell the police, for good measure. But assuming Linton believed her, this might only serve to make him more dangerous. He might bind and gag her and hide her in a cupboard, if not something even more painful and life-threatening.

An inner voice warned her to be cautious in what she said. Idle threats could easily backfire. Instead, she decided to find out more about what he was planning. 'You really expect to get Brockett's Farm, do you?' she said, once they were eating. 'In spite of Danvers and his Museum?'

He shrugged. 'Marie's on my side, still,' he said, as if it was all settled.

'So you didn't kill her brother?' The question was, she knew, a calculated risk.

His incredulous laugh was reassuringly convincing. 'Of course I didn't,' he chuckled. 'What an idea!'

'I'd like to believe you,' she said, fluttering her eyelashes girlishly at him. 'Because that's really the only reason I got into a state about the signs of GM. I mean – it isn't really my business what Knussens is doing.'

Linton gave this some careful thought. 'Do you mean you came here intending to accuse me of murder? Wasn't it bad enough that you plainly revealed that you think you have information that could ruin me and the company I work for? What did you think I would do? Just admit to it all and let you go off and tell the world?'

She hung her head, fiddling with the good-quality napkin he'd given her. 'I didn't think about it,' she murmured. 'I just wanted to hear your reaction.'

'You wanted me to explain it all away,' he nodded. 'And I think I've done that, to the best of my ability.'

'So can I go now?'

'Sadly, no. You must understand that I can't let you. At least not until the sale of Brockett's Farm has been signed and sealed.'

'But that could take weeks!' She stared at him in horror. 'Or months. You can't keep me locked in here all that time.'

'You're probably right,' he sighed. 'Don't you wish you'd stopped to think before confronting me the way you did?' He leaned towards her, his eyes suddenly hard, his mouth a tight line. 'You still don't understand how important this is, do you? How dangerous you could be to us, even if you haven't got your facts entirely straight.'

'So what are you going to do?' she asked in a small voice. Half her trout lay uneaten, and she knew she wasn't going to manage to finish it now.

'Nothing until tomorrow. You can spend the night here on the couch. And if you try to escape or attack me in any way, I won't hesitate to tie you up and gag you. It's all up to you.'

Rosemary contemplated the coming hours with increasing panic. Again, Linton seemed intent on maintaining normality as far as possible. To this end, he turned the television on, and within a few moments a news programme came on.

Rosemary watched it idly, her eyes drawn to it in the usual semi-hypnotised fashion. Suddenly a familiar face filled the screen. The news reader was saying something incredible, in explanation. *In a surprise development in the investigation into the murder by bow and arrow of a man in Baffington village, the local vicar, Reverend Keith Briggs, has confessed to the killing. He is being held in custody at Kingsminster police station, before appearing in court tomorrow.*

'What!' Rosemary screeched. 'Keith has confessed? He can't have done.' Her thoughts were in turmoil. Did Laura know about it? And Harriet? What did it all mean for the village? Surely Keith would not have confessed if it wasn't true? His obvious strain over the past days could have been the result of guilt. Sutton was an obvious threat to the well-being of Baffington, as well as a source of misery to Harriet Luke. All in all, Keith had several reasons for wanting him out of the way. Maybe he had experienced a moment of madness, and fired the arrow before he could stop himself.

Rosemary stared first at the television, then at Linton. 'I have to go to Laura,' she said. 'She'll be needing me.'

He smiled lazily, like a cat with an over-confident mouse to torture. 'No, no,' he disagreed. 'All this means is that everybody's going to be much too busy to worry about looking for you.'

Before she could react to this, there was a ring at the doorbell, which made them both jump.

Chapter Seventeen

At Brockett's Farm, Lyall prowled restlessly to and fro across the main bedroom. Every time he passed the window, he slowed his pacing and stared out across the fields and woodlands. Marie was out there somewhere, walking the dog and tending to essential tasks. When he had tried to go with her, she had pleaded with him to stay out of sight.

It wasn't long before he had to concede that she'd been right. At his next pause beside the bedroom window, he saw a car approaching the farm gate. Drawing back, he peered carefully around the curtain, and realised it was the police. Without thinking, he rushed downstairs, and through the house to the scullery at the back. From there, he let himself silently out of the back door, and crept across the vegetable garden to a small shed used to store flowerpots and slug killer.

He could hear no voices or slamming doors. The windowless shed was hot and stuffy, and full of cobwebs which got into his hair. The sense of being a fugitive irritated him and at the same time reminded him of some of the more peculiar exercises that had featured in his army training. His greatest fear was that Marie's labrador would betray him. If Bobby caught his scent, and started pawing at the door of the shed, all would be lost.

He waited a full thirty minutes, before cautiously edging the door open. All was still and quiet. Emerging from the shed, he waited for a shout, his skin flinching at the irrational idea that he might be in the sights of a gun or even a longbow, from a marksman hundreds of yards away.

It would be insanity to simply walk back into the house, in the hope that the police had gone away again, and yet there seemed little other choice. He couldn't just take off across the fields, abandoning Marie. Taking a deep breath, he retraced his steps to the scullery door. Listening intently, he went back into the house. Still no sound of voices.

'Oh, there you are,' said Marie in a bizarrely normal tone, as he went quietly into the kitchen. 'I'm making some cold beef sandwiches. Do you want horseradish on yours?'

'Have they gone?' he whispered.

'Who?' Then she smiled. 'Oh, the police. Yes, they've gone. I told them I hadn't seen you for at least a week, and wouldn't have expected to. I acted rather indignant at the very idea that you might be here.'

'And they believed you?'

'Possibly not, but they went away just the same.'

Lyall sighed. 'It's no good, pet. I can't stay any longer.' He brushed at his hair, shedding bits of dust and cobweb. 'I can't keep hiding like this. It's only going to make everything worse, in the long run.'

Marie looked stricken. 'No it won't!' she protested. 'They'll catch the real murderer, and then everything will be all right.'

Lyall gave her a look full of anguished frustration. 'You don't understand,' he groaned. 'I can't stay out of it another minute. It's cowardly. Besides,' he set his jaw aggressively, 'I've got a score to settle – and it's high time I got on with it.'

Without waiting for a sandwich, or any further discussion, he strode to the corner of the room. Standing against the wall was a longbow and a quiver of arrows. 'I might need these,' he said.

With a sense of operating in a parallel universe Rosemary and Laura were both at work in the churchyard on Monday morning. The conversation was in equal parts about Linton and Keith, although Laura did her best to give Linton the greater part of their attention.

'It was so clever,' sighed Rosemary. 'The way that police-woman simply stood there, asking that I come immediately on urgent business. No hassle, nothing Redland could do to stop us. He just stood and watched us go, his face like concrete.'

'You have Flannery to thank for that. His methods might be unorthodox, but they seem to work.'

'So what convinced him that I needed rescue?'

'I really don't know,' said Laura.

'Except,' Rosemary went on, 'it didn't quite feel like being rescued. I was just picked up and moved, like a pawn in a chess game. The police officer checked that I was all right, and then just let me drive myself back here, as if nothing had happened.'

'Mmm,' said Laura, very intent on the positioning of a cherub on the edge of a slowly emerging path through the middle of the graveyard. 'He still committed a crime. You can't just let him get away with it.'

'I know,' said Rosemary, with a low chuckle. 'I've been thinking about that.'

Laura gave her an enquiring look.

'Instead of pressing charges, with all the palaver that would entail, I think I know just the way to get my revenge.' Laura waited patiently. 'I'm going to send those slides, with an explanatory letter, to Professor Henry Owens. He'll know exactly what to do with them. I think we can safely assume that my friend Linton will be out of a job within the week, and Knussens will be under close scrutiny from all sides.'

'Brilliant!' Laura applauded. 'Direct action certainly has a lot to be said for it.'

Rosemary smiled, before turning thoughtful again. 'What time is Keith's court appearance, do you know?' she asked, a few minutes later.

'Ten thirty,' said Laura. 'Sandy and Digby have gone to stand bail for him.'

'Bail!' Rosemary was amazed. 'Not for a murderer, surely?'

'It seems they're making a special case for him,' said Laura. 'Flannery phoned and told me.'

At midday, Digby's Puma came carefully into the main street, and drew up outside The Holly Tree. Rosemary and Laura dropped their tools and trotted to the lych-gate to greet them. Three people emerged from the car.

'Keith!' exclaimed Rosemary. 'They let you go!'

'Very strict bail conditions,' he said tersely.

'My word! Have they electronically tagged you?'

'Not quite,' said Keith, looking pale but composed. 'My father has had to promise to pay just about all he has if I abscond.'

As they stood there, Harriet Luke came running towards them from the direction of her cottage. 'Keith!' she cried. 'Is it really you?' She flung her arms round him, and squeezed him in a fierce

hug. Sandy made a small clucking noise that seemed to indicate
surprise and disapproval.

When he'd been released, Keith looked at Harriet fondly, and
said, 'That's enough of that. We've got work to do. This Fayre
isn't going to happen by itself, and there aren't many days left.
Straight after lunch, we'd better go and see Franklin. There are
several things I want to say to him.'

'We'll come with you,' said Laura, eagerly. 'We need to consult
him about these statues. He's sure to have very decided views as
to just how they should be positioned.'

Keith gave her a blank look, making her think she'd been
insensitive to talk about the churchyard, when he had much
more important matters on his mind. Then he nodded. 'You
might as well come,' he said.

Sandy and Digby were hovering, at a loss what to make of the
talk about Fayres and statues. 'Lunch?' echoed Digby.

'Yes,' Keith said. 'I'll treat you, Dad. You and Mum have been
magnificent, dropping everything like this. I honestly appreciate it.'

Something in his voice only served to confuse them further.
Meekly the whole group followed him into the pub, where he
ordered lunch in the dining room for six. 'Is anybody else booked
in?' he asked the landlord.

'Mr Winthrop has a table for two. I think he's entertaining one
of his business colleagues.'

'Oh, good,' said Keith, obscurely.

Mr Winthrop had evidently seen the television news the previous
evening, and he stared at Keith in blank astonishment as the
party of six entered the dining room. The man with him clearly
had no knowledge of what had been going on, and was seriously
disconcerted when his host got up from the table and confronted
the new arrivals.

'What's all this?' Mr Winthrop demanded. 'You two ought to
be behind locked doors, after what you've done.' There was no
mistaking who he meant. He jabbed a thick finger first at Keith,
then at Harriet. 'I saw you,' he accused Harriet. 'I told the police.'

'Yes, I know,' said Harriet. 'And I don't blame you at all.'

'What did you see?' Laura asked him, in bewilderment.

'This young lady, sneaking about in the churchyard, the night after the murder. Rummaging in the undergrowth on the far side of the church, until she found what she was searching for.' His eyes widened in triumph. 'An arrow. She picked it up, and then slid it inside her slacks. I saw the whole thing.'

'It's true,' said Harriet, simply.

'And it proves that you attacked Malcolm Sutton. Your first shot must have missed him, so you fired another.'

Laura almost exploded. 'You stupid man, it proves no such thing! How dare you —'

Harriet put a calming hand on Laura's arm. 'It's all right,' she said. 'I think we should all settle down and have our meal. Mr Winthrop did what he felt was his duty.'

Rosemary had listened to them in silence, wondering why her thoughts were in such disarray. 'Hang on,' she said slowly. 'We found an arrow in the churchyard, as well.'

Keith laughed briefly. 'Arrows all over the place,' he said. 'Lyall will be cross with us for being so careless.' His words sounded stilted, uttered like a bad actor. Both his parents looked at him as if afraid he might be losing his wits.

Harriet's gentle forbearance with Mr Winthrop left the man looking foolish, not only in his own eyes, but in those of his client. Suspecting that he was being manipulated in some way, he sat down again, and tried to continue his meal with what remained of his dignity.

Keith leaned over towards him, after a few minutes. 'Please don't worry,' he said. 'The fact is, they let me out on bail. One of the perks of my profession, I suppose.' Next to him, Laura let out a peal of laughter, eliciting a look of surprise from Rosemary and Harriet.

'Ignore me,' said Laura. 'It just sounded funny, for some reason.'

Digby sniffed censoriously. 'Can't see much to laugh at myself,' he grunted.

The conversation was restricted to small talk until Mr Winthrop and his client had finished and left the dining room.

'Poor man,' said Harriet. 'He thought we were teasing him.'

'Serves him right,' said Laura. 'Silly old buffer. Fancy making such a wild accusation against you.'

'Well —' Harriet began, before Keith interrupted her to ask how she was after her accident on Friday. His distress and shock at what so nearly happened were still evident on his face.

'I'm fine, now,' she assured him. 'Although I don't know when I'll be able to get behind a steering wheel again. And it's a really horrible feeling, to know somebody deliberately tried to cause my death, or serious injury.'

'Do you know who did it yet?' asked Rosemary.

'It must have been Lyall,' she said, sadly. 'He's the only person who knew I'd come back early from London.'

'But why?' Rosemary insisted. 'What does he have against you?'

Harriet groaned quietly. 'I can only suppose he somehow thought I was an impediment to the plans for Brockett's Farm. He realised I knew about – well, I was privy to a secret, and perhaps that made me dangerous to him in some way.' She shook her head. 'I suppose he mistrusted me. He was always worried about what Franklin would think, trying his best to stay on his right side.'

'But —' Rosemary said, before Laura cut her off by suddenly asking Sandy whether she'd like to visit the church after lunch, or even see the vicarage.

'Well —' Sandy hesitated, with a glance at Digby. 'We thought we should be getting home now. We've already loaded up the car. The cat didn't get his supper last night, and Digby has a dental appointment tomorrow morning.'

Keith said little, except for a joke about food at the police station, and a comment about dentistry in the Middle Ages. His parents kept a close watch on him, wondering what the next surprise would be.

Twenty minutes later, as they all got up and went outside, there were several villagers idly standing about on the green, quite obviously there to catch a glimpse of the murderer.

Keith stiffened when he saw them, as if waiting for the first rotten egg to be thrown, but the mood seemed not so much hostile as confused. A woman stepped forward. 'Is it true, vicar?' she called. 'What they said about you on the telly?'

Keith merely smiled, and turned away to speak to his mother. 'I suppose we ought to be glad the press haven't arrived,' he said.

Sandy gave him another long searching look, as she had done repeatedly throughout lunch. 'You'll go to prison,' she said, in a flat voice, drained of emotion. 'For murder. This is just a short reprieve, which I must say I don't really understand.'

'Come on, Sand,' said Digby, giving her a bracing little pat on the arm. 'Never say die. We still haven't heard the boy's side of the story. If you ask me —' he gave Keith a sad attempt at a wink ' – he's got a trick or two up his sleeve. Eh, lad?'

Keith lifted his chin. 'I've done what I believed to be best,' he said, ambiguously.

Sandy sighed. 'I just wish you'd explain it better.'

Keith reached out and pulled her to him in an awkward hug. 'I'll see you again soon,' he mumbled. 'Thanks for coming. It was very kind of you, and I'm sorry if I've caused you distress.'

Sandy forced a laugh. 'Oh, well,' she choked, 'I suppose that's what sons are for.'

'Oh, Sandy,' said Digby, before grasping Keith's hand warmly. 'Bye for now, lad. We'll see you again soon.'

Even without Keith's parents, it felt rather like a delegation, as the four of them set out up the hill to Franklin Danvers' large house. Keith led the way, talking more animatedly about the Battle of Baffington and the enthusiasm with which the villagers had thrown themselves into the whole business of the Fayre, emphasising that his release from police custody had been largely due to his insistence that he was essential to the community festivities over the forthcoming weekend. 'They've really got into role, many of them,' he said. 'With all the clothes and contemporary language.'

'The language is all wrong, actually,' said Harriet. 'A lot of it is more eighteenth century than fifteenth.'

'Never mind. The important thing – and I want you all to remember this – is for the Fayre to continue, no matter what. Laura – you and Rosemary must be here for it. You promise me that, don't you?'

'Of course,' said Laura. 'We never expected anything else.'

'We wouldn't miss the Grand Banquet for a million pounds,' Rosemary confirmed.

'Franklin has seen us, look,' said Harriet, sounding nervous and pointing to a figure standing in the driveway. 'I wonder if Lyall's there as well.'

'Hello!' Danvers greeted them warily, his gaze full on Keith. 'What's all this then?'

Keith stepped in front of the others. 'Sorry to trouble you, Franklin, and it's obvious you're surprised to see me. The thing is, I'm out on bail, mainly so I can help you with the last minute preparations for the Fayre. It might be immodest of me, but I thought you'd probably have a struggle without me.'

Danvers quickly mastered his feelings and smiled. 'Well, I don't suppose I need worry that you'll murder me as well as Sutton, do I?' he said, with a forced laugh. 'But I must say I'm rather taken aback. You did it because of Harriet, I suppose?'

For a second, Keith looked as if this remark was too much for him. He went white and wrapped his arms around his own stomach as if in pain. He was very careful not to let his eye catch Harriet's.

'I've been asked not to speak about it,' he said tightly.

'I see,' Danvers nodded. 'But there's nothing to stop me speaking to the others, is there?' He looked from one woman to another in slow succession. 'I don't know how a man of the cloth could have committed such an act,' he said. 'Out of sheer common jealousy. Such a messy motive for murder. And stealing one of my longbows for the purpose! Not to mention damaging that doorframe in the church to get into position for a clear shot. I ask you – what a sorry business.'

Harriet interceded with a pleading note. 'Franklin, please stop. It isn't doing any good, and Keith's already said he isn't allowed to talk about it. We've come to discuss the Battle re-enactment. We have to draw up the precise formations and ensure there can't be any risk of people getting hurt.'

Rosemary had been fighting all morning to keep a grip. The events of the previous day repeated over and over in a corner of her mind, overlaying everything that was going on in the room, there and then. Linton's smooth voice, weaving together reason and extreme danger, whispered tirelessly to her. Despite her plan to expose his behaviour, the after-effects were still with her.

But something important was happening, here in Franklin Danvers' house. Laura was staring at Danvers with something like horror, while at the same time trying to send some sort of silent message to Keith, who was not receiving it. He had turned his back on them all, leaning over the table in the middle of the Great Hall, examining a large plan of campaign which Danvers and Harriet had constructed.

Danvers seemed to be similarly unaware of Laura's state of mind. He gave a harsh laugh at Harriet's words. 'But, my dear, this is all because of you. You understand that, don't you? Poor Keith was just one more of the local men to be nursing romantic feelings for you, and when it looked as if you might be going back with that swine Sutton, he just saw red. I must say, it was very noble of you, Vicar, to go along and confess the way you did. A relief to all concerned, I should say. And quite a surprise to me. I had Gordon Lyall at the top of my list of jealous lovers, rather than you.'

Just as Rosemary realised what had been nagging at her for the past few minutes, Laura finally spoke. 'Hold on,' she said. 'What did you say, a minute ago?'

'Yes!' Rosemary jumped in. 'I was going to ask you that.' She looked at Laura excitedly.

Danvers blinked at them. 'I beg your pardon?'

Laura took a step towards him. 'About getting a clear shot. Damaging the doorframe in the church. Nobody knew about that – not even Keith. Not even the police. Isn't that right, Rosemary?'

'Absolutely. I haven't breathed a word about it, and we made sure nobody would notice the damage.'

Harriet looked wonderingly from face to face, trying to grasp the implications. 'What are you saying?' she asked.

'We thought it was Lyall,' said Laura, in confusion. 'We were sure it was Lyall, protecting Marie's interests. But – my God! – it was you.' She looked at Danvers in horror. 'You killed Malcolm with one of your own longbows. You smashed open that little door to do it, and then hid the bow in the organ pipe, and strolled away as cool as a cat.'

Danvers did not move, except to glance from Harriet to Laura and back again. 'Harriet,' he said, not quite managing the tone he wanted. Instead of appealing to their years of comradeship, working together as a team, it emerged more as the whine of a little boy. 'Harriet, you don't believe this nonsense, do you? I wouldn't kill anybody, you know that.'

Rosemary spoke, with a hand to her forehead as if manually sorting her thoughts. 'Harriet told me in the hospital how several of the men in Baffington find her attractive. That includes you, doesn't it, Mr Danvers? You've been nursing a deep devotion to her all this time, and when she gave no sign of returning your feelings, you thought it must be because of Malcolm Sutton. So that's why you've attributed that same motive to Keith – and, of course, poor old Lyall. You tried to kill him as well, by sabotaging the brakes on your car, because you were afraid he'd take Harriet away from you.' She looked at Keith. 'You might have been next on his list,' she realised.

Keith made a pathetic attempt at a smile, but said nothing.

Laura was shaking her head in an effort to work out the puzzle. She continued to address Danvers. 'You must have been tremendously surprised when you heard that Keith had confessed. What did you think was going on?'

Danvers was moving slowly sideways, which nobody seemed to notice. 'I thought he really had fired at Sutton that same evening, and missed,' he said, in a more controlled voice. 'I thought he truly believed himself to be a killer. Why would he lie about it?'

Keith's startled gasp drew Laura's attention. She stared at him. 'That's it,' she realised. 'That is what happened. You and Harriet were larking about in the churchyard that evening, firing arrows at the side wall, and next morning convinced yourselves that one of you had managed to kill Malcolm by accident, especially when you couldn't find all the arrows you'd used. You fools,' she added affectionately. 'All that guilt and anguish for nothing.'

'But where's Lyall?' Harriet persisted, lagging helplessly behind in the rapid-fire realisations. 'I thought he must have tampered with the car, when he knew I would be driving it. Have I got that wrong?'

'He didn't do it,' said Rosemary, clearly and slowly. 'That was Danvers, trying to remove Lyall from the scene, because he was jealous. He thought Lyall would be driving the car, to fetch you from the station.'

Harriet nodded slowly. 'I see now.' She turned to Danvers. 'But whatever gave you the idea that Gordon and I were lovers?'

Laura cleared her throat. 'I think that might have been us,' she confessed. 'We said something, just in passing. He must have thought there was some truth in it. We were very careless,' she finished remorsefully.

Danvers made a choking sound, shaking his head. 'No, it wasn't you,' he managed. 'I saw them together, in the workshop, giggling and messing about.' His face twisted savagely. 'It made me sick.'

Harriet leaned weakly against the table. 'It was nothing,' she murmured. 'Just a bit of fun after a hard day's work.' She looked at Keith. 'It seems that every time I let myself go, it leads to trouble,' she said ruefully.

'But all the time Lyall has been in love with Marie Sutton,' said Laura. 'We realised that some time ago.'

Harriet nodded in confirmation. 'Oh, yes. I knew about it, but Lyall asked me not to say anything. He's been more or less living up at Brockett's Farm for months.'

'What?' Danvers' voice was a hushed whisper. 'What are you saying? But why would he keep it a secret from me?'

'Mainly because he was afraid you had designs on Marie, oddly enough. You have been very attentive to her lately, you must admit.'

'Only because I hoped to buy the farm,' Danvers choked.

'Yes, well,' Harriet said, 'Gordon wasn't sure, and he didn't want to get into a fight about it.'

Harriet had moved closer to Danvers, addressing him with a gentle accusation which held more than a dash of pity. Rosemary too found herself feeling sorry for the man.

'You really don't understand women, do you?' she said to him. 'You think they can somehow read your mind, without you needing to say anything. You must have believed that Harriet was deliberately snubbing you, when she really had no idea how you felt.'

Suddenly Danvers cracked. With a rapid lunge he grabbed a short-handled pike from one of the displays with one hand, and seized Harriet's upper arm with the other. He then pushed her against the wood panelling behind her, and held the lethal point under her throat. Nobody had moved in the seconds this took. Keith, who had had at least as much difficulty as Harriet in keeping up with the turn of events, opened and closed his mouth in bewilderment.

'Keep still, all of you,' Danvers snarled. 'I hope nobody doubts that I'll use this if I have to. If I can't have you,' he addressed Harriet, 'then why should anybody else?'

'Easy, easy,' said Laura, flapping a hand at Rosemary and Keith to prevent them from doing anything rash. 'Come on, now. This isn't going to help, is it?'

'He means it,' said Harriet in a choked voice. 'Please don't —'

'It's all right,' Laura said. 'Just keep calm.' Inwardly she raged at herself and Keith for being such fools as to let things reach this point. Keith had been unreliable from the start, she realised. Letting his feelings for Harriet rule him the way he did, and then being so slow to react when Franklin Danvers' revelation changed everything.

For several seconds, the whole room was like a frozen tableau. Everybody knew it couldn't continue like that. Something had to happen. Danvers was the first to act on this knowledge. 'I'm going to take Harriet outside now,' he said. 'You three stay here, until we've been gone for exactly five minutes. If I see or hear any movement, I'll kill her.'

The sudden shocking *thwack* stunned them all. The sound somehow came from Danvers, but he had done nothing to cause it. He was, however, standing at a strange angle, the arm holding the pike looking oddly stiff. He gave a frightened cry, as he realised what had happened to him. An arrow with blue and red flights was embedded in the panelling, having passed through the sleeve of his jacket. He was firmly pinioned, and as he wrestled to free himself, Harriet wrenched away from him and ran to Keith.

At last, Laura looked behind and upwards, searching for the bowman. Gordon Lyall was standing in the minstrel's gallery at the far end of the hall, still holding his bow. 'Good shot!' she called to him. 'Thanks very much.'

Lyall gave a formal little bow, and moved to a window at one end of the gallery. He opened it, and waved at somebody outside. Almost immediately, people came through the front door.

Laura approached Flannery slightly tentatively. 'We seem to have got there,' she said. 'Although I'm not sure quite how.'

Flannery gave her a patronising smile, and went towards Keith who appeared to be welded to Harriet. 'Vicar,' he said. 'May I?'

Keith gently disengaged himself, and held his arms out at his sides. With astonishment, the women all watched as the police detective slid his hands inside the vicar's upper garments, and after a short intimate procedure brought out a small black object, which he held aloft.

'He was wired!' Laura gasped, almost speechless with amazement. 'You've been listening to everything we've said.' Her shock was shared by Rosemary, who stood with the same slack-jawed astonishment on her face.

'Worked a treat,' Flannery smiled. 'Though we didn't reckon on poor Miss Luke being taken hostage. We weren't at all sure how much danger she was in, but it sounded serious.'

'It was,' said Harriet, in a weak voice. 'Franklin isn't just a keen historian – he has a completely medieval mindset. I've come to understand that in the last few weeks, with all this Fayre business. Women are chattels to him, you see. And it was quite true – if he couldn't have me, he might easily have killed me to stop me going to anybody else.'

'But you never imagined he'd killed Malcolm?'

Harriet shook her head. 'No. I thought it must have been Gordon, because of Marie and Brockett's Farm. Although I couldn't altogether believe he'd sabotaged the car, deliberately trying to kill me.' She looked up at the gallery. 'Sorry Gordon,' she said. 'I should have known better.'

Lyall threw her a quick salute in acknowledgement.

Chapter Eighteen

It soon became obvious that nobody really knew exactly what had just happened. Laura's admiration for Flannery's subterfuge with the microphone knew no bounds, despite a sneaking feeling that he might have taken her into his confidence beforehand. Rosemary was finding herself becoming more and more feeble, as people swirled around her asking each other questions.

The only clear and certain fact seemed to be that Franklin Danvers, local squire and famous historian, had killed Malcolm Sutton and attempted to kill Gordon Lyall by sabotaging the car brakes. The assumption was that by clinging to these unwavering facts, everything else would somehow fall into place, until the whole picture was in perfect focus.

'Did you see Lyall going up to the gallery?' Laura asked the Detective Inspector.

He shook his head. 'We weren't sure where he was, to be honest. We could only hope that when he heard that the vicar had confessed to the murder, he would come out of hiding, assuming he was safe. Which he did,' he added, looking smug. 'We were all set to jump him, when everything suddenly changed.'

'It's true he'd gone into hiding, but not for the reasons you thought,' Laura reminded him. 'He was scared because he'd worked out that the damaged brakes on Danvers' car were intended for him, not Harriet, and until he was sure who wanted him out of the way, he decided to lie low up at Brockett's.'

'Seems reasonable,' nodded Flannery.

'So why did he come sneaking up to the gallery, instead of just walking in normally?' Laura wondered.

The detective inspector raised his eyebrows. 'Wouldn't you?' he demanded. 'The poor man had no idea what might be waiting for him, after hiding away for two days. He and Miss Sutton had no real idea of what was happening down in the village.'

'So I suppose it's naïve of me to ask why he was carrying a longbow?'

'Because, like his boss, he respected it as a weapon, above all others. Silent, accurate, versatile. It helps to be an excellent shot, of course. The way he pinned Danvers to the wall like that was magnificent. Not a scratch on him, either. He can't have been sure of what he would find in here, but it made extremely good sense for him to be prepared for things to turn nasty.'

Laura had heard enough for the moment, and Flannery was impatient to complete his investigations. 'I'll ask you exactly when you realised Keith was innocent some other time,' she said, to his shoulder, as he turned to go.

Only then did she notice Rosemary, who had slumped into a squatting position, propped against the oak panelling. 'Hey!' Laura called. 'What's up with you?'

Rosemary turned a white face to her friend. 'I'll be all right,' she mumbled. 'I just came over a bit wobbly. Too much happening, too quickly.' She managed a feeble grin. 'I expect I just need a nice big steak and a pint of best local ale.'

Harriet and Keith, who after their prolonged hug seemed to be rather embarrassed with each other, came to Laura's side. 'Is she all right?' asked Keith.

'She will be,' said Laura. 'Let's get down to the pub, and have a nice sit down, shall we?'

They all felt rather like the audience departing after a particularly powerful and gruelling play. Their emotions had been ravaged – fear, anger, confusion, relief, had stormed through them, one after the other, leaving them drained.

The four of them walked down the hill in a ragged group, still asking questions, and noting sudden small explanations that had been overlooked. 'So many wrong assumptions,' sighed Laura. 'We really jumped to some silly conclusions in the past few days, didn't we?'

'Such as?' asked Harriet.

'Oh, well – mainly to do with Lyall, I suppose. He seemed such a sinister character, barking orders to people one minute, and being all red-faced and shy the next. He looked like a man with something to hide, which he was, of course – but not what we thought. Even when we suspected he had something going with Marie, that only seemed to increase the case against him.'

'Lyall's a good man. I admit I've grown quite fond of him in the past few months. But that's my problem in a nutshell.' She sighed. 'I do get fond of people. Even Franklin is a good employer, interesting and generous. I liked working for him. I told him when I admired what he did. And that must have given him quite the wrong idea about me.' She sighed again. 'Men do that, you see. They think I'm encouraging them to take things further. None of them wants to be just good friends.'

'And me?' asked Keith in a small voice. 'Is that true of me as well?'

'Oh, Keith,' Harriet laughed. 'Let's not go into that now.'

They reached the church gate before anybody noticed them. Everything was quiet and deserted, as if nothing unusual had happened. Then Mr Winthrop came hurrying towards them across the green.

'Oh, help,' muttered Rosemary. 'What do we say to him now?'

The antique dealer was scarlet-faced and breathless. 'That was a fine performance in there,' he began, jerking a thumb towards The Holly Tree. 'Making a fool of me like that. What's going on, that's what I want to know. There's some game afoot, and I don't mind telling you, I do not like it.'

Laura waved at the others to stand aside, as she confronted the angry man. 'Come and sit down,' she said, directing him towards his wife's memorial seat. 'You'll do yourself a mischief if you go on like this.'

Reluctantly he allowed himself to be ushered over to the seat. Laura sat down next to him, and carefully recounted the story, in summary. As she did so, she found it helped her to grasp the whole picture much more clearly herself. When she had finished, she leaned back. 'I think that covers everything,' she said.

Mr Winthrop was still flushed, and his mouth worked convulsively as he understood his own role. 'Oh dear, oh dear,' he mumbled, once or twice. Then, 'I was terribly mistaken, wasn't I? I jumped to completely the wrong conclusion. But it all seemed to fit, you see. Miss Luke was behaving with such irrationality, shouting at people and so emotional. And now I see why. Or I think I do.' He fixed a mournful gaze on Laura's face. 'The poor girl. I made everything much worse for her, didn't I?'

'Well,' said Laura, 'perhaps not. If it hadn't been for your testimony to the police, they wouldn't have taken Harriet for further questioning. And perhaps Keith wouldn't have been impelled to make his confession, and we'd never have caught the real killer.'

Mr Winthrop was somewhat consoled by this. 'Franklin Danvers!' he exclaimed. 'Whoever would have believed it? Not that I ever liked the man, of course.' A sudden new thought hit him. 'The Fayre!' he cried. 'What about the Fayre?'

Laura smiled reassuringly. 'I think you'll find the Fayre will go on quite well without him,' she said. 'That's one good thing about Mr Danvers – he was a very good delegator. Everybody knows what they have to do, and with Lyall and Harriet and Keith in charge, it's sure to be a huge success.'

Laura had expected Keith to explain the way things had turned out to his parents by telephone. Instead, he insisted that he should see them again face to face. 'I need to get some matters straightened out with them,' he said. 'It isn't something that can be done on the phone.'

'But when?' she had wondered.

'Tomorrow,' he said. 'I'll drive over there in the morning.'

'Oh,' said Laura, feeling oddly disappointed. Thinking about it, she realised she'd hoped to see her cousin's face when she understood the truth of what had happened. Sandy had a lot to apologise for, in Laura's opinion.

Then Keith said, 'You can come with me, if you like. I'd be glad of a referee, to be honest.'

Laura didn't hesitate. 'Right,' she said.

Rosemary continued to feel shaky for the rest of the day, but refused to let it overwhelm her. Leaving Laura sitting in the sun with Keith and Harriet, she returned to the churchyard, finding the rhythms of some last-minute pruning and planting both soothing and conducive to constructive thought. She cleared every last weed from around Sir Isaac Wimpey's tomb, intent on making it the grand centrepiece that it deserved to be. She examined again her efforts at repairing the broken date, worried that it looked botched and amateurish. But when she looked closer, she realised that somebody else had added some finishing touches, painting delicately around the figures, and blending in the edges of the filler she had used. The whole thing looked as good as new. 'Fairies?' Rosemary murmured, glancing around at the many statues of winged figures. 'Or one of these angels?'

A voice came from beneath the yew tree. 'Looks OK now, doesn't it?' said a man.

Rosemary peered into the shadows. 'Oh – it's you!' she said. 'Did you do this?'

Lyall stepped forward and nodded modestly. 'I've always had a soft spot for old Wimpey,' he admitted. 'He's actually part of my own family history, in an oblique sort of way.'

Rosemary's eyebrows lifted. 'Oh?'

'My mother's grandfather was one of his friends, who raised the cash for the tomb. Small world,' he laughed. 'But I never dared tell Mr Danvers. He wouldn't have approved at all.'

She scrutinised him again. 'Why are you here?' she asked. 'Shouldn't you be with Marie, reassuring her that everything's all right now?'

'Marie's out there, look.' He pointed at the green, where Marie Sutton was sitting on the grass, playing with Bobby. 'We're coming out, as you might say – letting people see that we're together. When I noticed you in here, I thought I should come and say thank you properly.'

'Nonsense,' scoffed Rosemary. 'We didn't do anything.'

'That's not how I see it,' he argued gently.

After he'd gone back to his girlfriend, Rosemary thought about Marie Sutton and her beautiful farm, with its woods and lake and ancient acres. If Knussens had got hold of it, how long would it be before the land was covered with regimental rows of commercially grown trees? Not to mention the likely new buildings and polytunnels and glasshouses. Baffington would never be the same again, if that happened. And Rosemary had to do her best to prevent it.

At last, exhausted both physically and mentally, she put down her trowel, knowing what she had to do. Without saying anything to Laura, who had gone into the vestry a few minutes earlier, Rosemary went up to her room in The Holly Tree. She plugged in her laptop, and composed a letter. She addressed it to Professor Henry Owens, who had convened the recent conference where she had first met Redland Linton. In it, she laid out, in unemotional terms, her observations from samples taken of young yew trees being grown experimentally at Knussens, and enclosed the carefully wrapped microscope slides. She then made copies, to be sent to David Billington, the ecologist, as well as the editor of *Nature* magazine. They would all be better placed than she was to take the matter further. They would know, between them, how best to address the issue. She closed the lid of the laptop with a satisfied sigh.

Keith drove only slightly less precipitately than his father. 'It never ceases to amaze me,' said Laura, trying to relax, 'how people change when they get behind a steering wheel.'

'Oh, sorry. Am I going too fast?'

'Not really. It's just not what I would have expected of you.'

Keith made an impatient *tck*. 'Everyone takes me for such a wimp,' he complained. 'Including my mother.'

'Not any more,' she assured him. 'You were very noble and brave in what you did. It must have been a dreadful dilemma for you.'

'Divided loyalties are never comfortable,' he admitted tightly.

Sandy and Digby greeted them cautiously, having been told almost nothing about the latest developments. 'Are they taking you back into custody?' was Sandy's first question.

'No, Mother, of course not.' Keith threw himself down in an armchair and heaved a deep sigh.

Sandy looked to her cousin for the whole explanation, instead of trying to get the story out of Keith. Digby fiddled with a bottle of wine, intended for their lunch. 'Are you here to protect him from me?' Sandy demanded of Laura.

'If necessary,' Laura replied, with a straight look.

'So – what's been happening?'

Laura moved to the chair next to Keith's and tried to decide where she should begin. Much of the tale seemed obvious to her now, and hardly worth retelling. It was difficult to remember how little Keith's parents knew of the people involved and the underlying motives for their behaviour. Starting from the very beginning was out of the question, if only because Sandy would never have the patience to listen to it all.

'Keith is no longer under suspicion,' she said. 'The real murderer has been caught and is now in police custody. Keith was acting with the police as a sort of decoy —'

'What!' Sandy glared furiously at her son. 'You did what? How could you be such a traitor? You tricked some poor wretch into giving himself away to the pigs, did you?'

'Shut up, Sandy.' The order came from the mild-mannered Digby, still standing at the sideboard on the other side of the room. 'Nobody calls the police "pigs" any more. Swallow your stupid adolescent prejudices and listen for once, will you?'

With a wordless gargle of shock, Sandy fell silent. Her husband took up the conversation. 'Was Keith in any danger?' he asked quietly.

Laura saw her chance. 'Very much so,' she nodded. 'The place was full of lethal weapons, and tempers were out of control. Keith put himself in the position of having to protect three women, at the same time as risking his own exposure as a police spy. He was spectacularly brave.' She paused, hoping she hadn't overdone it.

'Brave?' Sandy croaked. 'Keith was brave?'

'A hero,' Laura insisted. 'You should be tremendously proud of him.'

Keith had clearly heard enough. He reached across to Laura's chair, and patted her arm. 'Steady on,' he said.

But the message had been conveyed, and both his parents were gazing at him with new eyes. 'How did you do it?' Sandy wanted to know.

Keith took up the story from there on, prompted now and then by Laura when he threatened to sound overly modest. Under her tuition he seemed to gain in stature, his actions expanding in the retelling until he himself believed that he had done something heroic.

'But why did you confess in the first place?' Digby asked, when the account of Danvers' capture was complete. 'That's what I don't understand.'

Such was the extent of Keith's newfound confidence that instead of blushing with shame, he merely laughed at himself. 'It was when they took Harriet for more questioning,' he explained. 'I thought they'd found proof that she'd done it. I had convinced myself that one of us must have, you see.' He told again, in more detail, how he and Harriet had gone to the churchyard in the last of the evening light, with their longbows, and got into a childish competition. 'The churchyard is so big, you see, we could fire them quite a distance. It was extremely silly – we were just fooling about, to be honest. We both seemed to need some release of tension, after that disastrous meeting, and all the strain of the Medieval Fayre. Two of the arrows got lost in the undergrowth. At least, that's what we thought at the time. We got a bit carried away, and I jogged Harriet's arm as she shot her last arrow. It flew off in a completely different direction. Then we heard a car arrive right outside the lych-gate. We didn't want anybody to catch us behaving like children, so we escaped through the little gate at the back.'

Sandy cleared her throat, and Laura noticed that her eyes looked suspiciously shiny. 'Oh Keith,' she said, going to his side and giving him a clumsy hug, 'I never thought I'd hear those two words coming from you. You can't imagine how happy they make me.'

'What?' Keith blinked. ' "Little gate"?'

'No, you idiot. "Fooling about". I've always wished you'd done a lot more of that, and a lot less mooning over books and churches and all that stuff.'

Keith held her at arm's length, facing her squarely. 'Mother, you would never believe that I was doing what I enjoyed, even if it wasn't your own choice. People differ. You would never accept that. And the awful irony is that for ten minutes last Monday evening I was behaving more in line with your ideas, and see what trouble it landed me in!'

Sandy was silent for several seconds, and then smiled broadly. 'You're so right,' she said. 'I've been horribly unfair to you, ever since you were small.'

Keith began to reject this, but Sandy put her fingers over his mouth to silence him. 'All the same,' she said, 'I'm glad you can fool about sometimes. And I bet that Harriet girl's glad as well.'

Laura and Digby had watched the beginnings of a rapport between mother and son with great satisfaction, but Laura had not forgotten the earlier part of the conversation.

'The car you heard must have been Marie, arriving for her meeting with Malcolm,' she said. 'And he was lying dead under the yew tree by then. She saw you, you know. But she didn't say you were carrying longbows.'

Keith nodded. 'We left them behind the church. I went back for them before driving home, half an hour later. I'm afraid I even went so far as to wipe them thoroughly, so they wouldn't have our fingerprints on them.' He moaned. 'That just made things worse, of course. Later on, when Lyall called them all in, I just dropped mine and Harriet's at Highview, leaving my prints on them, but not hers.'

Laura was intent on sticking to her reconstruction of the whole story. 'So Danvers must have got there before you and Harriet even started your shenanigans. All the time, Malcolm was there under the tree and you never saw him.'

'Did Marie see him?' Keith asked.

'Oh yes.' Laura reported how Malcolm's sister had chosen to creep away again, giving the killers – who she believed to be Keith and Harriet – time to compose themselves, or construct an alibi.

Sandy interrupted at this point. 'A girl after my own heart,' she asserted.

Laura shook her head. 'She was very wrong to do as she did. If she'd raised the alarm there and then, the police would have quickly ascertained that Keith and Harriet were innocent. It would have saved them both a great deal of heartache and trouble.'

'Nonsense,' said Sandy. 'Sheer nonsense. They'd have taken the girl's word for it, and looked no further than Keith and Harriet for the culprits.'

Keith and Digby both spoke. 'She's right,' they said, and Laura found herself over-ruled.

Digby was in charge of the lunch, producing a glistening roast chicken that he boasted had come from his friend's free-range smallholding. 'You won't have tasted anything like this for years,' he assured them all, and they quickly agreed with him.

Sandy was subdued, apparently remembering with discomfort all the times she had been unreasonably critical towards her son. Keith was doing his best to reassure her, more by deeds than words. He asked her about her recent activities, taking great interest in a local campaign she was spearheading, to resist the construction of yet another large supermarket which would probably put the final few small shops out of business.

'We're not really so different,' he observed. 'We've just found other ways of achieving the same thing. You care about the general good, you put people's welfare at the very top of your list. I try to do the same, using alternative channels, that's all.'

'But all that mumbo-jumbo,' Sandy sighed. 'And the hierarchies, the rules and regulations. It's all so utterly alien.'

Keith opened his mouth to try to justify the traditions and systems that comprised the Church of England, and then closed it again. 'Never mind,' he said. 'I'm not going to try to convert you.'

'Thank goodness for that,' she sighed, and everybody laughed.

Rosemary and Laura worked long exhausting hours for the rest of the week, racing to get the churchyard presentable before the opening of the Fayre on Friday afternoon. Proceedings began with a fanfare of trumpets on the Green, promptly at two, followed by an opening speech. This would have been given by Franklin Danvers, and much debate had gone into the choice of his successor. Despite the short notice, one or two people had suggested Dr David Starkey or Simon Schama, but since nobody knew how such famous personalities might be contacted, these ideas came to nothing. In the end, the obvious person was Mr

Danvers' deputy, the person who possessed practical knowledge of most of the elements of the Fayre, and had become the village's most popular person during the past few days.

'Ladies and gentlemen, serfs and villains,' Gordon Lyall began, in a confident ringing voice, standing on a small stage that had been placed in the middle of the green, 'Welcome to the Baffington Medieval Fayre. We trust that there is something for you all, whether your interests lie in warfare, falconry, food or costumes of the Middle Ages. The success of this event depends on everybody who takes part. It is intended to be fun, first and foremost, but if some of you learn a little bit of history along the way, well – that's no bad thing.'

'Isn't he doing well!' Rosemary whispered to Laura, as they stood on the edge of the crowd. 'And aren't we lucky with the weather.'

'Absolutely,' Laura agreed to both comments. 'He's a different man from when we first met him.'

'Shh – what's he saying now?'

Lyall's manner had changed, and he was reaching his hand down from the platform to somebody they couldn't see. 'I hope you will forgive me for adding a personal note,' he went on, his words rather less clear than before. After a brief scramble, another person joined him on the stage. 'But we have a little announcement to make.' He put his arm around Marie Sutton's shoulders. 'Marie has consented to be my wife, and the two of us are to continue at Brockett's Farm, running it as an organic business. So – no Knussens, no Medieval Museum – just the same as before. And to mark the occasion, the Grand Banquet, which had been scheduled to take place in the Great Hall at Highview House will now be in the Big Barn at Brockett's. We trust we'll see you all there on Sunday evening, as the Grand Finale to this unique Baffington event.'

The crowd roared and cheered its approval at this. One or two shouted, 'And no new houses, either!'

'Ah!' sighed Rosemary. 'Isn't that sweet.'

'Mmm,' Laura said. 'I wonder what'll happen to Highview House now?'

'Who can say? After all, it still belongs to Danvers. He'll probably come back to it eventually.'

'Oddly enough,' Laura said thoughtfully, 'I think the village might welcome him when he does.'

'And make me feel I've wasted my time?' came a voice behind her. Spinning round, she saw DI Flannery, dressed in a brown monk's habit.

'Good grief!' she gasped. 'What have you got on?'

He grinned. 'I could hardly come in my usual clothes, could I? It's part of my job, to blend in. Besides, when I'm not catching murderers, I like to take part in a few re-enactments myself.'

Laura looked at him fondly. 'You never mentioned it,' she said.

His smile faded. 'No. There's a lot I didn't mention. It was a treat to meet you, Laura — and you, Miss Boxer. Your help here has been magnificent. I won't forget you.'

Laura met his gaze. 'Nor I you,' she said.

When he'd gone, Rosemary gave her friend a moment to compose herself, before saying, 'You wouldn't have wanted to get involved with another policeman, anyway – would you?'

'Of course not,' said Laura. 'Absolutely not.' Then she sighed. 'But he does like Ealing comedies.'

The Fayre proceeded with a zest and vitality that Laura found almost incredible after the limpness and apathy of the year before. Everything had been transformed, including the interior of the church, which had been vigorously polished and scrubbed by Joyce Weaverspoon and a regimented team of village ladies.

Seeking out Keith, Laura finally tracked him down on the Glebe field, once again firing arrows from a longbow.

'I thought the Battle didn't start until tomorrow,' she said. 'I like the costume, incidentally. Green tights are frightfully you.'

Keith grinned. 'Dressing up has become second nature to me, in my line of work. And you should see Mr Winthrop! He's volunteered to be the jester. And I've just seen him paying the most risqué compliment to Joyce Weaverspoon.'

'And Harriet?'

A voice behind her made her spin round. 'I'm getting myself to a nunnery,' Harriet said.

She was dressed in a wimple and long grey habit. Laura was struck speechless by the picture thus presented. 'Surely not?' she said.

Harriet laughed. 'It's tempting. But no, I think Keith has finally persuaded me to give the real world another chance. And I won't be wearing this throughout the Fayre. I just wanted to try it out.'

'What does it feel like?' Laura asked curiously.

'Hot, heavy and scratchy,' said Harriet. 'I don't know how they could abide it, year after year.'

'Keith, this is all such a triumph,' Laura said. 'Have your parents arrived yet? They're going to be so impressed when they see what you've accomplished.'

'They're at the vicarage,' he said. 'Dad's been painting the living room since yesterday morning, and Mum's making new curtains. They say they're not going home until they've made it a place fit to live in. I don't know what the Bishop is going to think – I'm supposed to get permission before I do anything like that.'

'Phooey to the Bishop,' said Laura.

'That's what Mum said, too,' Keith groaned.

'You must all come and see the churchyard,' Rosemary urged them, having taken some time to track them down. 'I've just put the very final touches to it.' She looked at Keith. 'I think you'll be pleased.'

Obediently, the little party followed her down the hill and into the churchyard. 'Da-DAH!' sang Rosemary, waving her arms in all directions. Although the work had been clear for anyone to see, in the final few days the whole village had been so preoccupied with spit roasts and costumes and battles and a dozen other medieval matters that they had scarcely glanced over the churchyard wall. Now, it was with genuine amazement that Keith and Harriet gazed around. Every gravestone stood proud, the grass around it shaved to perfection; paths meandered from end to end, bordered by young box and privet plants. The yew tree seemed to stand taller and straighter, and areas vivid with wild poppy, chamomile and feverfew had been left at strategic intervals. The Wimpey tomb sat squarely beside the church door, cleaned of moss and blemishes, magnificently flamboyant. To crown everything, the statues were squarely installed, looking as if they had always been there.

'It's utterly magnificent!' Keith applauded. 'You've worked miracles.' He looked to Harriet. 'Haven't they?'

Harriet nodded, wordlessly. Her eyes were damp, and her lips trembled. 'Hey!' Keith chided her gently. 'What's this about?'

'I know it's stupid of me,' she sniffed, with a flickering smile. 'It's just that I suddenly wished Franklin could see it. After all, it was thanks to him that it got done at all.'

'Not stupid at all,' Keith told her. 'It only goes to show what a generous heart you have.'

'You will keep it like this, now won't you?' Laura said, with mock severity.

'Absolutely. You have my promise,' Keith agreed. 'How long will it be before the new hedges grow?'

Laura wriggled her shoulders importantly. 'No time at all,' she said. 'Especially as I've given them a special infusion of yew, to help them get going.'

Rosemary rolled her eyes at this, but nobody noticed her.

'Yew?' echoed Keith. 'But I thought you said it was known as the Tree of Death?'

'Oh, it is,' Laura assured him. 'But it's also known as the Tree of New Life.'

Nobody had any answer to this, until Rosemary nudged Laura and pointed to a statue that the others hadn't noticed. Persephone, Greek goddess of Agriculture, had been positioned almost out of sight behind the buddleia that Rosemary had been so keen to retain. 'She'll keep an eye on them all,' Rosemary whispered.